Transience

Josef Peeters

Edited by: Rosemary Hillyard

Editing Services, rmhillyard@aol.com

ISBN-10: 0-6484561-1-0

ISBN-13: 978-0-6484561-1-7

DEDICATION

To Sandy

CONTENTS

ACKNOWLEDGMENTS

As an indie (independent) author, it is important to ensure that our books are of equivalent quality or better than traditionally published books. To that end, it is vital to vet our manuscripts scrupulously to ensure the reader is provided with an enjoyable experience free of flaws.

I would like to thank my editor, Rosemary Hillyard, for her invaluable assistance in delivering a quality manuscript from the rudimentary file I sent her. She made the entire process seamless and enjoyable.

I would also like to thank my Beta readers, Deborah Williams and Howard Jarvis, for their kind assistance in volunteering with a perusal and appraisal of the manuscript to give it the final polish before publishing.

CHAPTER ONE

He was on fire! He panicked. He ran for the first thing his young mind latched onto...water. Only, instead of hopping into the shower right next to him, he instinctively ran for the ocean.

In hindsight, Samuel, shortened in typical Australian fashion to first Sam Border then Sambo by his friends and brother, would remember that he shied away from entering the shower recess because the plastic shower curtain was ablaze. His first overriding impulse was to get away from the fire and to get to water, lots of water.

Charlie, attending to his ablutions in the corrugated iron outhouse, was so shocked by the sound of an explosion that he ran from the building with his daks around his knees, to see his beloved older brother running for the beach with his legs on fire, screaming hysterically. Further hindsight would have reminded Sambo of the reason they had returned to the house that day...the outgoing tide, the heat, and his need for a shower.

Sambo arrived at the top of the beach after his mad dash down the sandy path, then realised with dismay that the water was another kilometre away at least. Without thinking, he dropped to the sand, where he quickly doused the flames. Charlie finally caught up with him as he sat up in the sand attempting to come to terms with his situation. Sambo knew he had seriously injured himself, though he felt only a warm sensation on his legs moments after the incident. Both boys had suffered minor burns over the years from such things as touching a kettle after it had boiled on the stove, or an iron, giving them a healthy respect for fire and hot things.

After a few moments Charlie suggested they clean Sambo up, then put ice on the burns. It seemed the practical, calm, level-headed thing to do, as they had often enough witnessed their mother or father doing the same thing to them if they burned a finger. Sambo agreed to Charlie's sensible suggestion. As Charlie applied the ice gently to his brother's legs, once Sambo had donned his undies, both boys pondered the enormity of their problem. Sambo knew he would require medical attention, though he was not entirely mindful of just how serious his injuries were or the peril he faced if they remained where they were.

Enormous blisters were forming on his legs, restricting his movements. An insane idea was forming within his shocked mind. Without access to a phone or radio, not that they knew how to operate a radio had one been available, Sambo came to the inevitable conclusion that they would have to walk around to the resort where their mother was working to get help. Charlie, not knowing any better, quickly agreed with his older brother. Once the pair had dressed in protective T-shirts against the blazing sun, donned sunscreen, shorts, and thongs on their feet, they headed off.

The house was situated in the centre of the large horseshoe-shaped bay. Sambo believed that they should cut across the sandy/muddy flats to reach the rocky point of the bay, rather than using the soft sand on the beach all the way around. Halfway there, of course, the tide returned with a vengeance, stranding the pair atop a coral outcrop quite far from the shore. The incoming tide had submerged the burned areas on Sambo's legs, offering him a modicum of relief, but now the pain was asserting itself with pure intensity and menace.

By the time the water reached their chests, Sambo was screaming in utter agony, and Charlie was beside himself with worry. Charlie, crying unashamedly, had to slap his big brother several times to revive his senses. During one of Sambo's calmer, lucid moments, they saw a boat out in the bay at the same time. It was several hundred metres away and, while it appeared the captain of the boat had acknowledged their distress signals and screams, he did not make a move toward them. Up to their necks in warm waters notorious for shark activity, the two brothers were certain their time on earth had come to an inopportune end.

The boat eventually made its way to the stricken children screaming frantically for help. Onboard the vessel, the man their mother had met, whose house they hired for their holiday, was looking for an expensive diving watch he had lost over a year ago. His friend, a nurse, was diving for the watch, which was the reason the captain would not move the boat initially. He would not leave a diver stranded. Knowing exactly what to do, the nurse took charge to see that Sambo was made as comfortable as possible, shielding him with a towel from the destructive sunlight and constantly splashing cool seawater on his legs as they made their way to the resort to pick up the boy's mother.

After his mother recovered from fainting, a three-hour voyage aboard the same boat to the nearest hospital on Palm Island ensued, with Sambo screaming in torment all the way. Several times the boat had to be stopped while cool water was scooped up to douse the boy's legs. It was, by and large, the worst experience of Sambo's life. In later years he would come to think of it as perhaps the luckiest day of his life as well.

So many things occurred that day which helped save the life of the burned boy. The bottle housing the methylated spirits which heated the shower was plastic instead of the usual glass. A glass bottle subjected to the same conditions would have caused irreparable damage, probably death. The plastic jug used to add the spirits contained only a minimal quantity of liquid. Were it full, the burning liquid would have engulfed the boy in flames, causing burns to ninety per cent of his body or more. No one in those days survived burns of that extent.

The owner's son just happened to be looking for a watch he lost a year ago? Unheard of! A nurse on board the boat? The amount of time spent in seawater before the boat arrived, effectively beginning the healing process immediately while providing a soothing relief. Most burns victims die from shock or an infection. An infection was prevented by the saltwater immersion. That the boat was available to take them to Palm Island immediately after receiving fuel from the resort, effectively reduced the time for a rescue by half.

So many elements conspired to save the life of a fifteen-year-old boy that day that Sambo knew he was destined for something special, that life had a purpose in mind for him. He did not believe in anything as banal as God or religion, but he knew that fate did not want him to die that day. While he was not made privy to that purpose, he decided to remain alert and accepting of that purpose once it revealed itself. His life changed from that day. He also loved and cherished his little brother, his brave little brother, with all his heart.

CHAPTER TWO

Margaret and Benjamin Border, Sambo's parents, divorced a year before Sambo turned five. His brother, Charlie, two years younger than Sambo, suffered the separation from their mother greatly when their father gained permanent custody. The boys found some solace in their strengthening bonds of brotherhood, but yearned desperately for the return of their precious mother to their lives.

School holidays were generally an unhappy affair for the boys as they had to split their time unequally between the two parents. The periods with their mother attracted a further reduction because of travelling distances on the ubiquitous Sunlander, a notoriously slow train wending its way along the east coast of Queensland, Australia, stopping at every cowpat or outhouse on the way. To the young boys, there was no reason for the train to stop in the middle of nowhere with nothing but stunted Aussie scrub as far as the eye could see in any direction. They did not know that the train provided the mail, the lifeblood of the country, for the residents of the scattered communities, sheep stations and farms along the line.

Sambo and Charlie made a conscious decision to enjoy the ride despite the monotonous scenery 'flashing' by the window of their sleeping-berth cabin, paid for by their mother, who struggled with the expense. Margaret made sure to send them enough pocket money beforehand to purchase meals aboard the train. Sambo ensured they saved much of this money when he discovered his favourite card game, poker, being played in the club car until all hours. From the age of ten (the conductor saw only an innocent game of poker being played with matches), Sambo's winnings at the game ensured a comfortable ride for the boys with enough money (each match was worth a dollar), left over to enjoy the three remaining days of their week with their mother. Brisbane to Ingham on the train was a four-day return journey in those days.

Sambo took his responsibilities seriously. He had a younger brother in tow, who idolised him for reasons that Sambo had yet to determine. The two brothers developed an unshakeable bond from the moment they found themselves without a permanent mother. Sambo knew they were being used by their father as a means of revenge against their mother. This was exacerbated with strict rules such as calling their mother's new husband, "The Bastard". Their father would not allow any other name for the man to be uttered within his hearing.

The first time their mother heard Charlie referring to her new husband with that offensive moniker, she nearly fainted. Sambo knew enough to ignore his father's instructions while in their mother's home, but Charlie was just too young at first to understand. Charlie was also too fearful to go against his father's orders.

The boys had often enough copped a hiding with a belt or ironing cord for supposed transgressions. One only had to speak too loudly on a Saturday morning, when the old man was listening to the racing tips on the radio, to warrant an ear-bashing at best or a thrashing. Worse, in Sambo's opinion, was the cold, hard stare of absolute derision in his father's eyes at those times. It seemed that the boys were never able to please their father or do anything right, but were always on the receiving end of a tongue-lashing for one thing or another.

Christmas was the best of the holidays, enabling them to spend longer, a week, with their mother, who always managed to provide a special getaway location at those times. As well as the hostilities they experienced in their father's home, they suffered the humiliation and degradation of poverty through their father's excesses. Gambling, drinking and smoking took care of most of their father's meagre earnings as an unskilled worker, bumming around from one job to another with weeks-to-months in between of unemployment when no money was forthcoming.

These incomeless periods proved to be their father's undoing on the few occasions when he ran afoul of the law. He stole stuff, mainly to pay the rent when his 'sure-fire' bets didn't come off: the bloody nags still running, no doubt. Then there were the never-ending shortcuts. Their father was notorious for doing things just that little bit askew of the way anyone else would do them. Sambo learned that there were three ways of doing something in life - the right way, the wrong way, and his father's way. Benjamin Border, Ben, or Benbo to his friends, always had a scheme or two going. They weren't even good enough to be called confidence schemes. They were just useless attempts at defrauding the government or insurance companies or employers. Every get-rich-quick scheme he proposed ended up landing them all further in the shit.

Sambo had lost count of the number of times they had to relocate because his father failed to come up with the back-rent on a dilapidated shack in some shithole of a town, moving farther and farther away from their mother each time. His dad had the gift of the gab, though. Anyone that came into contact with their father was immediately drawn to him, befriending him and remaining loyal despite being ripped off by him.

"Loan us a tenner 'til payday, Bob?"

"Give us a loan of the car to get to work, Jim?"

"Wanna go halves in a sure-fire win on the fifth in Melbourne?" he'd ask the unsuspecting suckers.

Without fail, none of the 'loans' were repaid, and none of his tips ever bore fruit. Why anyone was taken in with his patter left Sambo baffled. His father could sweet-talk a bum into giving up his last fag. Anything of value the boys ever owned, compliments of their mother or earned by them, soon found its way to the pawnbrokers, never to be seen again. The worst of those infractions ever, in Sambo's case, was when they returned to live in Brisbane for a time.

Sambo managed to get a job as a paperboy at the age of fourteen. He would haul his newspapers behind him in a metal cart.

On Friday afternoons, he would sell *The Telegraph* at the stop-lights on Baroona Road, Milton. Saturday and Sunday mornings would see him struggling with his heavy load of *The Courier Mails* and *Sunday Suns*, as well as a smattering of magazines, in any weather, up the very steep Annie Street in Auchenflower, then across the top road and down Payne Street on the other side.

Sambo's unquestionable work ethic soon saw him extending his activities with the newsagent to collecting subscriber money for the papers thrown over the fence, after his Saturday morning paper run. Often he worked at rolling those papers for that service at midnight. Then he would finish his weekend by selling chiko rolls at Lang Park on Sunday afternoon to the footy crowd. In one year of working his little heart out, Sambo managed to save over two thousand dollars in a bank account set up for him with his father acting as trustee, as Sambo was too young to have one in his own right.

Sambo would often stare at the balance in his bank book with pride, knowing how hard he had worked to earn that sum. There were many times on blistering hot mornings with a cart-load of nearly a thousand papers, when he did not believe his under-developed little body would cope with the strain. He never gave up, though, determination and courage etched on his features to make it to the top of Annie Street come what may. Sambo did not attain his full height of 183 cm until well into his eighteenth year. Before that, he topped the tape at a little over 120cm, with a reed-thin frame.

One Monday afternoon, when a particularly successful weekend at the footy grand finals saw him earn in excess of a hundred dollars, he entered the bank just prior to closing time at three o'clock to deposit his earnings. He did not trust carrying that much money on his person on school banking day once a week, a Wednesday. He had taken his bankbook and his earnings from his desk at home after leaving school early without opening the book.

Sambo waited patiently in line for his turn to approach the teller window. He normally kept only a few dollars from his earnings each week with which to purchase a model aeroplane from the newsagent where he worked. His hobby had seen a collection of superbly painted models adorning his room's bookstand, and hanging from the ceiling.

"Excuse me, miss, there seems to be a mistake. That amount can't be right", said Sambo, upon hearing the young female teller declare the new balance of his account.

"It's right there in your bankbook, Master Border," declared the teller. "I put a stamp right next to the amount you just deposited to make it official", she said a little fearfully, hoping she had not made an error on her second day of employment.

"But it says that two thousand dollars was taken out on Friday. I didn't take any money out of my account, miss. I couldn't have. Bank closes at three, and I don't get out of school till then. I only get to leave a bit earlier on a Monday", insisted Sambo, close to panic.

It seemed an eternity waiting for the bank manager to be called to sort out the perplexing problem right on closing time.

"Master Border, sorry to keep you waiting. I had to find out which of our tellers was on duty Friday afternoon. You understand that it is always our busiest time of the week with everyone wanting to do their banking and drawing cash from their wage cheques before the weekend?" asked the manager, Mr Compton, with a friendly expression. Mr Compton was particularly proud of his young customer who diligently banked his weekend's earnings every Monday afternoon.

"Yes, well, it turns out that Mrs Roberts attended the windows on Friday afternoon and remembers clearly that your father, who is the trustee for your account, withdrew those funds. All quite above board, I assure you. Mrs Roberts was informed that you were aware of the transaction upon questioning your father about the rather large withdrawal. Was that not the case, Master Border?"

"Um, yeah, sure. That's right...I forgot. Sorry to cause a fuss, Mr Compton. I'm just a stupid kid, I guess. Forget my own head if it wasn't screwed on tight", Sambo laughed nervously, not for one moment convincing the astute Mr Compton.

"Master Border, the moment you turn sixteen I would like you to come and see me personally. I will set up a new account for you under your own name, eh? We'll keep your bankbook here at the branch so no one will know how much you have or be able to access your account. How does that sound to you?" The embarrassed manager patted the sweat off his bald head with a handkerchief.

"Thanks, Mr Compton. Probably won't be here then, but thanks, anyway," said Sambo, attempting to hold back the tears.

On his homeward journey, Sambo's shoulders shook with rage and despair. Those passing him became concerned for the young boy's welfare, finally conceding defeat at the lad's inconsolable grief. Believing he had suffered the loss of someone close to him, they offered their condolences before wandering away, uncertainly, shaking their heads.

Sambo quit his job at the newsagent the following week. He never returned to Lang Park to sell chiko rolls or watch the footy. Never in all his years to follow, did Sambo ever manage to salvage that lost zeal for business and earnest saving. While he managed to make substantial sums regularly in later years, he never regained the exuberance for hard work and its rewards. His old man had killed that spirit within him.

A few months later, in one of his rare moments of guilt, Sambo's father tried to mend some broken bridges with his son by offering him some silver bullion bars by way of reparation for the boy's 'borrowed' bank funds. Sambo finally accepted the bars under duress, knowing full-well the eventual outcome of the gesture.

Sure enough, to rub salt into the wound, two weeks later the silver bars went missing. His father attempted to chastise his son for being careless with his possessions, but Sambo wasn't fooled for a second. A trip to the local pawnshop soon corroborated his suspicions. There, in the window, among the items that were advertised as new stock, Sambo witnessed the two silver bars nestled within the satin-lined cigar box that he had fashioned for the items.

Sambo never forgave his father for that indiscretion, nor the continuing treatment he and his brother suffered under the yoke of his tyranny. Any respect he may once have expressed for his father withered to inexistence like a corpse consumed by eons of decay.

So, earning a little extra with his poker games during their train trips to visit their mum helped them out enormously to keep them well fed on the long journey. It was Christmas, and the boys were overjoyed to be spending an extended stay with their mum, who had organised a very special destination for their holiday.

Margaret lived and worked in Ingham, where she owned and managed a hairdressing salon. No longer married to her second husband, Margaret managed to squirrel away a fair sum to pay for what she believed would be a grand time with her children.

On several occasions over the preceding years, she had taken day trips to a resort on Orpheus Island in the Palm Island group. On one of those trips, she befriended a man whose parents leased a section of the island with a beach shack tucked away in their own private cove. Margaret negotiated a deal whereby she would holiday in the vacated house with her sons for a week, in exchange for his resort duties for a day, freeing the man to pursue other interests. The resort was nestled in a picturesque bay about three kilometres away, as the crow flies, from the private residence.

It was agreed that the boys, then fifteen and thirteen years old, would be dropped off at the holiday house while Margaret would continue on to the resort to perform her duties. She would then get a lift from the assistant manager, using a dinghy from the resort, to join the children the following morning.

The boys were enjoying themselves immensely throughout the hot morning upon reaching the tranquil bay housing the holiday home. No sooner had their possessions been stowed in one of the rooms and their mother departed, when the boys donned their swimming trunks to venture down to the beach. The tide was going out to reveal sandy and muddy stretches far out into the bay, ending at coral outcrops. The boys decided to explore the sandy flats and the coral at the edge of the water, more than a kilometre from the shore.

After the tropical sun had been beating upon them for hours, they decided to return to the house to freshen up and have some lunch. After discovering a shower, Sambo elected to rinse the salt and sweat from his body. Sambo and his brother had to endure many a cold shower over the years when their father was too poor to afford a home with running hot water. Luckily, it was Queensland, so it never became icy, but it bothered Sambo nonetheless. He detested cold water in any form. Charlie never had a problem with diving into the cold water of an inland creek or under a waterfall, but Sambo always shied from it.

Sambo was determined to have a warm shower. There was no electricity on the island. A diesel generator provided the minimal power required for lights and entertainment. The fridge and large freezer with blocks of ice ran on bottled gas, while the shower water was heated via methylated spirits. A tall stainless-steel cylindrical tube situated next to the shower, through which ran the water, had a metal tray located directly below it. In the tray, one poured a small quantity of methylated spirits, which was then lit. That produced the heat to warm the water.

Sambo had seen it done for him often enough by his father when they had a home with a similar set-up. He poured the requisite amount of spirits into the tray after undressing. He then lit the liquid with the matches provided, sitting on a shelf beside the cylinder.

With the water turned on, Sambo could not understand why it was not getting warm. The bathroom was bright with sunlight, as it was the middle of the day, and Sambo's inexperienced eyes could not detect a flame in the tray. Neither could he distinguish any fluid left in the tray. Believing the fluid had been used already and the flame had petered out, Sambo decided to pour some more liquid into the tray to repeat the process.

Anyone familiar with methylated spirits would know that it burns with a nearly invisible flame, indistinguishable to Sambo through the harsh glare entering via the window. When more liquid was added to the tray, the invisible flame travelled quickly into the bottle to cause a mighty explosion. The burning liquid fell directly onto Sambo's bare legs. Stunned by the concussion of the blast, Sambo peered down at his legs; totally aflame...

CHAPTER THREE

Sambo was wrong when he suggested to Mr Compton that he would in all likelihood not be around when he turned sixteen. He had no way of knowing that they would remain in Brisbane for longer than the usual eighteen months or so normally spent in one location. He had almost lost count of the number of schools he attended in his primary years. School was always a trying time for the boys, seen always as new meat for the seasoned natives. They were never around long enough to establish lasting friendships or join like-minded groups where safety in numbers precluded the normal hassles.

Sambo's diminutive stature did little to enhance his standing among his peers. The primitive and animalistic attitudes among the youth attending the lower socio-economic public schools assured the newcomers of a rough welcome and continuing discrimination. When Sambo advanced to high school, leaving his younger brother behind, he feared greatly for Charlie's safety. He need not have been concerned. Charlie's pleasant, obsequious nature usually won over most in his age group. He also tended to be a fraction taller and heavier-set than most boys his age, deterring all but the most determined.

On his sixteenth birthday, having received no more than a nod and a 'howdy' from his old man, Sambo planned to hit the pool at Ithaca, down on Caxton Street, in the afternoon. As his birthday fell in summer, it was certainly hot enough to merit a cooling dip in the pool. It was January 4th, 1974, three weeks before the worst floods in Brisbane's history on January 27th. The Ithaca pool, to which Sambo was heading, would be out of action for extended periods following the floods, as residents came to terms with the mountains of mud and silt on the streets and in their homes. For months the streets in the worst affected areas were filled with ruined furniture, bedding and carpeting, rotting and reeking in the hot summer sun.

With scant acknowledgment from his father on the morning of his birthday, (not that any was expected), Sambo happily accepted a gift from Charlie. When Sambo removed the plain brown-paper wrapping, he was delighted and distressed to see a box containing a model aeroplane kit he had sought for some years. Sambo was overjoyed at receiving the thoughtful gift but dismayed at the cost of such an expensive item. Upon questioning his brother, it was revealed that the boy had surreptitiously removed the amount required in small instalments from their father over the course of a year. That explanation caused Sambo to smile.

During the morning, with their father glued to a radio constantly blaring all the latest about horse racing, Sambo closed the door of his shared room to concentrate on building his model accompanied by his own listening pleasure. He detested the sound of the radio, or, rather, the subject matter. Charlie and he had invested a little of their hard-earned money on a portable record player, on which they played a variety of vinyl records. Sambo's favourite at the time was Suzi Quatro, whom he listened to most often. Sequestered in his room, building his model aeroplane, listening to the 'dulcet' tones (loud music on a Saturday morning was prohibited upon the promise of severe punishment), of his favourite performer, ensured a perfect start to his birthday in Sambo's opinion.

As he toiled at the task, entering a 'zone' where random thoughts occupied his mind while his hands moved on their own accord at the accustomed activity, Sambo recalled a haunting dream from the previous evening. Not a nightmare by any means, but a troubling dream nonetheless, though he could not identify the cause of those disturbing impressions. Part of the reason he wanted to venture down to the Ithaca pool was that it featured in his dream. He struggled to recall the exact details while retaining the essence of it in the emotions it evoked.

He was undecided whether the dominant emotion he felt was

happiness or an overwhelming sadness, as they seemed to be two sides of the same coin. Snippets of clarity mixed with blurred images made it impossible to make real sense of the dream. One scene, in particular, concerned Sambo. A house, a mauve house, played prominently in the scene. Then there were other aspects of the dream that engendered a heart-rending yearning that left Sambo aching inside without explanation or reason.

He remembered waking in the middle of the night in tears, sweating profusely. He tried desperately to recall the particulars of the dream, yet it was all so ephemeral. The only clear aspect he recalled was the emotion that tore at him like no feeling he had ever experienced. His heart was filled with an abundance of joy. Then, in a flash, the opposite emotion crushed him in a vice-like grip that threatened to squeeze the essence from his soul, leaving him a desiccated husk.

Try as he might while working away at his hobby, Sambo could shed no light on the mysterious dream or derive any sense from the resulting emotions. He had no difficulty reliving the intense feelings whenever he delved into the memories, but fell short of visualising the entire episode. He did not normally ascribe to any paranormal beliefs, portents or predictions other than the vague notion of his destiny after the accident a year earlier. He did not even place much store in the benefits or otherwise of those nocturnal theatrics. He was unable to explain the reason for dreams, particularly nightmares, and did not feel the necessity to do so. Dreams happened and that was that as far as he was concerned.

Walking along Heussler Terrace on his way to the pool, Sambo thought no more of the strange dream. After his pleasant morning spent in aeronautical construction, he was looking forward to an afternoon of relaxation by the pool. Weather forecasts had been predicting unprecedented rain in the near future with a weakened cyclone Wanda in the north playing a part, so he utilised the opportunity to indulge in aquatic leisure while it lasted. The day was steamy, in the high thirties and almost ninety per cent humidity, redolent of far north Queensland rather than the typically milder climate of Brisbane.

He noticed her the second he came through the turnstile. She sat on a towel wearing a very brief bikini. Her unblemished alabaster complexion contrasted dramatically against the black towel and matching swimsuit. Her auburn hair was tied back with a silken ribbon of black, topped off with a black sun-shade. Something about her just compelled Sambo to stare at her open-mouthed. There was an elegance in her repose that belied her youth. In Sambo's inexperienced estimation, she could have been anywhere from sixteen to twenty-something years-old. She had an open paperback on her lap, which she may or may not have been reading when Sambo first saw her. It was impossible to tell where her eyes were focused behind the popular, uber-large, dark sunglasses of the period.

Sambo stumbled to a place on the grass opposite her, the pool between them, without bothering to deflect his gaze from the magnetic vision. The crocheted bikini allowing tantalising glimpses of that pure alabaster flesh to peek through. He was too far away to actually see anything more than a hint of colour there, but Sambo's imagination was managing to embellish the reality. She had one of those collapsible lean-to beach chairs whereby she was able to support her back while sitting on the grass.

When Sambo reached his desired space on the green grass at the side of the pool, he was self-conscious about his need to remain in long trousers while swimming. His doctors had cautioned him about exposing his burn scars to sunlight. He worried how his uncool dress mode would seem to the most beautiful girl in the world.

At sixteen, he remained a virgin, though he had an inkling as to what sex was all about. He basically knew that appendage, A slotted into receptacle B, with a whole lot of sweating and panting in between. He had flogged himself enough since the age of fourteen to know exactly what all that sweating and panting was supposed to produce. However, that was fairly much the extent of his knowledge.

Sambo was a very pretty boy, never having any difficulty attracting the opposite gender in school. That was most likely part of the problems he faced during his school days from very jealous competitors who suddenly failed to maintain their beaus' affections once they had caught sight of Sambo. His unassuming, quiet and modest nature, coupled with his unblemished good looks, enticed girl, woman, or male to make his acquaintance. Unfortunately for Sambo, many a dirty old man made lurid suggestions to him over the years, disgusting him no end. He was unsure where appendage A factored into the equation in that scenario and didn't want to find out.

He managed to have a relatively steady relationship with a few girls during his high school years, but they had never escalated to more than kissing and cuddling. Several of his girlfriends had intimated they would be willing to extend that unsatisfactory limitation to their relationship, but for Sambo, none of his friendships had reached the point where he had wanted to share himself completely. He was not overwhelmed with the urgent desire he witnessed in most of his peers, who seemed to live for nothing else, speak of nothing else and most often, had nothing of intelligence to contribute other than sexual exploits.

The jocks in school scored with anyone they wanted. The drama students were in a permanent state of sexual arousal regardless of gender, seemingly willing to 'get it on' at the drop of a hat. Nerds were nerds in school and wouldn't begin their sexual journey until they appeared affluent, while Sambo simply drifted along without the burning desire to fuck everything in sight. He hoped to make his first time with a female a more dignified and poignant episode in his life, even though that notion was outdated.

He was able to communicate with girls on their level while his football-playing peers would recoil at conversation with the opposite sex. Sambo did not play footy, or cricket, or any other sport requiring gladiatorial prowess. He was fit enough and fast enough, but always lacked the size for those conquests of strength and brutality. He was frequently mistaken for, and often called, a poof by his peers even though he would almost exclusively be found in female company. Sometimes, when at his lowest, Sambo began to doubt his own sexuality when it seemed he did not share the uncontrollable lust exhibited by almost every other boy in school. He never acted on those doubts, however, recognising them for the falsehoods they were.

Eventually, he settled onto his towel to soak up the warm summer sunshine, allowing all but his legs to absorb the glorious abundance of nature. He lay on his stomach facing the pool. Only one family with a sevenish-year-old girl splashing away in the shallow end of the pool, and the perfect apparition opposite, were in attendance that day. The girl's parents, seated on towels a distance from the pool on his side, seemed to be in a heated debate. The girl splashed and sang happily by herself, totally absorbed in her own world. In those days, the Ithaca pool was in its infancy, with only a single pool, a brick kiosk, a couple of lean-to shelters and a small grandstand. It was early on a Saturday afternoon, with rain threatened for the following day, and so remained relatively unoccupied.

Whenever Sambo glanced at the figure opposite, legs slightly splayed, showing a patch of black bikini between the magnificent pale thighs, Sambo felt the reaction in his groin as it pressed hard against the ground. He had to force himself to look elsewhere so as not to embarrass himself when he eventually rose to have a swim. He was racking his brains to come up with a reasonable excuse to introduce himself, to strike up a conversation with the loveliest, sexiest female on the planet. He did not normally find it difficult to talk to girls. He certainly never indulged in those ridiculous one-liners that made the rounds once a day among the boys in school.

Finally, he managed to control his male impulses enough to risk standing. His intention was to casually walk around the pool to say hello, but he sensed that something was amiss. It was very quiet, with little traffic. Something about the unusual quiet struck a chord in Sambo. It should not have been that quiet for some reason that he could not immediately identify. Then it came to him. The singing! He had been hearing the singing and the splashing for the last hour. Everything had fallen silent. He cast his eyes about. The parents were still engaged in an animated conversation and he could not see the young girl.

He immediately concluded that the girl had gone off to the toilet, chastising himself for making too much of the silence. It was only a nagging sensation in the back of his mind that forced him to continue his careful observations as he walked toward the edge of the pool.

Upon witnessing the limp figure at the bottom of the pool, Sambo dove in immediately. When he rose to the surface with the lightweight parcel, he placed her gently on the tiled surface at the edge. As he hoisted himself out of the water he glanced at the young couple still too engrossed in their argument to take notice of their surroundings.

"Hey! Hey, folks. Your girl..." Sambo shouted as he crouched over the inert girl.

Without waiting for the pair to respond, Sambo sprang into action, following the protocols he had learned about pool safety in school as part of the bronze medal certification. He placed his mouth over the young girl's, blowing five quick, shallow breaths before turning his attention to chest compressions as his instructor advised. Fifteen short, sharp compressions, followed by another set of breaths. The girl started spluttering just as the frantic parents arrived on the scene, pushing Sambo roughly aside.

The father especially, seemed ropeable, as though he wanted to inflict pain and suffering on the boy.

"What the fuck do you think you're doing?"

"What, I don't..." stammered Sambo.

"How dare you touch our daughter, you pervert!" screamed the mother.

"No, I..."

"Come here you piece of shit," yelled the father as he advanced toward Sambo, who was backpedalling on all fours to avoid the irate man.

"Oy! He just saved your daughter's life, you idiot. You should be thanking him instead of blaming him for something that was your own fault. What sort of parents are you that you wouldn't keep an eye on your precious girl all alone in the pool?" asked the bikini-clad girl approaching the group.

"You keep out of it. We saw him kissing our girl, the..." started the mother.

"Yeah, kiss of life it's called. Your daughter nearly drowned, and if you hadn't been fighting all morning you would have prevented it. This boy just saved your daughter's life. Don't you get it? She nearly died!"

"Bullshit!" Spat the father.

"Yeah, right. You're feeling guilty as hell and are offloading that onto the boy, a hero. Both of you should be reported for negligence and have your daughter taken away from you as far as I am concerned. I will definitely tell the police that when they show up." As she argued the angel was enveloped in a wonderful, shimmering halo of sunlight as Sambo peered up at her from his position on the ground.

At that moment he knew, beyond a shadow of a doubt, that he was one hundred per cent in love for the first time in his life. He would walk over broken glass with bare feet for the goddess before him. There was literally nothing she could not ask of him. The vision of her captivated his attention to the exclusion of all else. Her velvet voice and statuesque figure, bathed in sunshine, infused his heart with desire and admiration.

An hour later, after the police had interviewed them all when the parents refused to accept anyone else's version of the events, Sambo recovered from his reverie. He was dismayed to find the girl was gone. The police had dismissed the parents' accusations out-of-hand. After speaking to the girl in black and the man behind the pool's kiosk counter, they were satisfied that Sambo was a hero and that the parents should be praising him instead of making up stories to cover up their own inadequacies as parents.

Sambo wandered home in a daze, cursing himself for not asking the woman of his drea... Then Sambo remembered the dream. The uncanny feeling he experienced the moment he set foot on the pool grounds, and the hairs standing up on the back of his neck, the shiver down the spine – they were all the signs one associates with dejá vu. The girl in the black bikini was the girl that appeared in his disturbing dream the previous evening.

CHAPTER FOUR

The heavens opened up that evening and continued for three weeks straight. An exceptionally wet spring meant that by the end of October most of the main southern river systems were at capacity. Cyclone Wanda pushed those systems to the limit by drawing the monsoonal trough southward. The Brisbane, Bremer and Stanley Rivers' catchment areas caught the additional rainfall to produce the state's worst-ever flooding. During a thirty-six hour period beginning the evening of the 25th of January, 642mm of rain fell on the city of Brisbane. The flood toll included sixteen fatalities, 300 injured, 8,000 homes destroyed and over 900 million dollars in damages.

From their home in Rosalie, Sambo and Charlie watched in dreaded fascination as the water level rose around their neighbourhood. The flood peaked at 6.6 metres, 22 feet, on the 27th. Benjamin Border had taken the precaution of moving all their furniture atop tables and such to prevent the ruin of the sofas and other vulnerable items. The carpet was lifted wherever possible and the nervous wait began.

They escaped the wrath of the flood waters by a mere two centimetres. The waves lapped at the underside of the floorboards but did not enter the house.

On the opposite side of their street, their neighbour's houses were all under water to the eaves, with only their roofs showing above the swirling brown maelstrom. Every wooden fence post or surface above the water harboured reptilian, mammalian or entomological refugees. Lizards, snakes, rodents and cockroaches huddled together to escape the deadly current threatening to wash everything away in its irresistible path.

The following days and weeks were filled with tears of hardship and grief for lost lives, livelihoods, homes and precious possessions.

Everywhere they looked along the streets of their suburb, the footpaths were lined with stinking, mud-soaked household goods and furniture. Sambo and Charlie joined the throngs of residents offering a helping hand to push mud from houses, remove furniture, carpet, lino, fridges, stoves, books and photo albums ruined beyond repair or recognition. The generosity of the Australian spirit was never more evident than in the aftermath of that tragic event. Complete strangers toiled for weeks to help one another for no more than a handshake or a thank-you from the grateful recipients.

Sambo lived in one of the worst affected areas because of its low-lying proximity to the Brisbane River. Insurance companies went broke, stranding policy-holders in limbo with nowhere to live. It was months before a semblance of order and clear footpaths returned to the region. Brisbane had taken a mighty beating, but the good folks prevailed to assist those less fortunate and helped restore faith in humanity.

When Sambo and Charlie returned to their home after the last time they were needed by their neighbours, they fell into bed to sleep like the dead. Only Sambo found it difficult to remain asleep very long because of the persistent dreams of his lost love. He had not been able to find the girl, though admittedly he did not have much free time to search. His nights were plagued by the recollections of that day at the pool. Every minute detail was played over and over in his mind until it set like concrete in his brain. He yearned desperately to know her name, talk to her, walk with her, hold her hand, and make love to her for the rest of his days.

Not long after the floods, Sambo left school to begin fulltime employment as a hardware assistant in the northern suburbs. The daily commute to his job in the peak-hour traffic on a combination of bus and train took its toll on his patience. He earned enough to perhaps live on his own in a small flat or room closer to his place of employment but remained where he was for two major reasons. His first obligation was to his younger brother. He did not want to leave his brother alone to suffer the tirades of their father. Nor did he wish to remove himself from the vicinity of the pool, which he visited every second Saturday.

During his rostered days off and Sundays, Sambo roamed the streets around his home endlessly in search of her. His dreams were entirely about her. He was obsessed with her to the exclusion of nearly all else, barely eating and sleeping enough to function normally. During that time, while purportedly remaining in the family home to offer Charlie his support, he tended to pay less and less attention to his little brother.

One Saturday morning about a year after he started his employment, while Sambo was dressing in light summer clothes to prepare for his morning exploration of a new section of a different suburb, Charlie was being unusually boisterous and noisy, playing his records at a higher volume than usual. The boys still shared a single room in the two-bedroom house, all that their father could afford despite demanding half of Sambo's take-home pay as lodgings. Charlie was playing out a battle scene with his toy soldiers, despite being nearly fifteen years old, with all the accompanying sound effects.

"Charlie, keep it down a bit, and turn the music off, will you? Old Benbo will hit the ceiling if his tips come on and he can't hear them properly. You're getting a bit old for all that stuff now anyway, mate. You're in high school, for crying out loud!"

"Bit old to be still looking for a fantasy girl who you flog yourself over most nights, aren't you?"

"If you're going be like that, you can get stuffed. Don't say I didn't warn you," said Sambo as he stormed out of the room.

As he walked through the short hall to the kitchen, he noticed his father setting himself up at the kitchen table with his usual assortment of Saturday papers and turf booklets, portable radio turned on, already blurting out the annoying racing rubbish. If Sambo never again heard another racing commentary, it would be too soon. He grabbed a bottle of Coke from the fridge before stalking out of the front door, careful not to disturb his old man.

He normally wandered the streets until at least lunchtime. His searches became a great way to gain some much-needed exercise and explore his neighbourhood. He would walk either side of the Milton railway line, depending on his moods. Sometimes he would find himself drifting towards the centre of the city to lose himself in the shopping crowds on Queen Street, or to stop at the Regent theatre to take in a movie when his enthusiasm flagged.

On that Saturday morning, he found himself on Roma Street, having lunch at a coffee shop. He could hear the trains rumbling into the busy Roma Street station across the road from the café. A never-ending stream of passengers poured in and out of the packed trains until lunchtime. After twelve o'clock on a Saturday, the city shut down in those days.

This was a symptom of the Bjelke-Petersen era, when a red-necked peanut farmer held the entire state in a perpetual time-lock from 1968-1987, when progress was halted by draconian, puritanical ideals. The state of Queensland was to become the laughing stock of the world with Joh Bjelke-Petersen and his wife Flo (of pumpkin scone fame), adopting the roles of clowns in a three-ring political circus. If it wasn't so pathetic, it would have been funny.

The despotic regime eventually came tumbling down amid reports and enquiries about bribery and corruption on a grand scale filling the news. Although the Bjelke clan was knee-deep in the proverbial, none of it ever really stuck. Their reputations were besmirched by accusations and innuendo, but they escaped the public condemnation and imprisonment of other high-ranking government officials during the inquests that followed.

It was not until the World Expo of 1988 that Brisbane finally matured into a modern cosmopolitan city. The development of the unsightly south bank into a prime commercial real estate concern, transformed the sleepy country town into a veritable jewel well-able to compete on a world stage, and open all weekend and some nights. Queenslanders flocking to New South Wales to play the pokies were able to gamble legally in their own state when the gambling laws changed.

On that Saturday afternoon, when Sambo sat down for a sandwich and a cup of instant coffee, (barista-style coffee being not yet in vogue), Brisbane was still in the thrall of its backward-thinking local government. After Sambo had finished his bad coffee, he made his way back to his house via a circuitous route that would allow him to investigate another part of the area.

When Sambo returned home an hour after leaving the coffee shop, he was puzzled to find the front door locked. His father would normally be home unless he was planning to go to the track, either Doomben or Eagle Farm. However, Sambo would always be warned if that were the case so that he would be home to care for Charlie, though it was hardly essential for a boy of fifteen.

The note attracted Sambo's attention the moment he stepped into the kitchen, being the only thing on the red laminate table, weighed down by one of Sambo's model aeroplanes; a Spitfire. In his father's scrawl, he read the ominous message that Ben had taken Charlie to hospital.

Sambo determined that they would have gone to the Royal Brisbane Hospital on Bowen Bridge Road. He knew he could get there on foot faster than if he waited for the bus, knowing the timetables as well as he did, and taking into account the hourly or worse intervals between buses on a Saturday afternoon. Sambo ran with his heart in his mouth all the way. His knowledge of all the streets around his home afforded him intimate details of the quickest route to the hospital.

When Sambo was finally allowed to visit briefly with his brother that evening, he put on a brave face for his little mate. Though by no means conclusive, as Charlie was still in a coma, the diagnosis of brain damage sat uncomfortably in Sambo's mind. When he entered the intensive care ward, where he saw the boy attached to tubes and wires, head and other body parts heavily bandaged, he broke down. He stood beside his brother's bed and whispered softly. His father sat in a corner chair holding his head in his hands, unable to hear what Sambo was saying.

"What happened?" asked Sambo when the pair returned home later that evening.

"He, he was playing with his soldiers and running around the house. I, I told him to go play outside, to, to give me a bit of quiet. I didn't even hear the brakes squeal, just the screaming afterwards..."

"Bullshit!" declared Sambo in a cold, quiet tone, the white-hot rage building within making him tremble.

"What? What did you just say to me?"

"I said 'bullshit', mister." He was nearly whispering, making it difficult for his father to hear.

"What are you talking about? Why, why would you say such a thing? You're upset..."

"Fuckin' oath I am. I'm upset at you bullshitting me and I am furious over Charlie's condition."

"How dare you talk to your father like that?"

"How dare you call you yourself my father? I know exactly what happened. Charlie didn't just run out of here and on to the road while he was innocently playing outside. He knew better than that. I've seen him out there...dad! He knew the score, knew not to venture onto the roads...daaaaad!"

"I'm going to allow you to get away with this just this once..."

"But I won't allow *you* to get away with it. Charlie was playing noisily this morning. I had to tell him to be quiet before I left. I warned him not to bug you. He did, though. Didn't he? He kept going after I left and he disturbed your precious horse tips, didn't he, Ben? You chased him. You got your fucking dander up because he spoiled your stupid race shit, and you chased him out of here and onto the road. The only reason Charlie would ever do that is if he was running for fear. For fear of you when he knows he will cop a beating from you."

"You ungrateful..." Ben advanced threateningly on his son.

"Touch me and you'll be sorry," said Sambo, standing his

ground. "Don't you dare ever touch me again, you bastard. If Charlie dies, I will kill you. No matter how long it takes, I'll find a way. You have abused us for the last time. If Charlie makes it, you'd better hope he never regains his full faculties, because I will go with him to the cops to see you behind bars for the rest of your miserable life when he corroborates my suspicions."

"Son..."

"Don't fucking 'son' me! I'm not your son; neither is Charlie. You abandoned us years ago. You tortured us with your vindictive games against our mother. You left us to rot and starve while you wasted our money on the fucking horses. You robbed us, stole every last cent we ever made to put on the gee-gees or whatever latest harebrained scheme you were cooking up. You abused us every chance you got, you fucking coward. If you say one thing more to me I will go straight to the cops with a long list of all the times you belted us kids. I'll make sure they marry up all those incidents with the hospital records. I have an 8mm recording of the last time you belted me in our room. I set up the camera I own when I knew I was going to cop it from you yet again.

"The only reason I haven't gone to the cops already is that you're going to pay for hurting Charlie, by providing for him for once in your rotten life. You are going to go to work every day, pay our bills like clockwork and deposit the rest of your wages into the bank account, which you will sign over to me. You won't spend one cent more on booze, gambling, or even smoking. One slip, you're going to face jail or worse. Don't believe me? Want to test me? Your own funeral. Go ahead. And make sure you never talk to me or Charlie again."

Sambo stormed from the kitchen, slamming his bedroom door, then fell onto the bed where he grieved quietly for his brother.

CHAPTER FIVE

Life changes in an instant for some. Tragedy or joy can alter someone's circumstances so dramatically that every dream or thought for their future disappears in the blink of an eye. Marriage, the birth of a baby, death and accident can all help to mould an entirely alternate destiny for the affected. Although Sambo believed he was meant for a higher calling or particular fate after his brush with death, he did not consider life as a full-time carer among those expectations.

While his job as a hardware assistant was hardly an exciting prospect as a career, it was a means of earning his own wage, with which to build his independence. After his younger brother was released from the hospital, upon waking from his coma, Sambo realised that his life could no longer follow the same path. His dreams and ambitions were no longer a priority or even a possibility. The severe trauma to Charlie's brain, when the bullbar of the Toyota Landcruiser struck him, left him a simpleton, unable to wipe his own arse, let alone achieve higher functions like dressing himself or attending school.

Sambo forced his father to refuse the offers of placing Charlie in an institution for the severely handicapped; essentially, a mental asylum. Sambo became Charlie's fulltime carer, assisting his little brother to live a life with as much dignity as possible. It was a messy, gut-wrenching, thankless task, which Sambo practised without complaint. He always kept a smile in his voice as he set about his daily duties, seeing to the comfort and cleanliness of his charge.

In those days, there was hardly any government assistance available for persons choosing to take on the responsibility of care for another. A pension as an invalid's assistant would have helped tremendously, but Sambo had to make do with Ben's meagre wage. He no longer referred to the man that made that wage as his father, or dad. As far as Sambo was concerned, the boys had no father. Their mother helped out as much as possible while she owned a hairdressing salon, but it was a token amount, all she could afford.

Even Sambo's mother often suggested that the burden he had undertaken was too much, that he should place his brother in a facility. Sambo's steadfast, polite refusal to relinquish care to anyone else gained him little respect or support from those around him. Charlie had very little control over his bodily functions, including mobility. He waved his arms around and managed to wriggle his legs a bit. His speech was limited to a drooling gibberish, which only Sambo could interpret, albeit with difficulty.

Before hydrotherapy became a popular method of rehabilitation, Sambo would wheel his brother down to the Ithaca pool in his wheelchair every Saturday afternoon to exercise Charlie's limbs. Regardless of the efficacy of such treatments, Sambo insisted that Charlie enjoyed the afternoons immensely. While it occasionally entered his mind that he might catch sight of the girl again whilst attending the pool regularly, his intentions were pure. He knew that Charlie loved his sessions in the water. Sambo could easily differentiate the moods of his brother by the facial tics and increased arm movements. Over the course of a year, Sambo noticed real improvements in his brother's motor control: he was even able to dog paddle on his own after a fashion.

Sambo's days were highly regimented, organised to a fault to ensure he spent as much quality time as possible with his brother. First thing in the morning, Sambo would see to Charlie's bath. He was able to leave his brother for a time alone in the shallow water while he removed his soiled bed linen, and pyjamas, which needed changing and washing every day. While Charlie wore nappies, they were ineffectual at retaining the contents during the night, when Charlie thrashed uncontrollably in his sleep.

Most nights saw Sambo having to comfort his young brother with soothing words and a song as the night terrors assailed the boy. Sambo knew that Charlie was reliving the horror of his accident over and over, as the boy almost mimicked the actions of being struck and run over. Sometimes, Charlie's voice became frighteningly lucid, uttering coherent sentences that described his thoughts as he relived his terror. Once or twice, Charlie would voice a shocking statement that would leave Sambo shaking with impotent rage. It was all he could do to prevent himself from walking straight into Ben's room and... He was never able to finish that line of thought. The fear Charlie voiced on those occasions confirmed Sambo's calculated assumption that Ben had chased Charlie out of the house that day.

Sambo knew that, one day, Ben would face a reckoning for his actions. Sambo was mature and intelligent enough to know that he would not bring that reckoning about because he had to be responsible for his brother. If something happened to Sambo, he knew his brother would no longer receive the level of care he deserved. He knew Charlie would end up in an institution where he would slowly die through neglect.

No one would or could stimulate his simple mind as Sambo did. No one else would read him stories or talk to him as though he were a real person with feelings and emotions. So Sambo stayed his hand, bit back the fury that consumed him at those times when Charlie was in the thrall of his nightmare, madly racing away from Ben, to be hit by a car over and over.

Sambo started to believe that caring for his brother was the calling for which he was intended all along. He could think of no higher purpose than the privilege of assisting the person he loved most in the world. He considered it an honour, an act he enjoyed instead of a duty. More than anything, he adored their time together on a Saturday afternoon. Alone, more often than not, or in a crowd, regardless of the amused or disgusted attitudes of anyone nearby, Sambo was thrilled by Charlie if he managed to propel himself across the breadth of the small pool. Sambo considered it a mighty achievement and applauded his brother enthusiastically every time.

Gradually, over the following year, due solely to Sambo's aquatherapy, Charlie regained a modicum of control over his limbs. Sambo believed that it was more a matter of retraining his brother's brain, to bypass the regular neural routes, to find new pathways with which to manipulate the unresponsive nerves. The hours upon hours that Sambo spent manually influencing the legs and arms while in the pool and at home, familiarised the new brain activity to accept the different neural messages.

Charlie's facial muscles were also gaining a semblance of normal functions, with Charlie able to mouth a garbled word or two. Best of all the glacially-slow improvements, in Sambo's opinion, was the renewed sparkle in Charlie's eyes. They were no longer vacant, limpid pools of non-participation. The eyes now followed Sambo's movements. At first, it was a mere glance, a hint of a reaction to something Sambo said, then a distinct movement as his face hovered above Charlie's while dressing or cleaning him.

Three long years after Charlie's accident, he was smiling. The first intelligible word Charlie uttered was "Thambo", which was repeated from morning till night. A few more words slowly crept into Charlie's repertoire. The agonisingly slow progress, often only witnessed by Sambo, had all the doctors shaking their heads in disbelief. Sambo had learned from the outset never to trust the word of the medical staff at the Royal Brisbane Hospital or any other quack. They either didn't care or didn't have the time or patience to believe that anything was possible. Before Charlie came out of his coma, they were urging the family to pull the plug on life support.

When Charlie survived the coma, they were adamant that a lack of brain activity meant institutionalisation was best for all concerned. Sambo fought the cold-hearted bastards all the way. The doctors and specialists urged Ben to 'do the right thing'. Ben had only to see the emphatic set to Sambo's shoulders and his icy stare to disregard the doctor's advice. Ben was beaten by Sambo's threats and the guilt he placed squarely on Ben's shoulders. He didn't attempt to talk to his son, scared senseless about what might happen if the truth came out. The guilt ate away at his insides until he found it difficult to hold down food to any extent. He lost weight and was often found crying pitifully during the night.

The conditions Sambo placed on Ben's behaviour saw him shaking and shivering with withdrawals in the first few weeks and months. Despite every fibre of his being begging him to forsake the sobriety, Ben overcame the weakness eventually. He refrained from booze, smoking and gambling to the best of Sambo's knowledge. Ben worked at his job, whatever it may be at the time, placing all the money into a bank account over which Sambo had complete control. The bills for Charlie's expenses, though onerous, were all paid on time.

Sambo did most of the cooking and cleaning so that Ben did not cop all the domestic duties on top of his employment. Sambo did not do this out of the goodness of his heart, it was his insurance that Ben would not use overwork as an excuse not to uphold his end of the bargain. Sambo learned everything from books he loaned from the library, or by watching shows on television. Any incident cropping up that required a specialist's attention for Charlie, or a tradesman for the house, Sambo would research thoroughly before attending to the matter himself. Sambo would trust no other person, medical or otherwise, to advise him about Charlie.

Sambo learned about bedsores, infections, and a myriad of general medical conditions pertaining to the invalid, which he attended to diligently. Thankfully, Charlie did not require constant X-rays or other treatments and tests. The medical profession had given up on the boy, believing his brain damage was irreversible and permanent. As far as they were concerned, Charlie was no more than a vegetable when Sambo bundled him into a wheelchair to leave the hospital. No amount of persuasion or instruction would sway the stubborn teenager and his father to listen to reason, so they washed their hands of the matter. Doctors were still viewed as demi-gods, despite much evidence to the contrary.

That the medical profession stuck to its guns, effectively negating the need to supervise continual testing, favoured Sambo in the end. He was left alone to administer his own regime of therapy, never believing for one second that his efforts were in vain. Regardless of the outcome, Sambo knew that his methods would at the very least inform Charlie that somebody cared and loved him. Even if Charlie was unreachable in the long run, Sambo knew that his efforts counted. When he eventually saw evidence of this, he was justifiably proud.

Of course, the moment the doctors became aware that improvements had been observed in a 'brain-dead' patient, the fraternity of celestials wanted a share of the notoriety, crawling over themselves to offer their educated and knowledgeable guidance. Sambo fended off one medico after another, hitting the books in the library in earnest to assess the value of all the reported therapies. His intuition and experience allowed him to pick and choose those methods that best suited his brother and himself. He could never be swayed by the rhetoric and guilt trips employed by the celestials to utilise their own award-winning, ground-breaking procedures.

Sambo saved every penny possible to purchase exercise equipment and all the necessary adjustments to their home to accommodate the semi-ambulatory boy. Ben would arrive home each day to find a new piece of equipment in the hallway: ramps, hydrotherapy bath, heat lamps and just about anything a hospital could provide. Space was at a premium in the tiny household, but Sambo would not contemplate relocation because of the convenient location to a public pool, still the ultimate in therapy as far as he was concerned.

While it appeared to all and sundry that Sambo was giving away his own life to bring about the reanimation of his brother, it mattered little to him. It was true that Sambo felt more than a little guilt for having left his brother that fateful morning to wander the streets in a fruitless search for his missing angel. Sambo raked over the coals of that incident in his mind almost every day, playing it out differently, analysing, dissecting and reconstructing the scenes. He knew it was wrong to place blame on himself when that rested squarely on the shoulders of the man parading as their father, but Sambo could not help it.

If he had remained in the house that morning, the 'accident' would never have occurred. However, that logic only went so far, for he knew it would just as likely have happened on another day, such was the state of Ben's propensity for violence. The accident may have manifested itself in countless other scenarios, all of which played out in Sambo's mind like a film reel of highlights and previews. Despite all the logical conclusions he attached to his role in the occurrence, Sambo still felt he was in some small way at fault. Therefore, it did not occur to him to question his complete involvement in his brother's rehabilitation.

That his own life of youthful pleasure and discovery was slowly ebbing into non-existence did not factor into his thoughts at all. Sambo concentrated every spare thought to extracting Charlie's trapped consciousness from within his damaged brain. No amount of internal or external interference would deter him from what he recognised as his destiny. He knew beyond a shadow of a doubt that he alone would bring Charlie into the light once more. He encountered evidence of his success in minute details every day. He learned to interpret the many inflections and nuances or repetitions of the way Charlie said "Thambo", to gauge his needs.

A series of three "Thambos" denoted a need for Charlie to go to the toilet. A long, drawn-out "Thaaaaaaambo", meant that Charlie was experiencing pain or was unhappy about something. A quick, staccato burst of two "Thambos", indicated a happy moment, always heard when they were swimming together. But when Charlie managed two particular words together, "Luh Thambo", it always melted his heart. To hear his brother say he loved him was his greatest reward. He knew he would never abandon his mission to release Charlie from the prison preventing him from joining the world.

CHAPTER SIX

"Thambo?"

"Yes, Charlie?"

"Chay thim guh?"

"Yes, Charlie swims good."

"Chay thim?"

"Of course you can. Off you go. Show me how you can swim to the other side."

"Thaaaaamboooo."

"No, you don't need me to help you. You've done it yourself lots of times, Charlie."

"Thambo, Thambo."

"Yep, it's good fun, isn't it? Charlie is a very good swimmer now."

"Thambo, Thambo," Charlie repeated exuberantly as he pushed off from the wall at the side of the pool where he had been standing with Sambo.

Charlie's motor skills improved dramatically. He was almost able to walk unaided, dress himself most mornings if he was able to concentrate - though he mostly mismatched his entire ensemble - and attend to his ablutions independently. Sambo discovered that his brother was growing into a deep thinker. If a particular thought entered his head, Charlie would cogitate on the matter until he arrived at a conclusion. Never able to fully express that opinion or conclusion with any degree of success, Charlie seemed satisfied having arrived there nonetheless. Success was usually pronounced with the "Thambo, Thambo", happy display.

Most profound of all the improvements in the ten years since the incident was the crystal-clear intelligence in Charlie's eyes. Those erudite portals to his inner thoughts and emotions contradicted his uncontrolled facial expressions and thrashing limbs. He knew that Charlie had an intelligence trapped in a brain that could not fully control his functions. But he saw the clear evidence of that intelligence shining through the eyes, often vexed with frustration at his inability to express himself properly.

It was a lazy Saturday afternoon nearing the end of summer. Sambo had accompanied his brother to the pool using only his walker. It was a long walk for Charlie, struggling over the bumpy footpaths with a sliding step motion that would eventually see him wear out his shoes and sandals at an alarming rate. Once Charlie managed to walk, he refused to be carted around in his wheelchair, pleading "Thaaaaambooooo" repeatedly until Sambo capitulated. While Sambo was tongue-tied with pride for his brother, the infuriatingly slow pace set by his him whenever they ventured to the pool tested his patience to the extreme.

Sambo would have to take Charlie down Baroona Road, then along Milton Road, to ensure a fairly flat path. The hills on Fernberg or Heussler Terrace, a far shorter route, precluded their use. Charlie's ambulatory prowess did not extend to hills, up or down. Crossing streets with gutter endings tested the friendship no end. It was an awkward affair requiring every ounce of Sambo's experience and guile. Often, on their return journey, the pair would stop by the park on Baroona Road, at Charlie's insistence, to observe a game of cricket being played by kids from the neighbourhood.

Charlie invariably became excited by the game and often made a spectacle of himself by shouting unintelligible encouragement from the sidelines. This did not impress the players or the spectators. More than once Sambo had to physically fend off an outraged spectator attempting to persuade the two to leave the park. Sambo, at age twenty-seven, posed a formidable barrier for anyone attempting to intimidate or ridicule his brother. At one hundred and eighty-three centimetres, weighing one hundred and ten kilos, Sambo had prodigious strength gained from lifting his brother many times a day for over ten years. There was not one ounce of fat on

Sambo's highly-toned musculature. Anyone with an axe to grind soon found himself planted upon the ground with a ringing in their ear or a very sore mouth where they had been spectacularly punched by Sambo.

Sambo could tolerate the furtive looks of annoyance, and even the blatant hostile stares, when people became upset about Charlie's loud and uncontrollable behaviour, because he knew they just didn't understand that Charlie was enjoying himself immensely, and voicing that exuberance in the only manner he was able. For the few who saw his brother as nothing more than a retard spoiling their day, he had no tolerance whatever.

Sometimes a more polite person would walk over to them and explain that the boy was affecting the player's concentration, and asked if they could move on. Sambo would politely answer that, as it was a public park, they would continue to stay exactly where they were. Sambo usually added that any player unable to block out a bit of sound would be of no use in a serious game, and that maybe they should consider other pursuits. Sambo knew he was inviting trouble when he should have demurred. At times he would: at other times he felt it his duty to educate the ignorant fools.

Most of the folks living around the suburbs learned to accept the pair, even welcoming them on rare occasions to picnic with them. Other times, strangers made a point of insulting or ridiculing them. Sambo was aware that, while Charlie did not let up in his enthusiasm of the game at those times, a slight pause indicated that he had heard and felt the barbs, striking deep into his psyche, regurgitating the cruel words for further cogitation once home and alone. Sambo stored those moments and etched the perpetrators on his mental list. Sooner or later, they would be served a piece of justice. Sambo only had to wait for the right time and place.

"Chay thim, Chay thim, Chay..."

"Yay, bravo Charlie," Sambo applauded. "Now, back you come. Come on back and then we can have an ice-cream. What do you think?"

"Ith-ceam, ith-ceam, ith-ceam. Thaaaaambooooo."

"No, not until you swim back here. Ice-cream when you get here, okay?"

"Thambo, Thambo."

"Good on you, Charlie. Bravo, mate."

Sambo waited for Charlie to make the swim back to his side. Charlie had learned the rudiments of swimming that paralleled the efforts of Eric 'The Eel' Moussambani, from the future 2000 Sydney Olympics. The world applauded and loved Eric for his courageous 100-metre swim, while Charlie attracted more derision than was necessary for his momentous achievements. Young children would snigger and point rudely at Charlie, while parents and older patrons of the pool voiced their concerns regarding the absurd possibility that Charlie might somehow infect them with his condition.

"Hello, Samuel," said a voice behind him.

Sambo turned, startled. He did not recognise the female owner of the voice, standing by the edge of the pool in a very revealing bikini for someone so young.

"I'm sorry, do I know you?" he asked with more than a hint of annoyance in his voice. The girl had called him a name he almost no longer recognised as his own. No one he knew called him anything but Sambo.

The girl sat down on the edge of the pool with her feet in the water, closer to Sambo than he deemed appropriate. He found it difficult to avert his eyes from the scantily-clad young girl who could not be more than fifteen or sixteen. Sambo was uncomfortable with the familiarity displayed by the brazen miss.

"I am so glad that I finally found you again," said the girl in a sincere tone.

"Why? How do you know me even?"

Sambo suspected a ruse by a group of youths to lure him into a false sense of security, and searched about him frantically, trying to identify from which direction the trap would be sprung. Charlie was slowly making his way across the breadth of the pool and no one else seemed to be noticing them at all.

"I am only here today because of you, Samuel."

"What? What are you talking about? How would you know I was going to be here today?"

"You're here every Saturday from what I have been told, but that's not what I meant. I mean, I wouldn't be *alive* today if it weren't for you. You saved my life when I was only seven years old, here at this pool. My name is Mary-Rose Darby, and you are my hero, Samuel.

Mary-Rose bent down to kiss Sambo squarely on the mouth. Sambo was so shocked at the public display that he was speechless for perhaps the first time in his life. The flush in his cheeks travelled to his chest and torso. Just then, Charlie arrived with a splash that swamped them all, squealing with delight at his antics. Mary-Rose laughed and joined the pair in the water.

"Chay thim guh. Chay thim guh."

"Yes, Charlie. You swim very good...I mean well," agreed Sambo with a cautious smile.

"Ith-ceam, ith-ceam, Thaaaambooooo!" Pleaded Charlie.

"All right, Charlie. You earned it. Go and dry yourself, and I will be there in a moment."

"Ith-ceam, Thaaaaambooooo."

"I will get you an ice-cream, Charlie, I promise. Just go on up and dry yourself and I'll be right there, okay?"

"Thambo, Thambo," said Charlie as he struggled from the pool. Appearing even more awkward, like a fish out of water, once ashore, Charlie crawled his way to the pair of towels laying a short distance away.

When Sambo turned around again he found himself firmly in the embrace of Mary-Rose, hugging him fiercely, pressing her firm body hard into him with one of her legs finding its way between Sambo's, pressing hard against his groin. Fighting to extricate himself from the persistent teenager was proving difficult. The harder he pushed, the closer she clasped herself to him.

"Mary-Rose, what are you doing? What about your parents?" Sambo asked in a near panic.

"They aren't here, Samuel. It's okay. I just wanted to thank you for what you did that day," said Mary-Rose with more than a hint of seductive amusement.

"All right, I accept. No need to keep hugging me."

Before Sambo could react, Mary-Rose had plunged her hand down the top of his trunks to grasp his growing member firmly. Sambo gasped, struggling vainly to remove her hand and her body without attracting the wrong sort of attention. While he felt panicked and frustrated, her hand movements were producing sensations in his body that he had forsaken long ago. Thankfully, there was no one in their immediate vicinity to witness his embarrassment. Try as he might he could think of no way to remove her hand without drawing unwanted attention.

Expertly, for someone so young, she fondled his granite-hard shaft within the Speedo briefs he now wore. Stroking it back and forth she evoked a muffled groan from Sambo, weakening his resolve. Were he not in public, and not wanting to make a spectacle of himself, he could easily have thrown off the girl. However, he saw no escape in his present circumstances, neither did he envisage a good outcome for either of them if she proceeded. Just when he thought the moment would arrive when he would embarrass himself, the girl disappeared beneath the water, where her mouth enveloped his penis after slipping it over the top of his trunks. Sambo almost died with shame: he grew redder and redder.

Sambo swore that all eyes at the pool were firmly fixed on him. He swivelled every which way to ratify his suspicions only to discover the few patrons minding their own business. Though he wanted desperately to find out if Charlie was okay, he simply couldn't force his mind away from the intense pleasure visited upon him from the girl below the water. Her mouth moved back and forth, lips tight about his member, tongue playing around, teasing him and sucking him harder and harder, until he exploded, unable to contain himself.

Mary-Rose broke the surface of the water to see Sambo with a look of shock and exhilaration. She ascended to wrap herself around him, face nuzzled into his neck once more. With one hand securing her position around his neck, her other hand sank beneath the water's surface to find his member once more, manipulating the stiffening object into her waiting vagina after pushing aside her string bikini. She took in the impressive length of him, moving her abdomen expertly, exciting him anew.

Sambo was incapable of resisting her, unable to extricate himself. The fire in his groin as he experienced his first sexual encounter threatened to overwhelm him. He joined in her motions, meeting thrust with opposing thrust to bury himself in her warmth. Gently, firmly, back and forth, they culminated in a mutual climax that left them both panting. Mary-Rose kissed Sambo's face and lips with pure gratitude and affection. She had dreamed of meeting her saviour for ten long years to demonstrate her gratitude appropriately. That Sambo turned out to be an absolute hunk added to the experience. That he was the most caring soul she had ever encountered, looking after his brother so lovingly, forced her to act on her impulses.

"Why don't you turn around to face the wall while I get us some ice-creams?" suggested Mary-Rose once she had removed herself and replaced his member, still as hard as a tent pole, within his trunks.

"Hmm? Oh, all right."

Of all the fantasies he had ever envisioned as a way for him to lose his virginity, none came close to the reality he had just experienced. It was without a doubt the sexiest, most risqué scenario he could ever have imagined for himself in a million years. He doubted anyone would believe him if he related the story in years to come. He was twenty-seven and no longer a virgin: not how he envisioned it, but wholly satisfying regardless. He watched as the girl raced away to her bag to retrieve a purse, then scamper off to the kiosk. Charlie was playing with some soldiers on their towels, having forgotten the ice-cream while his older brother was in the throes of ecstasy.

Sambo could not quite come to terms with the incident. He felt a great shame for his involvement with a girl so young. He thought she might have been about five when he rescued her. She said she was seven, making her seventeen, or thereabouts, depending on her birthday. Legal, sure, but only just: he felt a little dirty.

An unusual calmness descended upon Sambo, gradually removing the taint he felt. It was the dawning of a new sun within him, an awakening of a primordial sensation. His innocence had been lifted from him and his role among males had found a foothold. It was a rite of passage into the world of the adult male. A generous warmth suffused his body. Wholly sated within and without, he ventured from the pool to sit by Charlie's side when Mary-Rose returned.

"There you go, handsome," Mary-Rose said to Charlie, handing him a vanilla Drumstick.

"Charlie, this is Mary-Rose. She bought you an ice-cream, buddy."

"Thambo, Thambo. Ith-ceam."

"Hey, not fair giving Samuel the credit..."

"He wasn't. That's what he says when he's happy," explained Sambo, accepting an ice-cream. "Don't expect him to acknowledge you or thank you or anything. It takes a long time for him to find a face familiar or to learn a new word like a name."

"Yeah, I sorta get that."

"How could you have known?" asked Sambo.

"Look, I haven't been totally honest with you, Samuel..."

"You better call me Sambo, okay? No one calls me by my given name. What were you saying about lying?"

"I've been coming down here a lot over the last year. I watch you guys from the bus stop over there. Samuel...Sambo, I had the biggest crush on you from the moment you pulled me out of the water that day. The first thing I saw when I opened my eyes was you. That beautiful, kind face bending over me before my dad came rushing over to say horrible things."

"He was just concerned for you, Mary-Rose."

"Didn't give him the right to be mean to you. Anyway, my mum left him a few months after that. He was a total jerk. She got a job across town, so we had to move. The moment I left school and got my own job in the city, I wanted to come back here again. I've been coming down here to watch you and your brother, working up the courage to introduce myself."

"I don't get it. Why me?"

"Are you kidding? I mean, apart from the fact that you are, like, totally hot, I told you, and I've had a big crush on you. I would go to sleep every night thinking of you, adoring you, worshipping you for what you did. As I got older, I had it really bad. Started having wild fantasies about you from the first time I saw you here. Are you blushing again?"

"Well, I don't... It's just... You shouldn't be talking like that. I'm twenty-seven years old Mary-Rose."

"Yeah, awesome. I gotta tell you, though, when I saw how you looked after your brother, I just wanted to jump you, like, straight away. That made up my mind for me. I decided last night that, if you showed up today, I was going to do it."

"A simple thank-you would have sufficed."

"No way. Not for my guardian angel, the man of my dreams. Besides, wouldn't have been enough for me. I've lost count of how many orgasms I have had over you. I had to have you Sam...Sambo. I had to have you right here, today. I've never wanted anything more in my life, and I have to tell you, it was, like...wow!"

"Stop it. It's not right. It was embarrassing."

"Don't be such a prude. No one saw us. Sorry if you didn't like it," said Mary-Rose, feeling a little hurt, eating her ice-cream.

"It, it was incredible Mary-Rose," Sambo admitted. "I just...well, shit!"

"You can't be serious? That was your first time? Holy shit! I didn't think there were any virgins left in the world. Now I feel really great. That makes it very special. I can't believe it. Wow!"

"Keep it down, will you? I'm not really proud of it, you know."

"How come?"

"Well, it's pretty shameful being this old and..."

"No, not why you're ashamed, why you're a virgin? A good-looking stud like you should have the ladies climbing over each other for a piece of you."

"Are you always this...forward?"

"Nah. Usually a lot worse."

"Not very lady-like."

"Lady-like doesn't get you anywhere, even in the enlightened and semi-emancipated world we live in. A woman has to make her own way if she wants something. No point in waiting forever until it's offered. Shit, if I hadn't taken the initiative we never would have fucked."

"Would you please stop talking like that? It's indecent. It's..."
"Slutty?"

"A little liberal for my taste," suggested Sambo cautiously, fearing where the conversation was leading.

"I'm no virgin, that's for sure, but I don't sleep with just anyone. I already told you how I felt about you, how special you were to me."

"Thaaaaambooooo," whined Charlie.

"I got it, buddy. No harm done. Just a bit of dairy product on your towel which I can clean up. Here, why don't you finish mine?" said Sambo, handing his brother his ice-cream.

"Thambo, Thambo."

"Sooo?"

"What?"

"How come you were still a virgin at twenty-seven?"

"I didn't think about it. Been kind of busy with Charlie and the opportunity never came up. Besides..."

"Yes?"

"Well, there was a girl."

"And...?"

"She was here that day. I was on my way to say hello to her when I saw you at the bottom of the pool. After the police finished with me, she was gone and I never even knew her name. I went looking for her around the neighbourhood but never found her. It's sort of...well, partly..."

"What?"

"Ah, shit! I've never talked about this to anyone."

"Safe as a bank here. I don't gossip."

"Well, it's partly the reason Charlie is like he is. If I hadn't gone out looking for that girl, maybe..."

"Thaaaambooooo."

"Well, it's true, Charlie. You even told me that morning that I was chasing phantoms, dreams, or whatever it was you said. If I had been there, it never would have happened. I would have kept you quiet, Charlie. You wouldn't have been frightened. I..." Sambo trembled slightly as a tear escaped his eye."

"Luh, Thambo, luh, Thamb,." said Charlie weeping.

"I love you too, Charlie," Sambo said placing a comforting arm around the big man's shoulder.

"So, what happened to Charlie?"

"I don't want to talk about it. Never talk about it."

"Pretty obvious that you need to, though," suggested Mary-Rose as she sidled up to Sambo to hug his large frame.

Mary-Rose's proximity and the pressure from her small breasts against his chest made Sambo uncomfortable. The episode in the pool and the accompanying emotions flooded back into Sambo's mind and body. He was embarrassed by his traitorous body reacting in an inappropriate manner. He pounced on the one thing he knew that would kill the building sexual tension within him; to talk about the accident.

"I, I left Charlie alone that morning, to go on my rounds to look for her. I fell instantly in love with her the moment I saw her at the pool that day." Sambo did not register the shudder in Mary-Rose's body upon hearing his declaration of love, and did not place any importance on her pulling back from her tight embrace.

"I don't know what happened to me. I felt compelled to look for her like my life depended on it. I kept getting these flashes through my mind of a street or a house. Signs, I thought they were, even though I didn't believe in such things: messages in my dreams. You see, I had a dream the night before that day in the pool. She was in that dream, as clear as day. There was more stuff that I can't remember, but that part I know with certainty. I could never forget that perfect vision as long as I live.

"When I got home after my fruitless search for the umpteenth time, I knew something was wrong the second I stepped through the front door. When I saw the note on the table from our father, I knew what had happened before I got to the part about the hospital. I had been feeling it all morning, like an itch inside me that needed scratching. I wanted to go home, needed to go home, and couldn't until my search was complete. I had my usual cup of coffee afterwards, and the whole time I was thinking about what was bothering me.

"Ben, our father, was an alcoholic and a gambler. He would set himself up at the kitchen table every Saturday morning with about a dozen newspapers and turf booklets, listening to the radio give all the scratchings for the day and the 'sacred' tips from industry 'experts'. God help us if we boys disturbed his precious bloody tips. Before I left, Charlie had been playing with his soldiers and I told him to keep it down while I was gone. Ben had already downed a couple before I went out the door, so I knew we were in for a bastard of a day. I should never have gone. I should have fucking known."

"Thaaaamboooo."

"It's no use, Charlie. You will never convince me that I wasn't to blame in some part for what happened. Charlie didn't listen to me or simply forgot, got carried away with his game, whatever, and Ben went ballistic. He chased Charlie out the front door, onto the street, where a Landcruiser ploughed into him. He went under the wheels, broke a fair percentage of his bones, cracked his head against the bullbar before he went under, and that's what caused the brain damage. They had to cut out a large blood clot from his brain. Charlie was in a coma for months. I won't tell you what happened then, because I don't want Charlie to ever have to hear it." Sambo finished with tears flowing freely down his cheeks.

The three of them sat there in silence for many minutes, each lost in their own reflections. Charlie was still attempting to eat the rest of Sambo's Drumstick, vanilla ice-cream melting all over his face and hands in the warm sunshine beaming down on them. Sambo had never related the story to anyone, let alone a stranger. Although he guessed Mary-Rose was far from being a stranger after what had happened between them. It was only then that Sambo realised Mary-Rose had backed up a fair way from him after he had blurted out how he felt about another woman, after she had so tenderly elevated him from the lowly status of a virgin.

Sambo took her hand, though she offered some resistance. He grasped it firmly and smiled at her, instantly gaining her affections once more. He mouthed the words 'thank-you' to her and knew she not only understood the meaning of the words but registered the apology therein. Mary-Rose, far from being a naive child, smiled warmly at the gesture, though she was still pained by the revelation that her quest had been denied.

"And Crystal?" asked Mary-Rose sadly.

"Who?"

"Crystal, what about her?"

"Crystal who? Who are you talking about?"

"Crystal Montague, the girl you've been looking for."

"You, you know her name?"

"Mum told me and I've met her. Mum told me about everything that happened that day, over and over. I think, I think she sort of idolised you as well for what you did. I think she had a bit of a crush on you herself from the way she described you to me all those years. I only remembered your physical appearance from that day.

"Wow! After all these years I finally have a name to put with the face. Pity she didn't give you an address as well."

The ensuing silence made Sambo turn a questioning eye on her. "You know where she lives?"

"Not, not anymore. She moved about a year afterward. Mum would take me there to talk to her before that, just to be certain that we had the truth. That was when mum left dad, when she knew. Mum felt really guilty about it. She'd been fighting with my dad all morning about him having an affair with our next-door neighbour. He was trying to make her believe it was a one-off, no big deal. What with that and the guilt she was feeling about me, it was all too much for her. We moved away from him and I've seen him, like, twice since then."

"Where was she, I mean, the address?"

"Up on Given Terrace somewhere. I don't know the number or anything. I could probably show you if you really wanted to see it. Not much point now, though."

"Given Terrace, I've been that way a couple of times. I didn't recognise anything."

"Why would you? If you didn't know where she lived, why would you recognise anything? Why would you even give so much time to wandering around looking for her if you didn't know anything about her or where she lived? I mean, that's kinda weird, even for you."

"What's that supposed to mean?"

"Nothing."

"Mary-Rose, what do you mean?"

"Well, we just kinda had something going like, and now you're all 'where's this other girl' thing even though you know nothing about her. Not even her name."

"I've done something wrong, haven't I?"

"Yeah, duh! Not chopped liver here, you know!"

"I...I'm a bit confused."

"Typical male."

"Okay, truce, all right? Mary-Rose, you have to give me some latitude here, okay? I'm sailing in completely uncharted waters. Although I'm a lot older, you are so much more experienced than me in any of that relationship stuff. I have no idea what to do or say, or how to act. Never been there, don't know how it works."

"I wish you would stop making out like I'm some sort of nympho-slut or something. The only reason I did that with you was because I've wanted it since the moment I opened my eyes that day and saw your beautiful face, your magnificent body, over me. I have imagined you looking at me like that in my bedroom about a million times. It was a kid's crush at first. I get it. Not anymore. I have loved you with all my heart for many years, especially after watching you here on Saturdays, caring for Charlie with so much love and patience. You've developed into the most wonderful man I have ever seen or known. I love you, Samuel Border. I want to marry you and have your children, and Charlie can come live with us and we'll care for him together for the rest of our lives."

Sambo was stunned to complete silence. He had never experienced or imagined what anyone of the opposite sex might think about males in general or him in particular. He supposed females were correct in that regard. Males very seldom had deep thoughts about the machinations of the female mind. Emancipation had been fought for and bras burned for the cause, but few men still actually cared about or knew about the female mind.

He had always found kinship in female company going through school. He loathed all the crap males talked about, and so spent his recreational time largely within groups of females. That most of those females were undressing him with their eyes, or imagining themselves carried away in his arms across a threshold in a white dress, never entered his mind. That most of them simply wanted to have unabashed sex with him did not bear contemplation.

His experience with Mary-Rose that afternoon, although the

best feeling in his entire life, did not lead him to any deep feelings for her. Her admissions of love did not engender a reciprocal response in him. She was a very pretty girl with mousy-brown hair and a tanned, slim, firm body with perky little bumps on her chest which made her seem much younger than her years. A highly desirable female, in fact, but not one whom Sambo could love unconditionally. He could certainly maintain a fondness for her and had an indelible gratitude for her actions in the pool, but it fell far short of her expectations.

"Sam...I mean Sambo? Before you say anything more, I need to explain something to you. I have been planning this for a very long time, in great detail, right down to leaving my home, all my belongings in two suitcases, there in the kiosk locker. Today was it for me. Today was going to be the day I declared my love for you and win you over. It was all or nothing for me. I refused to believe in any other outcome, having gone over it in my mind a zillion times. My mother won't have me back. We had a terrible row over my decision and she told me never to come back. I think...I think she was actually jealous. I know that sounds really warped, but I truly think she wanted to get you herself. When I eventually told her what I was doing, she went crazy, right off her nut. Threw me out. Didn't matter to me, because I knew I was going to a new life with you."

"Thambo, Thambo, Thambo."

"Right now, Charlie? Okay mate. I'll take you to the toilet, huh?"

"Thambo, Thambo."

"Mary-Rose, I have to take Charlie to the toilet right now. I won't be long. Please stay. If you give me a chance, I'd like to...I don't know, repay some of the kindness you have shown me today?"

Mary-Rose nodded without much enthusiasm. While she wanted to run away as fast as possible from the embarrassing episode, feeling every bit the total fool, she simply had nowhere to go. She supposed she could either crawl back to her mother, or even worse, call her father, but neither scenario appealed to her. She had burned her bridges, believing with all her heart that she would succeed in her quest.

It never entered her mind that Sambo would not succumb to her ministrations. Never once did she consider any other outcome to her admissions of love and devotion. In her mind, he would accept her declarations like a gentleman, picking her up into his muscular arms, where she would remain until her dying days.

Though she remained, the temptation to run away almost overwhelmed her. Mary-Rose was nothing if not optimistic and quite stubborn. What hadn't occurred immediately required only careful nurturing to achieve the desired result. Time was all that was necessary to imprint herself upon her hapless Romeo. She would make herself indispensable and impossible not to love. Her overactive imagination and clever mind produced plan upon plan in milliseconds to counter the negative outcome of the first encounter.

CHAPTER SEVEN

When the group arrived home, Ben was sitting at the kitchen table with a shoebox and an 8mm camera, smugly sipping on a coffee as he listened to the races on the radio. Sambo led Charlie to their room, where he laid him on his bed to rest after the long walk back from the pool. When he walked back to the kitchen he stood still, watching Ben playing with the contents of the shoebox and several film reels, smiling. Sambo shook his head in disgust.

"Ever heard of copies? One with Mum, the other with her lawyer. Turn the radio off. You don't have any money to put on the horses, anyway. This is Mary-Rose. She's going to be staying with us for a while. She has a job and will pay her own way. Mary-Rose also told me that there is a government benefit available now for carers looking after invalids. Didn't know about that. If I can get myself on that, you can piss off. I will turn your bank account back over to you and you can go back to being a useless gambling drunk as long as you never come back here or try to contact us again."

It was the most Sambo had spoken to Ben in years. If what Mary-Rose said was true, and he was kicking himself for not having investigated the matter sooner, they could finally be rid of their unwanted boarder once and for all. He detested the man. He did not feel pity for a 'poor ill man' as was the common mantra among the do-gooders. Sambo harboured not a skerrick of respect or goodwill toward the man that had taken away his young brother's future.

Ben's face dropped like a bloodhound's droopy jowls at the mention of copies. He believed he had found his means of escape from the prison he endured. The years of servitude had taken their toll on his sanity. At times, it was all he could do to simply stay alive, tempted so often to take his life. However, he was a coward through and through. He faced up to that prospect long ago. Whatever guilt he possessed over his role in the events before the accident he had long since dismissed. The punishment meted out by his eldest son, with the lingering threat of imprisonment to keep him in line, had served to break him inside. He was an insipid shadow of the former man he once thought he was.

Ben was not aware enough of himself to see the truth. He could not identify the man he saw in the mirror each day as he scraped away the prodigious hair-growth. Ben would have to shave twice a day to control that growth if he wished to remain clean-shaven. He believed, wrongly, that he was once a strong man, a man among men. He did not recognise the tyranny he imposed on his children. He believed he was administering a normal amount of discipline. He could not conceive of what had come over his eldest son to attract such callous behaviour. Still, he did understand that a film of him serving up a helping of discipline upon the boy might be seen with different eyes these days.

Ben was a ruined man because of that inflaming evidence of his supposed brutality, especially if his youngest son recovered to testify against him. He had to remind himself every day that he could not let that evidence become public knowledge. If he was arrested for that and convicted of a crime against children, his life would become forfeit the moment he stepped into Boggo Road Gaol. His cowardice ensured he toed the line of Sambo's conditions. When he finally found the incriminating evidence after years of searching, he couldn't wait to rub the boy's nose in it, then give him a proper hiding for all the years of misery he had caused.

Ben walked toward the front door with drooping shoulders announcing his defeat...

"I lied, Ben. These *are* the originals and there never were any copies. You should have destroyed them straight away, but no, you didn't have even that bit of intelligence. I *will* make copies now, though. Thanks for making that obvious to me."

Ben lowered his head and walked out of the door. He now believed he could perform the act he had avoided for so long. He felt about as low as a snake's arsehole. He was at his wits' end. Should he fail in his endeavours, he would just walk away. There was nothing left for him.

Sambo led Mary-Rose to their bedroom, where he placed a mattress on the floor between his and Charlie's beds. It would be cramped for a little while, but, if Sambo guessed correctly, Ben's room would soon be vacant. In that event, he supposed he would move Mary-Rose into that room for the time being, as he needed to stay close to Charlie during the night. They went about the task of moving her in quietly so as not to disturb Charlie, snoring away after his big day out.

Sambo could not allow the girl to wander the streets, homeless, despite his belief that she could easily call her mother for help. It seemed best if she was allowed to reach such a decision of her own volition, and in her own time. He did not consider that she would remain in the house for long. He could not know the female mind, and he certainly had no idea about a creature called Mary-Rose. She was not a person easily dissuaded from her purpose, nor could Sambo fully comprehend the depths of her passion and resolve.

"So, anything to drink around here?" asked Mary-Rose, joining Sambo in the kitchen.

"If you are talking about alcohol, definitely not! With that mongrel being a drunk, I banned alcohol from the house. Yeah, don't look at me like that. I wouldn't have minded a drop or two over the years, I can tell you, but he just couldn't be trusted around it."

"Hope you don't expect me to be a teetotaller because I live here."

"Give it a couple of days, please, Mary-Rose. I think he'll be gone then. After that you can do as you like as long as you are careful not to leave it within Charlie's reach. I have to be real careful with him, because he gets into everything. You sure you want to stay here? He can be a real handful at times, and bloody noisy, 'Thambo-ing' all day long."

"He really gets that going, doesn't he? You understand all the different ways he says that?"

"Yeah, mostly. There are three major ones that he uses and you will get to understand those soon enough if you want to."

"Are you kidding? I'm looking forward to it. He's a darling. He loves you to bits, you know?"

"Yeah, I know. And I love him just as much. You want coffee or tea?"

"Cup of tea would go down well. You really think your old man will leave?"

"Yeah, I do. Did you catch all that I was saying to him when we came in?"

"Didn't understand much of it, but I heard it."

"I filmed him giving me a fair-dinkum belting one time. I threatened I would hand it to the police and press charges if he ever tried it again, or wouldn't back off the gee-gees and the booze. He found the bloody thing, even though I buried it in the backyard. Don't know how he found it. Haven't looked at it since I buried it. Tea is up here, sugar is over there on the kitchen bench next to the toaster. The kettle is there as well. Any dietary concerns I should know about?"

"You do the cooking as well?"

"Ben can't cook for shit and Charlie's not much chop at anything other than a Vegemite sanger. I'm pretty good. No one's died yet, anyway. You?"

"Yeah, mum taught me, and I took home-ec in school. Would you like me to help out a bit with the cooking while I'm here?"

"That'd be great, Mary-Rose. Have a seat, cuppa tea coming up. You prefer a bag or pot?"

"Bag'll do, and you better call me Rose. All my friends do. I think it might be easier for Charlie as well."

"I wouldn't hold your breath waiting for Charlie to say your name. Takes him months and months to learn a new word. Probably just call you a variation of 'Thambo' in the end."

"Is he, like, ever going to be better?"

"He improves every year, it's just so slow that you hardly

notice."

Rose peered through the kitchen window at the small backyard with the sunlight seeping through the leaves of an enormous camphor laurel in the next-door neighbour's yard. The dappled sunlight reminded her of their family's backyard, and her estranged father pushing her on the swing. Her experiences with the opposite sex had not been ideal, starting with the mothballed relationship with her father. Then came the few 'uncles' as her mother entered the dating game again, and her own misbegotten bunch of terrible relationships from the age of twelve onwards.

None of the boys or men she dated compared to the ideal she carried with her since that day in the pool. An Adonis of perfect proportions and beauty appeared in her line of sight as she coughed the water from her lungs, bringing renewed life to her body. His life, his breath, circulated through her lungs. No one ever came close to that vision of godliness. No one measured up, nor ever would. She dreamed of Sambo, ate of him and drank of him with every mouthful. He was the only reason for her continued existence, and she could not bear to be apart from him now that she had consummated that bond.

She watched intently as Sambo moved confidently around the kitchen, exuding a quiet manliness and allure. She wanted him more than she could admit, would do just about anything he asked. *Gosh, he could pretty much arse-fuck me right now and I wouldn't object.* One or two had tried that with her, much to their regret. In her mind, there was simply no alternative to her plan. She would get him to marry her, they would live together happily in a little house somewhere with Charlie, *and everyone else in the whole world could go fuck themselves.*

She smiled as Sambo placed a steaming cup of tea before her, sitting at the head of the table vacated by his father just moments ago. The shoebox and video camera still occupied the centre of the table. The domesticity of the little tableau made her heart warm with contentment. She almost sighed. She clearly saw herself in fifty years doing the same thing with this delightful, heroic, hunk of a man. She wanted to cast aside everything on the table to have him ravish her upon it there and then, if truth be told, but she tempered her cravings for the time being.

Compared to friends her own age, she actually did consider herself a bit of a nympho. They were all waiting for Mr Right and shit, while she could hardly wait to spread her legs and just have a good time, although, she chose her sexual partners carefully. If someone tried to get rough with her, the karate lessons paid off. Sex was always on her terms and timeline. She didn't see anything to be overly fussed about. Birds and bees did it, so why couldn't she? Damned if she was going to be all prudish about it.

Having made love to Sambo fulfilled a yearning so ingrained in her that she felt an insatiable desire to repeat it...often. It felt so right and so pure, that nothing could besmirch the experience for her. Of course, if it had happened in a bed after a glorious first date at a fine restaurant and copious amounts of champagne, she could see that as being more 'appropriate'. She would even have preferred that fairy-tale beginning, but she could see that the man of her dreams was never going to make the first move. Besides, he was too busy with his brother to notice anything around him, like the girl at the bus stop staring adoringly at him for over a year.

"What do you do?"

"Pardon?"

"For a job, I mean. What sort of work do you do, Rose?"

Rose listened to the honey-smooth voice in a dreamy state, unwilling to part from her fantasies, but glad to be engaging in conversation.

"Oh, I'm a sales assistant at Myer in Queen Street."

"Like it?"

"It's a job. I am at the bottom of the ladder with an old hag of a floor manager on my arse all day long. Actually, I think I officially hate it."

"Why stay?"

"You kidding? Too hard to get a job as an unskilled, practically uneducated female these days. I wanted to learn to be a window dresser ever since I first saw the Christmas windows at Myer when I was five. The magical North Pole scenes with Santa Claus and the elves? Wow, I just fell in love with all that. Then I started to notice all the other windows with the latest fashions. Classy; really, bloody classy. When I applied for the job, they said I had to learn the floor first and each of the departments before I could begin to assist in the windows. Jeez, that was like, two years ago, and I still haven't set foot in a window, even though I've been taking night classes in design and shit."

"Yeah, nothing ever works out the way we plan it," agreed Sambo wistfully.

"You regret the way it turned out for you?"

"Hmm, not sure how to answer that without coming across as ungrateful or foolish."

"Truth? No judgement here and Charlie is asleep."

"You think I meant that I could have done better than be stuck with Charlie? Nah, not by a long shot. When I told you that I loved Charlie, I wasn't pissing in your pocket. I don't have a single regret for taking on the role of caring for my brother. He cared for me once when he could just as easily have gotten away with doing nothing. Instead, he pretty much saved my life when I was a teenager and we found ourselves alone on an island in the Palm Island group. Long story, but I was burned pretty badly. I could have died for any number of reasons, but not because I had no one there to anchor me with their love."

"Is that what caused the scars on your legs?"

"Still noticeable, huh?"

"Barely. So, what do you mean then, if living and caring for Charlie isn't it?"

"My ordeal lasted quite a while in a burns unit in Townsville General. Stinking hot baths every fucking day! Can you believe that? Scalding hot baths for a burns victim! I was in a cancer ward and I saw people being shipped off under white sheets when they were discovered not breathing in the morning rounds. As the burns were healing, the muscles, sinews and tendons contracted to make me walk around the ward like a fucking crab. I couldn't straighten my legs one morning without feeling I was going to tear them. They gave me physical therapy until I wanted to die from the pain.

"Eventually, they decided to operate. My legs were straightened and placed in wrapping with hard plastic supports to keep them straight. When it was time to take them off, I had to take yet another fucking hot bath. When the nurse saw I was taking too long to peel the wrapping away from my legs to prevent skin coming away with them, she took charge by ripping them free without regard for my feelings. The pain from that episode haunted me for years.

"Anyway, after I survived all that and the awkwardness of attending school, I sort of figured I was here for a higher purpose, I suppose. I came to the conclusion that the purpose was looking after, Charlie. Now I'm not so sure. Once in a while, I used to get a tingling up my spine, and, strange as it sounds, it made me believe I was following the right path toward that purpose. Lately, I haven't had those tinglings. I feel I have strayed from my path."

"Wow, you talking in a, like, biblical sense?"

"Nah. Don't believe in all that crap. Have no respect for anyone who does. If that's you, best leave now. I have less respect for anyone religious than I do the medical profession, and that is really saying something."

"So?"

"Not religious, no. It is very hard to explain exactly. I get these sensations like déjá vu, and I immediately feel calm and sure, like an affirmation that I am heading in the right direction, like I know I'm on my way home. Whenever Charlie and I caught the train to visit our mother in Ingham, the moment we were past Townsville, seeing the familiar sights and locations leading up to Ingham, we got that warm feeling inside as though we were coming home. It's almost the same as that."

"When was the last time you felt that?"

Sambo was startled by the question. "I, I can't remember."

"That's not true, is it? When?"

"Never mind. It's stupid anyway. Just a superstition. You're right, it's as bad as religion and I should be ashamed. I'd better get dinner started and get some pyjamas out for Charlie. He'll wake up soon and need a bath. There's a TV in the lounge with some Nintendo games. It's a second-hand console, though. Can't afford a new one. Make yourself at home," said Sambo, rising from the table.

Rose watched Sambo with a curious expression and more than a hint of sadness. She knew Sambo was deliberately avoiding the subject of Crystal Montague: however, this time he was doing it to protect her feelings. That should have given Rose confidence. Instead, it made her feel sad.

CHAPTER EIGHT

Sambo was right, Ben did not return. No more money entered the bank account, which Sambo had not reverted back to Ben's name. He assumed correctly that Ben had quit his job. Thankfully, Rose had a close friend who worked for Social Security, providing all the help Sambo required to get his application accepted and processed quickly, with a full-time carer's benefits, rental assistance, bond guarantee and a host of other grants and benefits that the department did not want the general public to know about. There were many systems of help available if you knew which forms to fill in and where to lodge them in time.

With Rose's wage coming in every week to augment their government benefits, the threesome managed to live comfortably without Ben's wage or presence. Sambo was relieved to be free of the undercurrents that persisted while Ben skulked around, muttering under his breath. The open hostility between them, although it never again escalated, tended to wear down Sambo's reserves. A month after he left, the household settled into a welcome routine, with Charlie learning a new word to repeat every few minutes; "Roth, Roth, Roth". It meant that he wanted Rose to perform whatever duty was required.

The fact that Charlie allowed Rose to help him, since he rejected all others, gave Sambo a well-deserved break on a Sunday when Rose would be home from work. Most Saturdays, being the permanent junior, she was required to work until noon in the city. She would catch a bus to the Ithaca pool to join Charlie and Sambo, then walk home with them afterwards.

Brisbane, Queensland's capital city, played host to the Commonwealth Games three years prior, in 1982. While the city prospered as a result of the influx of capital, it kept its large country town feel, unlike its big cousins, Sydney and Melbourne. Brisbane remained behind the times where cosmopolitan chic was concerned. Antiquated laws and old-boy opinions ruled the state with an iron hand. Progress in real terms was a dirty word for the powers-that-be. The cash injection into Brisbane prior to and following the games did not come close to providing the progress that it desperately required to bring it in line with world standards.

Consequently, the little pool at Ithaca remained an obscure urban activity and recreation centre. Sambo was happy about that. It allowed him to frequent the pool with Charlie to continue his therapy in a familiar environment, which held particularly fond memories for him. Despite being extricated from his virginal status at the pool, while quite spectacular, he did not treasure that as the highlight of his experiences there.

Rose had continued to flaunt herself at him at every opportunity after Charlie's bedtime. Sambo found it increasingly difficult to dismiss her overtures or reasonably excuse himself from her affections. His chivalry was tested to the extreme most nights when she paraded around in the nude after having her shower. It was impossible for him not to be highly aroused by her nubile body.

She did not even seem to be attempting to seduce him. She made no moves toward him, no mention of any expectations. Sometimes, Sambo would be playing a game on the Nintendo when she would exit the shower looking model-perfect, to sit next to him on the sofa. She would then offer to turn the channel on the TV when the game was finished, so they could catch a show or a movie. She would deliberately stay on her haunches facing the TV while asking Sambo which channel he would like. Sambo could barely remove his eyes from the naked vision confronting him, the perfect derriere wiggling seductively, luring him like the song of a Siren, until he could take it no longer. He would go to his room to suffer torturous dreams.

It was impossible to avoid her and he didn't really want to. After all, she was a pleasant girl and highly desirable. It was just that he was unable to offer her the love she deserved. He could easily have used her shamelessly for sex and nothing more. She may even have accepted that less-than-ideal outcome, but he would not debase her by doing so. He would feel like he had taken advantage of Rose in such a situation. Ultimately, there was that elephant in the room; Crystal Montague. His thoughts never strayed far from his obsession with the girl he saw and with whom he fell in love. He often wondered if he was the male version of Rose and that if he ever found Crystal, she might treat him or feel about him the exact way he felt about Rose. It was a troubling thought.

Winter was on its way and it would be a while before Sambo would bring Charlie back to the pool. Charlie did not take to the cold water as he used to, so they took advantage of the waning summer warmth. Charlie was splashing at the shallow end of the pool with Sambo close by when Rose waltzed through the turnstiles after work. She appeared bright and cheery despite the severe black skirt and white blouse of her Myer uniform. Holding the black uniform coat over her shoulder, she made her way to the towels where the boys had a bag with her change of costume.

Sambo watched as Rose flounced happily to the changing rooms with a youthful exuberance. Sambo struggled with his intention to inform Rose about his decision. He knew she would be very upset, and he also feared that Charlie would be equally upset. Charlie had taken to Rose with great affection. He even seemed to accept Rose bathing him, after being highly agitated initially whenever she saw him undressed. Sambo discovered in himself a degree of jealousy in that regard. He had relinquished some of his duties to Rose, and it seemed Charlie accepted that enthusiastically. While Sambo felt tremendously relieved about that, he secretly harboured a little sadness at possibly being relegated to a lesser role in Charlie's care.

Sambo groaned inwardly as Rose appeared from the dressing rooms resplendent in the briefest string bikini he had ever seen, clearly showing her pubic hair through the wide, loose patterns.

After placing her neatly bundled clothes on the towels, she ran straight for the side of the pool, diving gracefully into the deep end with every male eye glued on her all the way. She swam swiftly to Charlie at the opposite end and hugged him joyfully.

Sambo watched as the two sat huddled together laughing at something Rose said. Sambo watched the interplay with a smile. She really was very good for him. Seeing Sambo smile at them as she turned, Rose made her way to him. She pecked him on the cheek as she said hello. She then turned around to watch Charlie. It became very routine for Rose to maintain a constant surveillance on Charlie. A single moment's lost concentration could mean a disaster, of which she was only too aware.

She moved to place herself directly in front of Sambo, backing up to him as she watched Charlie. She casually grabbed Sambo's hands, to wrap them securely about her as she backed up further into him. It was an innocent enough gesture for any two people who were affectionate with one another. Sambo found it to be more than a casual embrace, especially when her bottom ground into his groin playfully. She placed his hands, covered by her own, on her breasts. Sambo again found it difficult to remove her or extricate himself without causing a kerfuffle.

She continued to wiggle her firm bottom against his growing erection. Sambo was becoming uncomfortably embarrassed. He feared they would be thrown out and banned from the pool if their lewd behaviour were discovered. Anyone with a pair of swimming goggles would plainly see what was occurring below the water. He was effectively pinned by her against the wall of the pool where she pushed hard against the bottom with her feet to keep herself pressed firmly against him.

In an instant, Sambo used his superior strength to swing her around to face the wall, with him firmly behind her. Rose felt confident that her man was going to assume the leading role at last, feeling his hardness against her flesh, her bikini riding high up her backside with the applied pressure. She sighed audibly as he pressed harder, face leaning into her neck, hands fondling her breasts. She released his hands to reach behind her, grasping his head. When she felt him pushing himself off the wall, away from her, she knew she had failed.

"It's her, isn't it?" she turned back to face him. He moved just out of her reach.

"I don't know what to tell you, Rose. I know how you feel about me and I...just don't feel the same way. I like you a lot. I would be honoured if you stayed my friend, stayed on with us, and I can never thank you enough for what you did for me, but I refuse to hurt you more by allowing you to believe something that isn't true. I promised myself that I would tell you so today. I would much rather be totally honest with you."

"Then be honest with me. Is it her?"

"Rose..."

"Is it her?"

"Yes, all right? It is her. It has always been her. I can't get her out of my mind. She haunts my thoughts and my dreams. I thought I could ignore it, lose it, force it away from me, but I can't. Don't think for one moment that I haven't been tempted to sleep with you, Rose, because I have. You are a bloody sexy gir...young lady, and anyone with half a brain would fall over himself to be with you."

"Except you?"

"I was never known for being smart." Sambo tilted his head and smiled kindly.

Rose felt her heart breaking in two. She found it impossible to hate him for rejecting her. She had known how difficult it would be to win his heart. She had failed miserably. She supposed that she might have played it differently, not flaunted herself so brazenly. She couldn't think of another method to capture his heart, falsely assuming that lust held the key. Once united in flesh, she hoped she would succeed to entice him with her sexual overtures. She knew, however, deep down, that it was not possible, that Sambo was not like most men. He had a depth that revealed itself at times and she was drawn into that irresistibly. He would not be swayed to partake of her delights which normally had boys stumbling after her.

She could not blame Sambo entirely for the fiasco and her subsequent humiliation. He had admitted as much at the beginning. He was smitten by a woman he had never actually known. He hadn't even known her name until she blurted it out. It was her own fault. She had inadvertently opened the wound by mentioning her name. The mission to find her was reborn from that point. It was an unsurpassable barrier between them that no amount of obstinate persuasion could penetrate. She admitted her defeat reluctantly. She did not hate him for it, could not find anything in him to blame. She had simply failed. *Build a bridge, get over it.* She said to herself, while inside she was twisted into knots.

"Still want to know where she lived?"

"You don't have to do that. I'm really sorry, Rose."

"What the fuck? Get over yourself, big boy. Not the only fish in the ocean. I'll take you there after we leave today. It might help to get it out of your system once and for all. Now I need to go see my other man; Charlie."

Rose swam away from him trying to hide the tears, but Sambo wasn't fooled. Her brave face could not hide the pain he had delivered. He watched as she swam to his brother, who beamed as she approached. Sambo hoped that she would not leave them because of the way he had upset her. She was good with Charlie and it relieved him from being a carer 24/7. The brief respite afforded him when she assumed the role of the sitter enabled him to relax more than he had in the preceding decade.

Truth was, he liked her very much as well. They had shared many a fine moment in conversation and games with one another. They also shared some of the cooking, washing and cleaning, making Sambo's life a tolerable existence. Until she came along, he did not realise how exhausted or lonely he was. He loved his brother with all his heart, but secretly longed for another soul to talk to, with whom to share his days and voice his frustrations without it sounding like petty complaints. Rose filled a void in their lives that would be sorely missed should she decide to move on.

Clouds gathering overhead, blocking the afternoon sun, heralded the possibility of a storm front. Sambo shivered slightly as a breeze made its presence known. It was time for them to leave. Charlie would soon be too cold. It was another half-hour before Charlie could finally be convinced of that. They dried themselves and dressed in their casual gear for the return journey home.

"Maybe another time, Rose? I think there is a storm coming and I think Charlie is probably too buggered to make it up the hills today."

Rose lifted her eyes heavenward, "Nuh. Not going to rain for a while yet. We need to do this today, Samuel, or I may not have the courage to offer it again."

"Sambo."

"Samuel," she repeated emphatically.

Rose, dressed in tight jeans and a loose yellow cotton sweater, hair swept back over her tiny ears, clear skin and mesmerising dark eyes, made Sambo decide he was an absolute fool and a bastard. He could not reverse his decision to rebuke Rose's advances, but he berated himself just the same. He may well live to regret his senseless choice. Any other man would be eternally grateful to attract such a splendid female. The choice was not in his control. It had been made for him the moment he laid eyes on the mysterious and glamorous Crystal Montague.

He saw her clearly in the dream of the night prior to their encounter. Over the last month, other portions of that dream had surfaced, some of which he shared with Rose. The insistent emotions in that dream continued to erode his resolve to forsake the woman and the dream, to simply let her go. He could just as easily have a great life if he married Rose and shared their lives with Charlie. Conflicting thoughts assailed his troubled mind. He was tempted to resist the impulse to walk to the house in which Crystal lived at the time, but he was unable. He was drawn to her inexorably, infinitely.

"You finally going to tell me about it?"

"What?"

"The dream, of course," said Rose as they made their way along Given Terrace. "You only told me a little bit so far. Had to be more to it to make you get this horny for her."

"That's unfair, Mary-Rose. You shouldn't belittle what I feel just because of what happened between us."

"If something actually happened between us, I might agree with you. But it didn't, so I think I am qualified to make an observation or two about your weird obsession?"

"Wouldn't go so far as to call it an obsession."

"What the fuck else would you call chasing after a phantom and a dream?"

"She wasn't a figment of my imagination, Mary-Rose. She was real, there, at the pool that day. You've seen her since, spoken to her and knew her name. How can you call her a phantom?"

"You said you recognised her from your dream."

"No, not straight away. What I did mention, was that I had a strange tingling sensation, a déjà vu. It was only later that I realised she had appeared in my dream."

"So?"

"So what?"

"So, the rest of it, the dream. What happened to get you this scuzzy about it all?"

"Scuzzy?"

"Yeah, all freaky, weirdo shit. Scuzzy, like fuzzy, scummy shit."

"Wow, not very nice."

"Busting my hump getting this boy up this fucking hill after being rejected by you is not my idea of a good time, okay? You owe me Samuel. Spit it out!"

After a moment, "In my dream, what I remember is going down to the pool that day. An ordinary day, nothing special to mark it as different from any other day. I don't see her straight away. Don't become aware of her until we almost bump into one another as we swim laps. We laugh and apologise for getting in each other's way. Before long we are talking. She is a vision. The most beautiful girl I have ever seen, an absolute..."

"Yeah, yeah, yeah, I get the picture already. Do me a favour? Skip that sentimental shit, okay? I can't...handle that right now. Just cut to the chase."

"Sorry, Mary-Rose."

"Rose."

"Mary-Rose," said Sambo pointedly.

"Touché."

"In my dream, we got along like a house on fire. Couldn't get enough of each other. Sorry, Mary-Rose, but I have to say this. We both fell instantly in love. I remember so clearly when I first kissed her..."

"Ugh!"

"She was lying on the side of the pool watching me as I swam to her. I reached the edge where her head was in line with mine. We kissed. Next thing I see in the dream is walking her home after we left the pool. I recognise this road now, this footpath, all cracked and old with grass growing through. We were holding hands as we came up this way. A bit farther around that bend at the top, there is a bus stop seat where we sit and talk. We also cuddle and kiss a bit before she tells me she has to get home.

"We walk a little farther and we come across this telephone pole: that one just up there. Shit, I remember it exactly from my dream. I stopped to carve my name and hers in the pole, in a heart. I'd never done that before, but it felt right."

"Oh, please, you're making me ill."

Taking no notice of Rose's comment, Sambo made his way to the telephone pole, where he gasped. Thinking he was having a heart attack, Rose rushed to him. Sambo was shaking. She finally realised what he was staring at, causing him to tremble. Rose could clearly see a set of initials carved within a heart.

"I thought you said this was in your dream?"

"It, it, it was."

"So, when did you do this?"

"I...didn't."

"Bullshit!"

"I didn't know her name, Mary-Rose. You told me that only a few months ago. Look at that carving: does that look fresh to you?"

The carving did not appear fresh. It appeared to be positively ancient, in Rose's opinion. Peering up at the mauve house in which Crystal once lived, Sambo shivered in recognition. Then the heavens opened up to release their heavy burden.

CHAPTER NINE

For many months afterwards, Sambo would relive that day and the dream, reconciling the inconsistencies and discrepancies, separating fiction from fact. Something elusive escaped his introspection and no amount of cajoling would release the answer. He revisited that damn pole every chance he could and the dream haunted his restless nights.

Rose had relented in her pursuit of him, for which he was extremely grateful. He did not hold out much hope of disregarding the sexual temptation she posed, had she persisted. Gradually, she assumed more and more responsibility for taking care of Charlie, who began to prefer her help. While it troubled Sambo occasionally, he believed it would benefit them both in the long run. Charlie had only ever had his older brother for company and Rose appeared to be filling a void in his life.

Rose did not exhibit any outward signs of melancholia or worse for having failed to capture his heart. In fact, she seemed almost relieved, if Sambo was reading her correctly. He fervently wished that he had not managed to crush her feelings, falsely believing them to be little more than infatuation or puppy love at first. The correlation and irony between himself and his 'love' for Crystal and Rose's love for him did not go unnoticed, yet he would not fully admit that they were the same. He did acknowledge that life was often cruel and unjust where love was concerned.

Sambo hoped that Rose would have little difficulty finding a replacement for him in her heart. She was far too beautiful, exuberant and resilient to stay on her own for long. Under her guidance and loving care, Charlie was making some visible progress, which delighted Sambo more than he could admit. He used a few more words, had improved in mobility, and seemed much happier. There was a constant sparkle in his eyes and fewer 'Thaaaambooooos' of late.

When Sambo entered their shared room to get Charlie ready for his favourite TV show, 'Alf', his world came crashing down about him. He was so shocked by what he saw that it left him speechless and gasping for breath. Never could he have envisaged a scene such as he witnessed when he opened the door of their bedroom that evening. That he remained unobserved by the pair, cavorting on Charlie's bed in the throes of ecstasy, presented an opportunity for him to withdraw from the room as quietly as he had entered, an opportunity he was not predisposed to follow.

Rose, eyes closed, on top of his naked brother, riding him with wild abandon, caused Sambo to quake with fury. Barely managing to control his ire, Sambo slammed the door behind him as he exited the room, seething. He walked unsteadily to the kitchen, where he retrieved a half-bottle of whisky from an overhead cupboard. He did not bother with the soda water or the glass, he swigged straight Scotch from the flask. He could not control the thunderous pulse in his head, and the blood coursing through his veins was on fire. He knew he couldn't remain in the house. He had to leave before he did something he would truly regret.

Sambo slammed the bottle down, shattering it, to leave its contents spilling down the front of the cupboards beneath the counter. He grabbed his jacket by the front door before stalking out of the house with no clear agenda other than removing himself from the slut taking advantage of his innocent brother. Every instinct was urging him to shake the shit out of the charlatan and boot her out of the premises immediately. He wanted to strangle her, make her see how wrong it was, punish her. For all those reasons, he could not afford to stay in the house to confront them...her. It wasn't Charlie's fault. It was all on the whore's shoulders.

Sambo stormed down the street into the night. He walked for hours, in whatever direction his feet took him. The night sounds of the city did not penetrate his troubled mind as he passed through it until he found himself in The Valley. Fortitude Valley was a seedy, dirty, dingy part of Brisbane which most decent folks avoided during evening hours in the 70s and 80s. To walk alone in that part of town after dark was pure madness. Sambo didn't care, didn't know where his feet were taking him. At one point, a sudden sound broke through Sambo's deep concentration. He saw a bloke standing before him with less than polite intentions etched on his grubby features. Sambo growled at him like a mongrel dog protecting a bone, and the stranger fled the scene as though strapped to a rocket.

Past the nightlife, past the houses of New Farm, onward and onward he walked, a fever of emotions boiling within him. Everything, every injustice or slight he had ever experienced rose within him and manifested itself in a desire to crush and maim the perpetrator. He walked all the way to the end of the road; Myrtletown. In those days, it was nothing more than a smattering of derelict homes near the mouth of the Brisbane River, a place Ben had taken them fishing a couple of times when he'd managed to get the rods and reels out of hock.

At the end of Kingsford-Smith Drive, there was nothing but a gate leading to a dirt road that wound down to the dirty river. Sambo followed that track until he came to the banks of the river, illuminated by the brilliant halogen lights from the oil refinery opposite. Sambo slowed his determined pace as he neared the water's edge, soothed by the sound of the waves lapping upon the muddy banks. A foul smell of decay filled his nostrils from the mangrove swamps farther seaward, thwarting his progress.

Spent from the exertion of walking a great distance, with his emotions applying their energy-sapping toll, Sambo dropped to his knees, finally able to release the torrent of tears that had built up in him. He remained in that position until well after midnight, as the chill of the morning air, drifting lazily over the surface of the river, settled about his trembling body.

Seagulls screeched and night birds made their presence known. The wind, building in intensity, whistled through the rubbish and the long grass by his side. The area had been a dumping ground for derelict vehicles and white goods, along with household garbage, adding to the effluvia invading his nostrils. Sambo seemed to recall sewerage outflow pipes around the area as well, pumping their malevolent product directly into the ailing river, adding considerably to the miasma assailing him.

Disregarding the sounds and smells, Sambo sat quiescent, his mind in turmoil. An alien sound eventually worked its way through the barrier of familiar auditory accoutrements. Its singular distinction of being so foreign to its surroundings enabled it to invade Sambo's consciousness. He raised his head in an effort to gauge the direction of the sound. It was a primal sound that evoked a reaction in most humans. It could not be ignored, nor dismissed, and almost never endured for long.

Slowly Sambo raised himself to his feet, aching in body and mind, and made his way around the vehicular skeletons rusting away in the long grass, wary of snakes that might find his intrusion to be less than desirable. The metal shapes littering the desolate landscape in the shadows of the halogen bulbs from the refinery also attracted the ubiquitous red backs, nasty little spiders hiding in all the nooks and crannies provided by the rusting hulks, just itching to sink their fangs into the unsuspecting.

It was near impossible to determine the location of the pervasive noise among the wind sounds and other nocturnal utterings by insect, reptile and mammal; frogs and crickets drowning out almost everything else. Only a sliver of moonlight augmented the light filtering through from the refinery. Sambo had to stop frequently when the noise abated, unable to pinpoint the source. Stumbling about in the near dark, among a bunch of wrecks where any wrong move might see him slice and dice himself, made Sambo reluctant to continue.

He fought with himself, his conscience arguing that it was not his duty to investigate, that if he hadn't blundered into the vicinity he would not have heard it, anyway. He could not, however, refute his recognition of the sound. His admission, refusing to allow him to ignore it, compelled him to search as long as necessary. Just when he believed it had ceased permanently, the wind died sufficiently to reveal the weakening sound achingly nearby. He finally discovered the source near the open rear door of an old Holden Sandman, sans front end, wheels and most other bits. At the rear of the panel van's open doors, on the grass, lay a newborn baby.

The baby boy was naked and slowly losing his voice, shivering with the cold, still smeared with amniotic fluid and trailing an umbilical cord. A quick search of the area failed to reveal the mother. Sambo removed his jacket to swaddle the mewling child in its warm lining of flannel. Leaving only the face exposed to allow it to breathe, Sambo used a piece of sharp metal to sever the cord from the placenta, tying the end with a shoelace. A disturbance from the darkened interior of the van startled Sambo.

Working by touch alone, he found a pair of legs first. Sliding his hands up the legs he found the rest of the naked body, barely breathing. He assumed it was the mother, but she felt odd. He saw nothing in the pitch-black interior, but knew that any woman who had just given birth was bound to be bleeding, and possibly suffering post-partum complications. She might require stitching or...well, he wasn't really sure about what else. His knowledge of females and complications arising from birth were profoundly inadequate.

It did not take Hercule Poirot to deduce that the mother was unwell. It did, however, need someone cleverer than he to implement a means by which to render assistance to the woman and her child. While he had heard rumours regarding portable telephones the size of concrete blocks that rest in a cradle inside a vehicle, he had neither the vehicle nor the said telecommunications device at his disposal. The former was parked outside his home in Rosalie, the latter was priced well out of his reach for the foreseeable future.

Knocking on the doors of the few scattered homes in the vicinity did not warrant further consideration, as he did not feel like copping a beating or a bullet for disturbing the miscreants that drifted to the bottom of the heap to end up in Myrtletown. It was a quandary beyond his scope. If he left them where he found them to seek help, they would probably perish. They would probably perish, anyway, but action of any description seemed the more positive choice. He placed the baby at his mother's breast. She would be more suited, even unconscious, to provide succour to the baby than he. Before deciding to venture out of the van to find an alternative, he tested her neck for a pulse. Weak, but steady, he thought.

"Lady, I have got to get you to a hospital," Sambo muttered more to himself than to her.

Suddenly, an arm shot out to grasp his wrist in a death grip. "Nugh!" She garbled. "Nugh, no, hos… hospital. No, c… c… cops.

"Lady, you are going to die without proper care, and so is your baby."

"No hosp...ital. No cops. No...cops!" The voice trailed away.

He saw nothing of the woman's features inside the van but knew she was experiencing difficulty in forming her words. Not able to get her mouth around them, possibly an injury? He was flying blind and totally out of his depth. Outside, he began to feel chilled by the building wind. *Any wonder the baby was shivering,* thought Sambo. He felt the first pangs of panic developing in his harried mind. *No fucking hospital! No cops? What sort of trouble is this woman in, and why am I willing to get involved?* What was he supposed to do? Find a flying carpet to take them somewhere? No, not somewhere. He had to go back home, regardless of the risk in leaving them alone, to return with supplies.

Sambo guessed that it wasn't impossible for a woman to be so ashamed of having a baby, say, out of wedlock, even in the present day, to want to avoid hospitals and the police. It beggared belief that she would risk the lives of herself and the baby to keep the authorities away, though. Sambo knew he couldn't leave her in the condition he found her. She was naked as far as he could tell and she would soon be suffering in the chill wind. The baby would be fine for the time being wrapped in his jacket, but he had to find something to keep her warm while he was gone. He would also have to get some water with which to wash her down.

He had some matches in his coat pocket. He always carried matches for the kitchen stove. He could not afford to leave them around on shelves or window ledges because of Charlie, so he carried them on his person at all times. He could build a small fire at the entrance to the van. It would provide a little heat, and sterilise some water if he could manage it. It would also shed some much-needed light into the van.

Sambo got to work without further procrastination. He started a fire easily, finding enough dry scrub branches and bracken to get it roaring in no time. He discovered a hubcap in which he fetched water from the river. The water wasn't very clear: in fact, it was positively murky, but he was in no position to be ultra-fussy. When the fire created enough light within the van for Sambo to see, he drew in a sharp breath. The woman was black and blue from arsehole to breakfast time. He had never seen someone look as bad as she did. She was battered, bruised and bloody with scarcely one inch of her body clear of abnormal colouring. Her eyes were swollen to mere slits. Her bedraggled hair was matted with dirt and blood. She would have broken ribs without a doubt. Sambo saw clear signs of her being belted with a bat of some sort, maybe a cricket bat, he judged.

He retrieved his clean handkerchief - another essential item when travelling with Charlie - from his jeans' pocket. Once the water in the hubcap had heated sufficiently, he began working on the woman. He gently moved the sleeping baby from her chest to her side so he could clean her all over. It took a great deal of time and many trips to replace the water. Once he had cleaned the woman, it became obvious how close to death she teetered. If she were haemorrhaging inside, she would not last long. Her skull appeared to be intact despite its brutal assault. Only minor cuts and abrasions were revealed once the dried blood had been wiped away.

The next problem he faced, after returning the sleeping infant to his mother's breast, was containing the fire. The wind was beginning to whip at the flames threatening a possible conflagration. Luckily, only a few metres away, he found the remnants of a small galvanised-iron water tank. It retained the circular shape of the sides, while the top and bottom had long ago rusted away. It provided the perfect wind-break to ensure the fire did not get away. An old coir-wire single bed base, resting atop the low walls of the fire-break, acted as the perfect spark arrestor.

There was nothing lying around with which he could cover the woman, and he felt certain that anything he might have found would be too filthy and insanitary in any event. He was left with no choice but to remove his thin cotton T-shirt. His shirt was large enough to cover most of her smaller body. Without unduly disturbing either mother or infant, Sambo eventually had her dressed in the flimsy garment, affording her a modicum of modesty and some feeble protection against the chill. He debated long and hard before deciding on a course of action.

As he walked away from the pair, his guilt at seemingly abandoning them was slightly assuaged when a familiar tingling sensation crept along his spine. He started to jog along the dirt road, mainly to get warm. He also needed to get back home in the quickest possible time, so he called on his memories of every road and street he had ever traipsed to gauge the fastest route. While the urge to simply stop in at the closest police station to report his find gnawed at him, he resisted, though why he did so was a mystery. He guessed he had made an unvoiced pact of sorts with the woman when he accepted her protests without comment.

He hoped with all his heart that the broken-down claptrap of a car that Ben had bequeathed them upon his abandonment would actually start for once. The old Holden Kingswood station wagon was lucky to be firing on three of its six cylinders when it did cough into life. Sambo read all the literature available to breathe new life into the ailing beast, but believed it to be beyond the realm of mortal folk to resurrect it. Ben had purchased the car near brand-new, when one of his trebles paid off one Saturday, many years ago. The car had been abused and kept in poor repair for so long since then that it had no choice but to cough and wheeze like an old man with emphysema.

CHAPTER TEN

Peeking through the open door to his shared bedroom, Sambo allowed the scene to soak in for a precious moment. In the light provided by Charlie's night lamp, Sambo observed his brother in restful repose for perhaps the first time since the accident. With Rose tucked under his big arm, Charlie appeared to be in a deep, contented sleep, escaping the night terrors that normally saw him threshing within his bedclothes all night long, leaving them a sweaty mess.

He closed the door quietly to return to the kitchen where he was gathering supplies. His anger over his earlier observations had abated sufficiently to continue with his task. He knew that he could trust Rose at least to ensure Charlie's safety and health once they woke to find him gone. It was the longest time he had been away from Charlie and that played heavily on his mind. He had always been there when Charlie awoke in the morning or night. He had to submerge those nagging doubts to be able to proceed with his arrangements.

"What are you doing?"

Sambo whirled at the startling question to see Rose standing at the kitchen archway, completely naked.

"Go and get dressed, for fuck's sake!" said Sambo through clenched teeth, his anger returning.

The fierceness of his voice brooked no argument from Rose, who dashed back down the hallway to her own bedroom. She re-emerged moments later, appearing quite contrite. She sat at the kitchen table watching as Sambo placed a curious assortment of articles in a bag upon the table - first-aid kit, clothes, food, torch and more.

"I want you to pack your gear."

"I, I understand. I'm sorry, Samuel. I'll leave straight away if you want."

"No, I meant pack your gear and vacate the room. I need it for someone. You can move in with Charlie seeing as you're fucking *him* now."

"Oh. I, I guess I deserve that."

"I don't have time for this right now but we will finish this conversation in the very near future. You are free to leave, of course, at any time, just not until I return, please? If the bloody car decides to start for once, I'll probably be back in a couple of hours, depending on traffic. If it doesn't start, I may be gone for most of the day. You all right to stay with Charlie if that's the case?"

"Of course! Why would you even ask?"

"Who the fuck knows what goes on in that slutty head of yours, Mary-Rose? I know for damn-sure that I don't. No, I'm not getting into it," he insisted when he saw her about to repudiate the statement. "I have an emergency to deal with, and you are at the bottom of my list of priorities right now. All I need to know is that you will take care of Charlie until I return. And I am not referring to his sexual needs! Clear?"

"Samuel, I..."

"I will not tolerate a debate on that point at the moment. If you agree to that condition until we can discuss the matter, then you are invited to remain. If you disagree with those terms, you may leave upon my return."

"Okay, Samuel," Rose agreed reluctantly with her eyes cast downward. "Who are you bringing home?"

"I don't know."

"Huh?"

"I don't know who she and the baby are."

"Baby?"

"Yes, a newborn."

"You...you're a father?"

"Don't be ridiculous, of course not. When would I have had the time to meet someone and make a baby?"

"Then whose?"

"Look, I don't know anything at the moment and I don't have time to explain. If I don't get back to them, they will die."

"Die! What on earth are you talking about? If they need help of some sort, you should get them professional help. I know you don't trust the hospital, Samuel, but you have to believe that they can do more good than you if this woman and her child need medical attention. I don't understand why you haven't already. It's not like you to neglect someone. I thought you cared for people, Samuel. I know you do, otherwise I wouldn't be alive."

"It, it's complicated and I don't have time. How soon after a baby is born does it need to be fed?"

"A mother's regular milk doesn't come down for two to three days. The baby feeds on colostrum while it matures enough to digest the normal milk as it becomes available. Colostrum also delivers the antibodies a baby requires to survive diseases."

Sambo was surprised. "That was a very detailed answer for someone who has yet to experience childbirth."

"I studied everything I needed to know when I was hoping you would be my husband, so that I could make myself the best wife possible."

He ignored her efforts to cause him guilt.

"In theory, then, as long as there is some of that stuff in the mother's breast at the time of birth, she should be able to satisfy the baby's needs? I don't need to rush out and get formula or anything?"

"How can I answer that? I don't know the condition of the mother, whether the baby is premmy or not. A woman can go through some major shit during and after childbirth, Samuel."

"She's been through much worse than anything childbirth could throw at her. Make sure you are out of the room before I get back."

"Why? What happened to her?"

"Beaten black and blue, probably with a cricket bat. Probably broken ribs. It's not obvious that anything else is broken from what I've seen."

"Shit, you've got to tell the cops, let them handle it. Why you?"

"Dunno, just feel like I have to. See you later. Mind what I said about Charlie and you."

"Fuck you!"

"Yeah, as long as it isn't *him*."

Before she could retaliate, he rushed out of the rear door. She heard him cursing a few times as he loaded more gear into the car before she made out the irregular growl of the ill Holden. She followed the sound all the way into the street, where it turned right to head up towards Paddington. After a moment, she returned to her room to start packing her belongings.

Sambo stuck to the speed limit despite the early hour and little traffic. He did not want to risk being delayed by a cop, who would not be able to stop at a mere speeding ticket. There were too many faults with the car to disguise the fact that it was totally non-roadworthy. A cop would have a field day with him and would probably decide to impound the death-trap.

Making his way along the shortest route he knew, Sambo pondered his motives for agreeing to go solo with his rescue of the woman and her child. He had no definitive reason for doing so. It was against his better judgement and his character to ignore common sense in favour of some absurdly gallant gesture of honouring the lady's wishes. If it were not for one thing that occurred earlier, he would not have consented to the foolish suggestion that the authorities were not to be involved. That one minor reaction in him caused him to ignore his perceived responsibilities upon finding a fellow human in need.

He began to doubt his decision once he debated the ramifications of the obvious injuries she had suffered. She may die; have died already, as a result of his actions, or inactions, as the case may be. If he found two corpses upon his return to the site, he would never forgive himself. If they remained alive, he might well just ignore her request, delivering them both to a hospital where they would receive the treatment they required. His torn emotions provided an escape from the mundane task of driving the distance to decrepit old Myrltletown.

The morning light was barely peeking over the eastern horizon as he drove onto the dirt track through the open gate. The graveyard of rusted bodies, discards from a bygone era of automotive history, loomed in the headlamps of his vehicle. Sambo knew where he could deliver his own piece of automotive junk when the time arrived. He pulled up as close to the van body as possible. The fire was all but out, the wind had dissipated, and the morning was deathly still and silent. Sambo hoped it did not portend a bad ending to the evening.

When he found the pair alive within the shell of the panel van, he breathed a sigh of relief. While they were not yet out of danger, they had not perished during his absence, and for that, he was profoundly grateful. Sambo managed to spoon a little chicken soup into the woman's mouth after raising her gently to a sitting position. The baby was fast asleep on her lap. The woman's eyes had completely closed up, making her fearful of every touch. Only his calming voice mollified her enough to allow him to assist her.

With daylight creeping into the interior of the van, Sambo observed the serious condition of the woman, wondering how on earth she had survived the horrific beating. Her lips were impossibly swollen and he noticed several teeth missing where the bat or boots had obviously struck her fair in the mouth. Hardly one square centimetre of her body was unaffected by discolouration, swelling or injury. Where Sambo had attended her injuries earlier, he noted that he had succeeded in staunching the flow of blood, particularly on her head, the most worrying site.

Sambo spent the best part of an hour tending to her injuries and cleaning her thoroughly in an effort to determine the extent of the damage. Most, if not all, represented superficial concerns, requiring nothing more than bandaging. She did not appear to be suffering unduly from internal injuries. He could not be certain as to how seriously in need of medical care they were. All the while, the baby slept soundly, prompting Sambo to check on him constantly. When

Sambo had done all that was possible to attend to her immediate concerns, he took a moment to relax before contemplating the removal of her person from the van to his car.

Sambo had laid down the rear bench seat of the station wagon and prepared the area with a blow-up air mattress, sheets and blankets. He moved the baby first, after convincing the woman to relinquish her control. Though barely conscious and terribly weakened by the assault, she retained a formidable strength, and was gripping the infant for dear life. Sambo feared that her hearing may have been adversely affected by the beating, as she didn't appear to understand his intentions, despite him relating in great detail what he wished to do. He eventually removed the baby from her arms to place him in the car.

"All right, lady. I need to pick you up to put you in the car. Do you understand? Can you hear me?" Sambo imagined he perceived a slight nod of the head. "It is going to hurt like fuck, and I'm sorry for that. So very, very sorry, but if you don't want the cops or the ambulance here, then that is what I have to do."

"Ngh cop. Ngh cop," she muttered.

"I was afraid you'd say that. Okay then, up we go."

He winced when she screamed, almost reversing his decision. Reluctantly, he continued until he held the lightweight woman securely. He carried her over to the car in his powerful arms, and laid her as gently as possible within the rear compartment. He crawled in beside her to move her forward until she was all the way inside the vehicle. He then placed the baby back in her arms. She relaxed noticeably the moment she and the baby were reunited. He tried to imagine what it must be like for the woman, suffering a life-threatening assault, giving birth, probably prematurely as a result of the beating, then trying to ascertain the intentions of a stranger she could not see and most probably couldn't hear too well either.

Although Sambo had been giving her a running commentary on all his actions and plans, he doubted she heard much of anything. She could only do a bit of a 'Helen Keller thing', relying solely on touch to judge the quality of the person attempting to care for her. It would be extremely difficult for the victim of any such beating to trust anyone, let alone someone she was unable to identify through normal channels of sight and sound. Sambo covered her in warm blankets and tucked her in as best he could for the trip home...if that's where he decided to take her.

Sambo trundled down to the river after closing the rear tailgate and winding up the window to keep the occupants as warm as possible. At the water, he dipped in the bucket he brought with him to fill it with the murky brown liquid. He used that to extinguish the remnants of the fire. Once complete, he scouted the area in the dawn's light to find any evidence pertaining to the woman's presence. He removed the afterbirth, which was attracting flies and other insects to the scene, dumping it in the river. He removed any signs that the van or the immediate area had been used by them before leaving.

When he entered the driveway to his home a while later, he debated his decision for the hundredth time or more. As he was parking the car in the carport, it seemed he had made up his mind or had his mind made up for him. He dropped his head to the steering wheel, almost succumbing to sleep as he rested his head for a while. It had been a long and troubling night for him and he doubted he would be able to relax for some time.

Charlie was awake and watching a program on the black-and-white TV in the living room. Mary-Rose watched from the kitchen as Sambo entered through the rear door, carrying a bundle wrapped in blankets. She could not make out a person or a baby within the package. She did not offer her assistance when Sambo appeared to struggle with the door to her former bedroom, knowing her presence might not be appreciated. She turned around to continue washing the dishes. She had fully accepted the fact that Sambo did not view her with the same affection she felt for him, but still felt a pang of regret knowing how he reacted to catching Charlie and her together.

When Sambo finally emerged from the room at around

lunchtime, Rose was attending to Charlie's lunch in the kitchen. Charlie, seated at the table, was pretending to read his favourite book, turning the stiff pages enthusiastically. Since Rose had purchased the new *Cat in the Hat* book, Charlie was rarely seen without it. The awkward silence stretched out while the pair went about their separate tasks.

"Found out who she is?" asked Rose, to break the tension.

"She can barely open her mouth, let alone make herself understood," answered Sambo tersely. "Charlie, can you take your book into your bedroom, please? Good boy. Mary-Rose will bring your lunch in there, okay?"

"Roth, Roth, Roth."

"Yes, I just said it would be Mary-Rose bringing it in."

"Thambo, Thambo."

"Good, off you go then."

Sambo waited until Charlie was well out of earshot. "Okay, let's hear it."

"I'm not sure what you want me to say, Samuel."

"An apology might be a good start, don't you think?" Sambo said as he seated himself in his familiar position at the head of the table with a ham sandwich.

"Nothing to apologise for, Samuel. Charlie is old enough. He's only two years younger than you."

"In body, perhaps, but not in mind."

"Not according to you."

"What's that supposed to mean?"

"You told me that Charlie had a mature mind in there, just that he wasn't able to get past his physical limitations."

"Hardly a good reason to take advantage of a disabled person."

"Advantage? Me? Jeez, you don't know anything, do you? You're such a stuck-up snob about sex that you think the whole world is as old-fashioned as you. Why do you think Charlie has been wanting me to bath him lately? He gets off on it, that's why. Sits in the tub with a raging hard-on just begging for some sexual relief.

There may well be some things that Charlie can't do, but *that* is not one of them. He has normal, *adult* urges and feelings like the rest of the world, except for you, that is. You've been...stifling him."

"How dare you? I have done everything for him, given up everything to be there for him."

"How dare you accuse me of taking advantage of him? Not everyone is as uptight about sex as you are. You were a virgin before I came along, weren't you?"

"That has nothing to do..."

"It has everything to do with it. You are a big strong male, not the least bit disabled, yet you didn't push me away, didn't stop what we were doing in the pool. You really believe I could force either you or your brother into doing something you found unpleasant? Dream on."

"Have you been rehearsing your answers long?"

"No, Samuel Border, I haven't. I didn't really think I had to. A man and a woman had consensual sex. The man needed it and the woman didn't mind one little bit, just for your information, seeing as no one else took up her offer. So, get down off your high horse Mr keep-it-for-the-right-woman Border. No one does that any more. Wrong century, buster."

"He has the mind of a child, he..."

"No, he doesn't. You were right, he's trapped in a part of the brain which he is fighting every day, and sometimes winning. He hasn't found the control yet to sound like a mature man, but I can see it inside him."

"*Cat in the Hat*?"

"He's not always in control. He allows his child to rule him at times when it doesn't matter. He's not ashamed of what he is, why are you?"

"I am not ashamed of him. I love..."

"He needs more than just a brotherly, dutiful love. He needs inspiration and challenge. He needs..."

"You've been here five minutes and suddenly you're an expert on what my brother needs?"

"I'm not going to sit here defending myself. Maybe you should read what Charlie writes some time before you run off at the mouth and embarrass yourself."

"What are you talking about? Charlie doesn't write, he can barely talk."

"See? You know bugger-all, big shot. He keeps a diary. On the days he feels able, he writes in it, labours at it, and a lot of it is really good. He showed it to me a couple of days after I arrived and I have been encouraging him to keep it up. He writes at a greatly superior level than his speech. It's just that he can't maintain the concentration very long. He lapses back into 'Thambo and Roth' and *Cat in the Hat*."

"Really?"

"Are you honestly that surprised? You were the one who railed against the medical profession, declaring to everyone that Charlie had more to offer, that he could progress. Why are you so shocked when you are presented with proof of that?"

"Show me this book," demanded Sambo.

"No. You need to ask Charlie if you can read his book. It's not up to me. I won't betray his trust in me."

"You care for him, don't you?"

"I have come to love him dearly, in my own way. I won't apologise for the sex. It was pure, clean, wholesome love-making, nothing the least bit dirty or smutty. If you can't accept that and want me to leave, then I will go. I won't even ask Charlie what he thinks. You are his official carer and I will honour your decision."

"I...looked in on you when I came back to get some things."

"I know, that's what woke me."

"Charlie, he...looked peaceful for maybe the first time since the accident. He normally tosses and turns like a wild man in his sleep. For that alone, I can see that you are good for him. I won't say that I like what I saw, but I don't want you to leave because of my so-called antiquated views."

CHAPTER ELEVEN

"How is our patient this morning?" asked Sambo several days after bringing home the woman and her baby.

"Managed to nibble a bit of toast," replied Rose as she entered the kitchen.

"Oh, that's great. Must mean the swelling in her mouth is going down."

"Samuel? How on earth did you find *her*?"

"I told you how it happened. I heard the baby and..."

"No, I mean, *her*."

"She was with the baby, of course."

"You're not understanding me. I know you found a woman and a baby, and how you came across them. That is weird enough on its own. What I mean is; HER! How could you possibly find her?"

"You're right, I have no idea what you are talking about. Her, who?"

Rose looked at him askance. "You really don't know, do you?"

"Don't know what, for crying out loud?"

"Who she is?"

"Of course not, she hasn't been able to tell me her name yet. I have no idea who she is."

Rose shook her head, "Men!"

"What has gotten into you this morning, Mary-Rose?"

"I wouldn't have believed it possible except for everything you've said to me. Sometimes, I guess, it's just inevitable. After all, I found you, didn't I?"

"Mary-Rose, you're talking in riddles. I feel I could get more sense out of Charlie right now."

"The universe has somehow decreed it and made it happen for you, drawn together by the powers that govern chance."

"Now you are starting to freak me out. What the fuck are you talking about, Mary-Rose?"

"Her, Samuel. By some quirk of fate or destiny, or whatever you want to call it, you managed to find the woman of your dreams, beaten to shit and left in some swampy dump at the end of the road. You rescue the woman you most desire in all the world, Crystal-bloody-Montague."

Sambo stared at Rose with incredulity, trying to gauge the depths of her depravity to engage in such a hurtful lie. Just when he thought he would blow his top, he began to recall a few odd things that had escaped his attention during the rescue. Paramount among these was the tingling sensation he had experienced, that unforgettable perception that always indicated a friendly path to him, a going home, a harmonious familiarity that followed him in connection with her.

"No," he said uncertainly.

"Yep," Rose said with a heavy heart.

"No, it isn't possible. You couldn't know."

"She may be all beat up and shit, but there is no mistaking that beauty spot above her lip on the left side of her face. Once I saw that I started looking for other clues. Skin colouring was a bit hard because of all the bruising. More green and yellow now than the perfect milky complexion, but you can just make it out. Hair colouring and body size, but the eyes are the real giveaway; emerald green. Game, set and match right there. Never seen eyes like hers anywhere else. Revealed for the first time this morning. I really thought you must have known for you to bring her here. But you really are a total gentleman, aren't you? Rescued a complete stranger, never knowing that she..." Rose was unable to continue for the tears rushing down her cheeks.

"Rose?"

"Now he calls me Rose. Just when I have no hope in hell of ever winning him over, he finally calls me Rose again. Oh God, I wish you had left me on the bottom of that bloody pool, Samuel." Rose rushed out of the kitchen.

Sambo sat in stunned silence. He had initially accepted Rose's attention as nothing more than an infatuation, a young girl's crush on someone she identified as a hero: a man who had saved her life as a child, a man she had fantasised about and built into an image suiting her immature memories. That she had grown into a woman was undeniable, and a beautiful woman at that, but she was still a young woman with her whole life ahead of her. Sambo was profoundly grateful to her for delivering him from a world of sexual ingenuousness. He could not, however, feel more for her than gratitude or fondness. He could not reciprocate her feelings, which he now recognised as being far more substantial than a childhood crush.

To Sambo, it seemed that, whatever he did in his life with regard to the opposite sex, it always ended up wrong. Without any effort, he seemed to foul up his few relationships with remarkable consistency. He knew he was an absolute rube when it came to sex. Rose had taught him that. That he was a no-hoper when it came to matters of the heart as well left him feeling disgusted with himself. He regretted many of the things he had said to Rose. She was in love with him...still, and he continued to find new ways to break her heart.

He admitted, reluctantly, that Charlie was a grown man as far as bodily functions were concerned. He did not want to admit that Rose was actually doing them both a great favour with her seemingly wanton behaviour. Charlie had been sleeping calmly, requiring far less medication, ever since Rose had begun sharing his bed,. He would never openly condone her less than romantic relationship with his brother, but he no longer felt it his duty to interfere. He always knocked now before entering their room, affording them the privacy they deserved.

As it was only a two-bedroom house, he had taken to sleeping in the lounge when he was not attending to the woman, often sitting by her side until he fell asleep. The baby slept well, never causing any real problems. He woke, he fed, and he was cleaned by Sambo or Rose, then placed back on his mother's bosom to feed or sleep. A few days had passed and it seemed that mother and baby were doing as well as possible in the circumstances. Her injuries, while remaining severe, no longer appeared as life-threatening as first believed.

Sambo rose unsteadily from the table to walk to the room that Rose had vacated at the front of the house, with a window overlooking the street. It was a corner house with two street frontages. The front of the house bordered on a major thoroughfare, and the side street was quiet enough to allow them to reverse their car without undue delays. He entered the room, which was kept mostly dark to allow the occupants the healing rest they required. He walked softly to the chair he had set up beside her bed and eased himself down into its old leather, which creaked slightly with the weight.

"H'llo, Sham."

"Shit, sorry. I didn't mean to wake you. Wait, what? You, you know who I am?"

"Y'sh Sham. Know, y..."

"You shouldn't try to talk. I know how much it must hurt. Had to try to talk through a few busted lips myself at times. Just nod Or can I give you a notepad and pen until your mouth heals?"

"Wan' shpeak...Sham. Wan' th, thank...y. B, baby an' me."

"No need to thank me. Nothing anyone else wouldn't do."

"Not, not tchew. Did more, Sham. Thank y, you."

"Let me ask you something. Do you just know my name, or do you know who I am? That we have actually met before?"

"Know, who...know you, Sham. Easy, know you, Sham."

"So, you really are Crystal? Crystal Montague?"

"Y'sh." She nodded and answered between clenched teeth, avoiding the pain and effort of opening her mouth as much as possible.

"Wow! That is just...just...well, it's freaky. After ten years of...well, and here you are. I can't quite believe it."

Sambo felt like a twit. His chest was near to bursting and his heart was pounding as though he was running a marathon. If he didn't know better he would swear he was about to cry. It took all of his self-control to fight the impulse.

"Sh, Sham?"

"Hmm?"

"Baby?"

"Yes, a good looking baby, all toes and fingers accounted for, and doing well as far as I can tell, but then, I'm no expert."

"Baby name. Sham Jun...Jun-ee-or."

"No, you mustn't. Give it some time, okay? No need to name him right away, and certainly no need to name him Sam Junior, if I heard you correctly? Surely you want to discuss that with the father first?"

Crystal began to shake uncontrollably at the mention of the boy's father. She trembled with fear so much that it woke the boy. Sambo stood immediately and hushed her with a soothing voice, promising not to mention the father again. After a while, mother and child settled sufficiently for the baby to suckle the exposed nipple. It became clear to Sambo that the child's father was responsible for her condition. Sambo could not imagine the type of personality it would require to inflict such harm on the mother of his child. What sort of sadistic arsehole must he be to beat a woman, a woman bearing his child, to near death?

"Okay, Crystal. Sam Junior it is. Would you mind if we just called him Junior or Little Sam, though, to save any confusion while you are here? Yes? All right. Well, welcome to our humble home. I live here with my brother, Charlie, and his...friend Mary-Rose. She prefers Rose, by the way."

"Rosh luh y' Sham."

"You, you can't possibly know that"

"Wom, woman knowsh."

"Whatever Rose feels for me, I don't feel the same way."

"Shome...shomeshing, 'ere."

"I can't help but feel something for her. It is very easy to like her, that's for sure, and she has been great for Charlie."

"Y' should luh her, Sham."

"Good grief, listen to you. Hardly a day or two from death's doorstep, and you're playing matchmaker. Won't do any good, though. You see, someone else stole my heart a very long time ago. I have never been able to move past that. Never wanted to."

"Who?"

"Would you like to hear a story? You may not quite believe it all, but I promise you that every word is true."

Crystal nodded her head slowly, unsure what to expect from the dear, dear man who wore his heart so noticeably on his sleeve. She listened intently as the bizarre story unfolded. She knew about the pool, of course, and about Mary-Rose's rescue. She did not know of his relentless search for her afterwards. Through slitted eyes, which she could barely keep open for long periods, she watched the enigmatic man, now grown from the boy she once knew, retell his fantastic tale, including the haunting images of his dream, ending at the mauve house upon the rise.

The tears ran freely down her face before the completion of his story. His declaration of unrequited love for her tore at her soul. She witnessed the desperation in his voice as he explained how he had longed for her to the exclusion of all else for over ten years. The words tumbled out of his mouth in a torrent of abject misery for having lost her, and untold happiness at finally being reunited. Breathlessly, Sambo unloaded the decade of loneliness and despair at her bedside, while she listened with trepidation and an innate sorrow.

He could not know that she had dreamed of him often during the years since they first met, felt the same intangible connection, pulling at her inexorably across the ether. He could not know that her father had been called across the ocean to troubleshoot at remote oil rigs and mines across the globe until she finally left school to fend for herself. He could not know the terrible mess she had made of her life after that, when she finally returned to Brisbane. If he knew how low she had sunk in terms of humanity and depravity, he would look upon her with utter disdain, a look she could not bear to see.

She could never reveal the truth of her life to Sam as he had. She could see nothing but gallantry, courage and generosity in the handsome man before her. He would see only the ugliness and sordid horror of her existence if she told him the truth. One thing, though, above all else, she did not think it wise to convey to him her own troubling dream.

CHAPTER TWELVE

Crystal's resolve weakened dramatically in the following months, leading up to the happiest period of her life. Desperately attempting to hide her emotions while falling in love was proving almost impossible. Keeping the knowledge of her sullied past and her dreams a secret from the man she loved threatened to widen the emotional gap between her and Sambo.

Rose had relieved Sambo of most duties where his little brother was concerned, allowing Sambo to devote his attention to the woman of his dreams and his namesake, Little Sam. Sambo remained undecided as to whom he felt more drawn, the baby having won his heart and devotion as assuredly as his mother.

During the first few weeks of her recovery from serious injuries, Sambo rarely left their side, either sitting in a recliner at her bedside or in the lounge with her once she became mobile. He spoon-fed her soups and soft foods while her mouth recovered. He doted on the pair, as proud and nurturing as any father and husband might be. Without wishing to usurp the role of the biological father or interfere with any emotional attachment the woman may have retained for the father of her child, Sambo threw himself into the role of caretaker and surrogate father with gusto.

Sambo displayed all the qualities of a true gentleman and reliable provider. He was too good, too pure and naive of the other side of life for Crystal to allow her affections to be made known. Slowly, as the weeks following the birth of her wonderful gift passed, as her eyes gradually healed and allowed a better view of the life around her, listening to her benefactor declare his feelings for her without reservation or regret, she came to know the man, her child and herself.

In the beginning, she avoided all questions of her past or the boy's father. Crystal did not want to reveal the sordid experiences leading up to her discovery by the man she grew to admire and cherish more with each passing day. Though still in pain from broken ribs whenever she moved, or from a sudden intake of breath, she responded to his ministrations quickly, gaining a healthy glow before long. As her bruises ebbed and her pure alabaster complexion returned, along with the clarity and depth of colour in her eyes, she regained the vitality and lustre Sambo first envisioned in his dreams.

The serendipitous ambience was to continue for a year as the strange little unit found solace in each other's company and mutual friendship.

Sambo knew a happiness and contentment he would never have considered possible. Though he never once shared a kiss or other intimate moment with Crystal, despite all the times he had to bathe her and the baby in the first few weeks, his heart continued to fill to overflowing. He was gentle, kind, observing and respectful at all times of his ward's needs and considerations. He felt foolish enough for having confided his innermost secrets to a relative stranger, revealing his love so swiftly. To compound his foolishness by attempting to force his emotions upon an unreceptive target did not bear consideration.

Sambo knew that his aspirations for a life with Crystal, should he succeed in gaining her affections, required the utmost delicacy, restraint and patience on his part. He watched in silent amazement as the purest vision of beauty emerged from the chrysalis of black and iridescent blue-green-yellow bruising while Crystal recovered. His heart leapt within his chest, bursting with love for the delicate creature materialising before him every day. The dull tones of the grey walls appeared all the brighter and friendlier for her beauty gracing the room.

Sambo watched with pride and elation when mother and son were coupled at feeding times. Crystal was unable to hide her pure adoration and love for her son at those times, smiling at him like the enigmatic Mona Lisa. Little Sam, for his part, displayed little effects from his brutal birth, sleeping soundly and contentedly for most nights. He gave no trouble other than the general duties and obligations of an infant to provide dirty nappies and demand a feed at irregular hours.

The longer she was under Sambo's spell, the more difficult it became for Crystal to suppress her feelings towards him. She also came to know Rose well and suspected the love she carried for Sambo persisted. It was yet another reason for her to keep her feelings buried. While she knew that Rose's love was not reciprocal in Sambo's eyes, she did not want to come between the pair, valuing their friendship above her petty desires.

"Wow! Even your feet are bloody perfect," said Sambo while applying nail polish to Crystal's toenails.

"What are you talking about, Sam? How on earth can feet be anything more than what they are?" Crystal smiled uncertainly, waiting for the punch line.

"Oh, well, you obviously don't hold much store in feet. A human foot can have quite an allure if the proportions are correct and the form pure. The toes have to be in a graduating order of ascendance from the little to the big. Many a foot has a digit out of place, shorter than the preceding toe. Heels may be cracked and gnarly, toes misaligned or misshapen, feet distorted by shoes, etcetera. A dancer will often have the ghastliest of feet, despite enabling their owner to perform the most graceful pirouette. A foot may be too large, too small, or a host of other variants, making them appear less than perfect. You have, without a doubt, the most perfect feet I have seen."

"Oh, no, Sam. You cannot be serious." Crystal laughed. Little Sam, whom she was nursing, temporarily dislodged from his suckling, gave a cry of protest.

"No, it's true. Why do you think men have foot fetishes? That wouldn't happen with just any old foot. It has to be a beautiful foot. Hands are also a source of admiration for me. There is more to attract a male than a face and a torso displaying the right attributes."

"I think you are a minority, in that case, Sam. Most men are unable to see past the tits, and usually the bigger the better."

"I can't be alone, surely? I see nothing sexy in breasts that have had enlargement procedures making the recipient appear top-heavy. The term 'more than a mouthful is wasted' had to come from somewhere? I thought all women agreed that bigger is not necessarily better," offered Sambo, pouting.

"You obviously haven't seen the size of the dildos available in European and Asian sex stores, as I have."

"Oh? You visit stores like that?"

"Don't look at me like that, Sam. Sex is not frowned upon overseas as it is in Australia, especially here in Brisbane. We are so archaic in our views in this country. You have no idea what it is like elsewhere, Sam, and that is probably best. It might spoil you. For that reason alone, you should ignore your feelings for me."

"I could never do that, Crystal. It would go against everything I am. From the moment I saw you at the pool and felt the tingling up and down my spine as though someone was rolling a low voltage apparatus along it, I knew where my heart belonged. I did not recognise you straight away, but eventually I knew you were the woman from my dream. I can see you so clearly now, in that dream, walking with me from the pool that day..."

"From town, Sam..."

"What?"

"Nothing, never mind," said Crystal, too quickly.

"No way. What is it, Crystal? Why have you suddenly gone deathly pale? Come on, you owe me that at least. I haven't asked anything of you, nothing. Can you not give me that at least? You have been holding something back from me, I...I feel it. You corrected me. You said...'from town'? What does that mean?"

"Please don't ask me, Sam."

"I have to. I have to know. Won't you please tell me? Don't you think I deserve to know?"

"You deserve everything, Sam. I can never repay your kindness to me. You deserve far better than me, that's for sure."

"I don't get a choice in these things. It is what I feel, what I am meant to feel. I am following a path by being with you, a path that is right for me, for us."

"Stop it, Sam."

"I won't. I can't help it. As sure as I need the air to breathe, I need to follow this path that my heart decrees, that my dream assures me is..."

"Wrong."

"What is? What's wrong?"

She sighed. "Your dream, Sam. It's wrong."

"It's my dream, so it can't be wrong. It's not possible for a dream to be wrong."

"It is when it is shared. I...know the dream, Sam."

"Of course you know the dream. I told you about it in great detail."

"You told me about *your* dream, Sam. I am talking about mine. In my dream, you and I do not walk home from the pool, we are walking back from attending the cinema in Queen Street, the Regent Theatre, after seeing a double feature, Charlie's Aunt with Jack Benny and Under the Doctor's Spell. It is Saturday night, the seventh of October, 1944. Newspapers proclaim that the allied forces in Holland are menacing the Hun. You are walking me home after the show. It is your last night of leave before you must return to the war in your bomber. You were a pilot, walking home his sweetheart during the latter stages of world war two.

"The streets were very dark still because of the war. You had a torch which we used to find our way along the unlit footpaths. You were so tall and handsome in your RAAF pilot's uniform, a smattering of medals on your chest. Before we got to my house, we sat on a bench, a bus seat. We were holding hands in the starlight. After a while, in silence, while I hoped you would find the courage to kiss me, you got down on one knee and proposed.

"I was crying as I accepted your proposal, knowing full well that you might never return from Europe. Then, I saw you take out a pocket knife. You were so excited about us getting married that you wanted to shout it out to the world and you were making an awful racket. You didn't have a ring yet, so you wanted to make sure there was some tangible evidence of our engagement. Near the bench was a telephone pole. I watched you carve our initials as I held the torch: SB loves CM, within a heart."

"Samuel Border loves Crystal Montague."

"No. I was Camille Matthews. Your name was Sydney Burton"

"Then we kissed?" asked Sambo, tentatively.

"Then we kissed," she agreed, reluctantly.

"Then?"

"I don't know, Sam. I don't recall any more of the dream if there is any. That's where it always stops for me, at the kiss."

Little Sam had fallen fast asleep while she related the tale. She was embarrassed after the telling of it, never attaching much importance to the baffling nightly episodes. Crystal had never given much credence to providence, extrasensory perception, fate, destiny or any other spiritual occurrences. Despite those leanings, she did fall deeply in love with the man in her dreams, with the face and physique of Sam and the name of Sydney.

The night she gave birth, when she believed her end had surely arrived, the voice of her dream lover brought her back from the brink of oblivion. She recognised the voice eventually, though through a haze, having heard it every night of her life since she could remember. As a young girl, she swooned at the sight of him in her dreams, melted as he gazed into her eyes with gentlemanly desire. Her romantic evening trysts with Sydney Burton accompanied her throughout her childhood and into her teens until she finally saw Samuel at the pool that day.

She could not believe her eyes when she spied him coming through the turnstile with a look of astonishment on his features. She could not be sure what had captured his attention but guessed it might have been herself. She hoped it might be the case. Unfortunately, the large youth with the superbly bronzed and sculpted musculature, peering in her direction often enough to make her heart race, did not seem to care a whit for the forlorn lady on the opposite side of the pool.

Just when she thought he might be walking over in her direction, he suddenly dove into the pool. It was only a second later that she noticed the absence of the girl who had been playing by herself, with her parents arguing all the while. Everything turned to mayhem at that point, with the dreadful parents making ridiculous accusations to cover their guilt for having neglected to properly care for the girl. Had it not been for her statement, Samuel might well have been charged with a heinous crime. She managed to slip away quietly while he was still embroiled in statements and such with the police.

She had every intention of returning to the pool the following Saturday in the hopes of meeting the young man properly. When her father was called away to Kalgoorlie on urgent business, her plans were postponed indefinitely. Their house was placed on the market within a year, as it appeared they would not return to Brisbane in the foreseeable future. Oddly enough, it was on her return to Australia, nearly a decade later, that she decided to visit their house, making sure to touch the carved letters in the pole for good luck. In all the years she had repeated that simple act while they lived in the house farther up the hill, there had never been an incident. On that particular day, while brushing her hand lightly over the carving, she acquired a nasty splinter, causing her to yelp.

That was when she met the striking Tommy Duggan. Thomas Sean Duggan, exiting the house where she once lived, heard the sharp cry as he walked down the front steps. After copping a tongue-lashing from his da, he was in no mood to be inquiring after the young lady's well-being, but sauntered off in her direction, anyway.

"Y'all roit then?" he asked as he neared Crystal, who was waving her hand around.

"I'll be fine. Just a splinter, but it hurts like crazy."

"Bleedin' loik, too, oint it? Oil have a looky?"

Crystal nearly fainted when he produced a large-bladed knife from nowhere, fearing her life was in dire jeopardy. With a vice-like grip on her wrist, she was unable to move away from him or the deadly blade hovering insanely close to her face. She watched in dreaded fascination as he deftly used only the tip of the hunting knife to carefully remove the large splinter. It required a small incision to be made in order to remove the entire length of the invasive timber. Leaving even a tiny portion of the wood deep in the finger would invite a nasty infection in just days. When the young man gently wrapped the wounded digit in his clean handkerchief, she was immediately impressed by his charm and Irish swagger.

"So what does it mean?" asked Sambo, interrupting her daydreams.

"What?" She rose to place the baby in his bassinet at the side of her bed.

"The dream. What does it mean that we share the same dream?"

"We don't really, do we? I mean, mine is completely different to yours. It doesn't mean anything."

"Come on, Crystal. Bit more than a coincidence don't you think?"

"What do you want me to say? I don't believe in fairy tales and neither should you." She settled back into bed.

"I believe we were meant to be together, Crystal. Every time I am near you or see you, I have this tingling down my spine. I have faith that it means I am on the right track, that I was destined to be following a certain path leading to you."

"You never struck me as a religious person, Sam."

"I'm not. My conviction is based solely on my own intuition, a calling of sorts to follow a path that is right for me. Some would probably explain that as being guided by God, but I don't agree. It is something entirely different that I feel. I am probably not explaining it very well."

"Sam, you have to stop thinking that way. You and I will never be together like that. You have to give up on the notion of being with me. It won't go anywhere but bad, believe me. Besides..."

"Yeah?"

"Never mind."

"It's him, isn't it? Tommy?"

Crystal stopped breathing as she stared at him with shock. "How...could you know?"

"Cried out his name in your sleep a couple of times during the first few nights. He the one that did that to you?"

Crystal nodded when she decided she could not lie.

"He the father?" another reluctant nod. "He should be locked up for the rest of his life for what he did."

"Sam, listen to me. This is very important. Never, never speak his name to anyone, especially the police. Promise me?"

"Why?"

"Promise me," she insisted.

"Okay, okay, I promise. But tell me why?"

CHAPTER THIRTEEN

Tommy Duggan was without a doubt the mangiest cur to ever broach Australian shores. He had the devil's own smile with which to charm the birds from the trees, and the persuasive ability to have a dog surrender its bone, but his charm expired soon thereafter. At one-point-seven metres tall and thin as a rake, he was hardly a poster-boy candidate, yet that did not sway his propensity to lure the opposite sex into the most depraved activities imaginable. His Irish brogue and enigmatic smile soon charmed the pants off any girl he chose; when he chose it.

Charismatic, magnetic blue eyes peered through the long flame-red fringe, a continuing tribute to Beatle mania, to pierce the intended with their allure and open desire. His black personality did not emerge until his victim was under the pall of his influence.

When the handsome man successfully removed the offending splinter from Crystal's finger upon her return to Brisbane, she immediately felt a compulsion to discover more about him. She did not fully understand the sudden affinity she felt, yet acted on that impulse to allow the man to escort her to dinner that evening.

Over dinner in some unknown restaurant in Fortitude Valley, she discovered that Tommy Duggan, his father, Shamus, and grandfather, Paddy, had purchased their house from her father the year they left Australia. Her father had never mentioned the names of the buyers to her, so it came as quite a surprise. She did not witness Tommy's descent down the front stairs of her old house when he came to her rescue. Small talk and general conversation about their lives had Crystal ignoring the poor state of the building they were in or the tasteless food served therein. Had she taken the time to truly observe her surroundings and the state of the repast before her, she may well have put it down to the fact that the man lacked sufficient funds to afford a higher-class establishment.

Crystal, despite her father's status as a highly-ranked mining overseer/engineer, affording them a relatively profligate lifestyle, never adopted any airs about their wealthy station in life. While not overly wealthy in comparison to the magnates of the world, they were generally a station above the neighbours. Her father could not abide living among the affluent in their shady estates, preferring the company of real men and women with whom he associated freely and openly. That down-to-earth character rewarded her father with lucrative management positions across the globe, with competing mining companies offering exorbitant salaries to gain his services.

Wherever Tommy escorted Crystal in the following weeks, he was accorded a curiously deferential manner by the hosts of the restaurants or nightclubs they frequented. Crystal remained in the thrall of the enigmatic young man while retaining a minor reticence to surrender herself entirely. While she readily admitted to herself that sex would not have been out of the question, he had yet to approach her in that manner, playing the part of suitor and gentleman with consummate grace and ease. Her blinkered outlook did not fail to recognise that Tommy Duggan preferred the seedier side of life to be found in the darkened streets of Fortitude Valley, seemingly avoiding the bright lights of the central city district.

Crystal had yet to determine Tommy's occupation or manner of earning a living. Approaching the subject was usually met with avoidance or distraction. Her initial impression that he may lack the funds to treat her to a better class of fare faltered at the sight of the permanent roll of cash produced from his trouser pocket each time it came time to pay for their outing, always at night. She never saw Tommy during daylight hours apart from the first occasion of their meeting. Sometimes she fancied he might be some sort of vampire or something. He certainly shied away from bright lights or sunshine, preferring to stay up till all hours of an evening.

Tommy Duggan was not often seen to be drinking to excess or partaking of other 'entertainments' in her company. In truth, there was nothing at all to alarm Crystal about her boyfriend after a few months, yet she still harboured an inexplicable restraint, withholding a measure of affection. She never gave one hundred per cent of herself, physically or emotionally.

When the night finally arrived, when Crystal felt sure that her beau would instigate intimate relations with her, it came as no surprise when Tommy invited her inside his home for the first time. His father and grandfather had taken a holiday to far north Queensland, Cairns, where they hoped to indulge in a life-long ambition to hook a record-breaking marlin. Of course, any other of the highly-prized pelagic species would suffice while waiting for a billfish to strike.

Entering her old house had a peculiar feeling for Crystal. She remembered the house as being bright, joyful and always vibrant with music, mainly the classics, Beethoven being her favourite composer. It seemed an entirely alien ambience under the ownership of the Duggans. Dark and foreboding was the initial impression that came to her mind when Tommy led them down the hall to the living room. Heavy drapes on every window defended the interior against the slightest invasion of external light. Immaculately clean as far as she could tell, however, the room bore a lingering scent of stale booze and cigarettes which pervaded her senses and sullied that impression.

Tommy proceeded to turn on two table lamps, eschewing the brighter overhead fixtures. Leading Crystal to the leather sofa, Tommy slunk into the kitchen to fetch a bottle of champagne, a 68 Laurent-Perrier. Not the champagne of the elite, preferring the likes of a Dom Perignon, yet not the worst, like the inferior, cheap Australian version of the period; Great Western. Tommy returned with the open bottle nestled in a silver ice bucket, a damask napkin wrapped about the neck to protect against the condensation, and two champagne flutes.

Irish music played softly from an overhead speaker that Crystal had not discovered, as Tommy settled beside her on the sofa, the leather creaking slightly as his light, wiry frame eased into the stuffed cushions. He poured her champagne suggestively, almost leering at Crystal over the rims of their glasses.

"A torst?" Tommy suggested after filling the flutes.

"Very well, what shall we toast to?"

"To de future Mrs Duggan. Welcome to de formily."

Crystal wasn't sure she had heard right, "I beg your pardon?"

"Oi want ye take ye clothes off now so I can see me noo broid."

"Tommy? What has gotten into you?"

"Oil be one gettin' into ye shortly, woman. Take ye fooking clothes off," demanded Tommy, with a face devoid of all human expression.

Before Crystal could voice her indignation, the first of many backhands was delivered to her face: it landed with a mighty crack, sending her sprawling on the floor. In a flash, a demonic rage igniting within the man saw him pouncing on the bewildered and hopelessly defenceless woman cowering on the floor, where he proceeded to accost her with a flurry of well-aimed punches to her body. He tore off her clothing as she lay stunned upon the Persian carpet. Blood from a split lip where he had backhanded her dripped freely onto the carpet. He slapped her hard again.

"Don't ye be bleedin' on me fookin' carpet, bitch!"

Tommy hoisted her roughly from the floor, turned her and pushed her down again, positioning her on all fours in front of him, while he pulled his swollen penis from his trouser fly. His enormous beast was barely capable of erection due to the considerable quantity of blood required to engorge it sufficiently. He poured the contents of his champagne glass onto the bared backside of the shocked female before him.

When the behemoth was forced brutally into her rectum, Crystal screamed in agony and tried desperately to crawl away. Tommy easily pressed her to the floor, where he inserted the full length of his rigid shaft into her torn bottom, bleeding profusely from the damage. Though Crystal fought with every ounce of her energy, her strength was no match for the steel-hard muscles pushing her ever deeper into the carpet, while the thrusting, aching, merciless carnage of her posterior continued. To add to her litany of woes, he then bit her savagely on the shoulder, her pure white skin immediately separating as the teeth tore through her flesh.

Her recent thoughts of vampires spiralled through her mind as she endured the terrible agony forced on her by an evil presence. However, sucking her blood for survival or satiation was not on her malevolent attacker's agenda. Try as she might she had difficulty recalling any movie where Dracula or his converts coveted brutal anal sex. No, the horror making use of her was not a paranormal phenomenon, it was all too human and, at the same time, animalistic to be considered in such a romantic vein.

The assault on her continued for what Crystal thought of as an eternity. Accompanying the debilitating sex to her savaged rear end was a consistent barrage of stunning blows to her back and head, coupled with torturous bites to her shoulders and neck. Tommy finally reached his climax in a shuddering explosion of fluid entering her arse, shoving his cock even deeper if that were possible.

While Tommy raised himself to the sofa, where he refilled his glass, then reached for a cigarette from his jacket pocket, Crystal remained on the floor, crying pitifully, too sore to attempt to move. She wanted nothing more than to shrivel into an invisible ball. She ached all over, inside and out. Never had she experienced such violence and evil in a human being. Her senses were so battered that she was unable to process thought, move or contemplate flight.

Her ordeal was to be repeated interminably over the following months. She was locked in a sound-proofed room, handcuffed to a bed, any notion of rebellion knocked out of her by the constant blows raining down on her. She was used and abused day in, day out, by the ugly man, spewing his vile vitriol to produce the shame and control he desired.

Estranged from her father living overseas, unmissed by any friends since she returned to Australia, Crystal remained a prisoner with no hope of a rescue.

Total subjugation was his goal. Total subjugation was his reward. Any signs of defiance or retaliation were met with harsher and lengthier punishments. Whips, studded leather belts, metal irons and cricket bats were all used in her treatments.

A year later, Crystal was reduced to a quiescent, obedient vassal performing every task demanded of her without objection or pause. Only one bone of contention remained between the pair that Tommy was unable to force. She refused to marry him no matter how bad the punishments, how foul the verbal abuse, how deep the cut or bruise. Short of murder, Tommy found no way of inducing her cooperation in the matter. In the end, it didn't matter to Tommy, he knew he could wait her out, that he would own her completely in time.

Tommy dealt in the underworld of life in Brisbane. He, along with his father and grandfather, carved out a fiefdom of illegal activities that saw them commanding a fearful respect in The Valley. They owned brothels masquerading as strip clubs and massage parlours because prostitution was illegal in Queensland. Gaming dens, because gambling was outlawed, drugs, extortion, stolen auto parts, chop shops and anything else the trio could dream up, saw them swimming in ill-gotten cash.

Anyone found to be suspicious, or maybe thinking of turning into a squealer, soon found themselves feeding the enormous pike eels at the mouth of the Brisbane River, in the suburb of Pinkenba, at the end of the line in lowly, desolate Myrtletown. The father-son team ruled with absolute fear, ensuring a strict adherence to their edicts. The reputations afforded the pair were born of a sadistic and aggressive history stemming from their grandfather, the patriarch, Paddy Duggan, the worst of them all.

Everything they were, they inherited from Paddy. Reaching a mere one-point-five metres tall, Paddy balked at nothing, feared no one, winning every encounter through dishonesty, brutality and by thinking ten steps ahead of the competition. Before a traitor had a chance to betray Paddy Duggan, he found himself, or herself, broken into tiny pieces to be used as bait on the end of his fishing line at Myrtletown. Paddy spent an awfully long time with his rod and reels near the mouth of the river, hauling in one huge river monster after another, some weighing as much as fifty kilos.

Paddy loved reeling in the giant eels found scrounging and slithering around the muck of raw sewage and river silt at the mouth of the dirty river. Every stinking, rotting carcass, bits of garbage or household effluent entering up-river ended up floating down upon the banks of the river at Myrtletown, including industrial waste from any number of factories based upstream. It was a toxic brew that defied logic and law if anyone had taken the time to investigate the deadly soup. But that was Brisbane and the rest of the world back in the day, displaying total ignorance of pollution until it was too late.

The Duggan family was made up of only a male lineage. Females were merely the apparatus by which the male heir would be conceived and carried. Once that act was performed to their satisfaction, the broodmare, always carrying the Duggan name to ensure absolute legitimacy in the eyes of their God, was summarily discarded. It was always assumed that Paddy's wife ended up on his fishing hooks. Shamus' woman ended up as dog food after being placed in the industrial mincer of a butchery they owned. Shamus had been urging Tommy, his only boy, to provide them with the next heir apparent. They had been arguing about his father's constant goading and harassment over the issue when Tommy emerged from the house one afternoon and spied a young lady flinging her hand about as though swatting wasps.

Tommy knew the family tradition well, having been made to observe his mother's demise, upended live into the maw of the mincer. He still grimaced at the distasteful end to the woman who nurtured and loved him unreservedly through the first five years of his life. He had not yet found a suitable candidate. Truth be told, his proclivities in that regard were not entirely clear-cut. Not that he could confide such to his father and grandfather. When the opportunity presented itself so fortuitously that afternoon, he did not hesitate to begin the quest of dominion over the hapless woman, applying a charm and innocence difficult for anyone to reject.

Over the course of a year following her abrupt and painful initiation to the Duggan clan, Crystal bore the brunt of her captor's disappointment and despair at being unable to sire an heir. A doctor in the sole employ of the Duggans failed to identify any reasons for Crystal's infertility. Whenever the doctor visited to examine Crystal for evidence of a pregnancy, and none was forthcoming, she suffered brutal assaults at the hands of Tommy, who, in turn, copped more and more pressure and abuse from his father and grandfather.

Tommy stubbornly refused to 'be rid-o-the fecken whore' to find a woman who would bear him a son. He found the whole prospect of finding another female to be totally abhorrent. He suffered the ignominy of her barrenness because he could not abide the thought of placing himself in another woman. She served a purpose beyond the progeny so desperately sought. The fact that he could use her in other ways assuaged most of his constant urges. The pursuit of a preferential alternative did not bear contemplation lest he ended up feeding the eels himself.

Several years after her capture and capitulation, her total obedience, Crystal missed a period. The Duggan clan was jubilant at the doctor's proclamation of pregnancy. That jubilation turned to rage when it was discovered through an 'unlucky' ultrasound during the third trimester, with the baby facing the right direction, that Crystal was carrying a girl. None of them knew that the inverted genitalia of the baby would eventually find its own way out of the body to present as perfectly normal male genitals once the baby was released from the womb.

Only a month before the baby was due, Crystal suffered the combined wrath of the entire Duggan clan in a free-for-all that visited blow after blow upon her while she cradled her stomach protectively. Crystal was unsure of the passage of time, inured to the violent treatment she received. Her mind had completely switched off except for one overriding directive, to protect her baby.

Later that evening, barely alive, she was unceremoniously dumped at Myrtletown, left to die until Paddy returned later to prepare her for his fishing lines. Sending his useless grandson in his stead when urgent matters required his attention, Tommy arrived there at his grandfather's behest. He was, however, unable to locate the woman at his grandfather's favourite position on the banks of the Brisbane River.

A cooling wind was gathering from offshore, travelling atop the river to find its way into Tommy Duggan's face, making him shiver. After an hour of fruitless searching with a faltering torch, Tommy abandoned the task, too cold and tired to continue. He would relate a tale to his family whereby he finished the job and threw her to the eels and crabs. He was glad to be rid of her, but loathed the upcoming quest for a replacement. As he walked to his car he stopped momentarily to listen to a faint sound carried on the breeze. Unable to place the sound or the direction from which it came, he muttered to himself as he opened the door to his Holden, igniting the throaty V8 before leaving the scene in a flurry of dirt and dust as the powerful vehicle sped away.

CHAPTER FOURTEEN

Sambo could hardly believe his ears as the story was narrated to him over the course of the following months. He found it difficult to fathom the extreme circumstances that forced Crystal to remain quiescent for years. That she willingly accompanied the monster around The Valley, on the occasions when he felt magnanimous, without attempting to escape or seek help, defied Sambo's innocent concepts. He tried to imagine the horror she must have endured to ensure her obedience and loyalty to such an evil arsehole.

His blood boiled at the thought of her brutal rapes and consequent torture at the hands of the vilest piece of shit he was ever likely to encounter. His mind thrashed through a million scenarios whereby he might exact a revenge on the thing that dared to defile and deface the body and visage of a pure angel. Crystal had to shake him out of his reveries at times with dire warnings not to take any form of action. She feared for all their lives should the Duggan family ever discover evidence of her survival and the birth of her perfectly-formed son. Their proximity to the Duggan house sharpened her fears to a razor edge, and she made sure that she and the baby never ventured out of doors during the night.

During daylight hours, she decided that they were relatively safe, considering the night-owl habits of the Duggan tribe. She still needed to avoid the immediate area around her old house, regardless of the hour. The Duggan family home was monitored fiercely by their neighbours, always on the lookout for curious police patrol cars scouting the streets. Cops not on the Duggan payroll numbered few, but enough for the Duggans to remain circumspect and vigilant. In The Valley at night, they were constantly surrounded by a wall of protectors seeing to their welfare, ensuring they had ample warning should anything occur.

Despite all her trepidations and misgivings regarding an

intimate involvement with the man of her dreams, Crystal was drawn ever deeper into his charming, innocent spell. He was the antithesis of all that she had come to know of the Duggan clan. All that had been forcefully instilled in her by torture and drugs gradually subsided as his goodness filled her heart. Having seen this gentle, loving man in her dreams for most of her life, it was inevitable that she succumb to his patient affections and all-encompassing love for her.

It did not seem real or even possible at the start. While she was slowly recuperating from her life-altering ordeal as a sex slave and incubator, recovering from her life-threatening injuries, she listened and watched the wonderful man caring for her with acute interest born of suspicion and fear. In glacial timescales, she lowered her guard to allow his ministrations to comfort and guide her recovery of mind and body. She examined him closely for imperfections when dealing with either herself or her baby. What she saw, she could scarcely comprehend. His love was of such purity and honesty that her heart dissolved eventually, while her eyes fought back a constant stream of joyous tears.

Allowing herself to love again after her vile experiences, allowing a man to hold her and her baby with affection and adoration, melted the stoic resolve she had erected as a safeguard while in the clutches of evil. Every day in the front room of that little house in Rosalie brought new light and emotions into her world once more. Layers upon layers of well-constructed defensive walls came tumbling down as Sambo reignited her passion for life. His deft control of her fragility knew no bounds of patience and care. His undying love never once asserted itself to pressure Crystal into anything she was unwilling to accept.

Sambo permitted her all the time and privacy she required to work through the turmoil in her mind. It was an immense task to wear away the indoctrinated, brain-washed impressions from a true demon, to find the original, angelic personality concealed therein. In their second year together, their love blossomed on the emotional level. Sambo did not dare approach the physical aspect. He could not broach either the subject or the act without a clear and unmistakable sign from her.

Crystal regained the healthy glow and vitality of her alabaster complexion, with most evidence of her physical assault disappearing naturally. Her internal injuries of broken ribs did not cause lasting problems or complications to other organs. The bruises were soon gone, leaving only broken teeth to mend at the dentist. Scraping together and saving their combined monies enabled Crystal to gain porcelain crowns eventually to produce the happy smile Sambo remembered and cherished so vividly.

Brisbane came alive around them with the big one; the World Expo, in '88. The Bjelke-Petersen government was finally ousted unceremoniously in '87 among alleged bribery and corruption allegations leading to the humiliating dismissal of the police commissioner. Brisbane matured into a state capital city, gaining a healthy respect on the world stage.

While Sambo devoted most of his waking hours to Crystal and Little Sam, Rose grew more attached to and responsible for his brother, who showed remarkable behavioural progress and rehabilitation. His speech had improved dramatically and his ambulatory motions were greatly increased: he required his walker less and less. It came as no surprise when they eventually announced their intentions to marry. While Sambo still felt a smidgeon annoyed at the concept of Rose's calculated induction to their circle, he gave his consent readily enough. Her methodology for inspiring advances in Charlie's progress demanded his respect and admiration.

It was agreed that they would continue to reside together and that, eventually, Rose would assume the formal role of Charlie's carer, when Sambo's pension would be transferred to Rose. The loss of the government pension saw Sambo scrambling madly to find suitable employment, and, while Brisbane prospered, he found gaining a job as an unskilled, uneducated man a difficult task. It was during a friendly game of poker, where Sambo cleaned up as usual, that he developed thoughts of taking his talent further.

Gambling had still not been legalised in Queensland, so finding enough poker games of sufficient quality to fund their lives proved more difficult than he first imagined. Inevitably, the games were found only in the seedier parts of town or among the less than legitimate townsfolk. Naturally, Sambo avoided Fortitude Valley like the plague, though most of the best games were to be found there. Sambo played conservatively in order to risk as little of his stake as possible, yet it was not his natural game to do so. He found himself losing more often as a consequence.

Sambo eventually realised the folly of not playing his usual game, with a mixture of common-sense, careful observation and a large portion of luck to win more pots than he lost. That required a certain amount of risk with larger bets to scare off the opposition in some instances. It was calculated risk, a law of probabilities utilising an innate instinct and observational skills. By studying the players at the table, Sambo was able to identify their playing routines, their 'tells' (giveaway signs), indicating a good hand or bad. It was not a game of guarantees. There were no absolutes. It was simply a game of probabilities, whereby if he stuck to his methods long enough and gained enough experience of the other participants, he would eventually gain the lion's share of winning pots.

His preference was five-card draw, where five cards were dealt to each player for the first round. Players then discarded however many cards they deemed suitable to gain an improvement on the original five. For instance; if a player held a pair (any two of a kind), they usually discarded three cards in the hope of gaining a third or fourth to the pair. Sometimes a player would disguise the fact that they had a pair by retaining a third card, usually a high card such as an ace. That allowed them a dual possibility of gaining either three of a kind or two pairs with one pair being high.

Entering a game with new players required a careful investigation of everyone's methodology when it came to betting. It usually wasn't hard to pick the ones bluffing almost all the time.

Finding the cheats was not always so easy. Once found, he made sure to reveal the offender by demonstrably throwing in a winning hand, cards face up to show all the other players what he thought of the deal. Nothing showed up a cheat as easily as throwing away a full house or a straight so that everyone at the table knew what was happening. If the cheat reoffended, Sambo would leave the table without a word.

Spotting collusion among players, accomplices sitting behind him to reveal his cards with hand signals, mirrors above, behind or beside him, marked cards and any other of the innumerable methods of cheating, were all commonplace to the astute. Sambo knew most, if not all, of them. He had learned them all the hard way, losing his precious money in the process, so it became essential to recognise them as soon as possible after seating himself.

Sambo did not openly expose cheats or confront them angrily. If he found himself in the unenviable position of knowing he was being cheated but unable to identify the means, he simply halted his contribution to the play. If questioned why he was abstaining from play he simply remarked that until play resumed at an honest level he was not willing to donate his hard-earned funds.

That was usually sufficient to force the person responsible to amend their game to one of legitimacy. Sambo never partook of alcohol while playing poker, whereas some found it almost obligatory and voiced their objections at anyone abstaining. Sambo pleaded an intolerance on those occasions, claiming a debilitating allergy to fermented beverages. If that were not accepted, he would voluntarily remove himself and his plentiful stake from play.

His size and physique were usually enough to deter most potential thieves from foolishly attempting to part him from his wallet if he was found on the streets at night. When that display of superiority failed to impress, he called upon his strength and agility, coupled with a confident skill at boxing and martial arts to dissuade the unsuspecting. If a weapon happened to be employed as a last-ditch means of persuasion, Sambo soon dispelled such silly notions, handing out a sound thrashing after disarming the assailant.

The routine of playing poker three or four times a week during the evening while spending most of his waking hours in the delightful company of Crystal and her son, rewarded Sambo with the happiest period in his life. He usually earned enough to cover the bills, keep them all well-fed with good, wholesome food, and allow them to enjoy a matinee movie or late lunch/early dinner.

Crystal continued with her adamant stand on not appearing anywhere in public after sundown. If ever Sambo mentioned an outing 'after hours', it was as if a blind were drawn over her soul. It caused a glaze to dim the lustre of her brilliant eyes, a dark shadow almost blotting out her features, leaving a blank look of desolation. Her pain and sorrow ran to depths that no one could plumb. The spectre of her ordeal remained firmly entrenched in the nether regions of her mind where they could be dredged up to the surface with the most inconsequential remark, suggestion or stare.

Crystal devoted herself to her son despite his origins. Little Sam was the sole light in her otherwise bleak existence, excepting Sam Senior. All her efforts to avoid any involvement with him or any other man were for naught. He had won her heart without ever demonstrably pushing boundaries. His gentle manner and quiet devotion sought their way deftly around the major barriers she had erected around her personality. The pure, bright and honest love that shone within him required no vocalisation to make itself known to her. No amount of protestation on her part could influence the earnest man from his quest to gain her affections.

It was perhaps the most artful and cunning subterfuge in the annals of romance, in that his love for her conquered her battlements without any sort of conflict having ever been waged. The antagonist wove his way in and out and around her defences, all the while declaring that he had no intentions of pursuing a physical interest with her. A friendly peck on the cheek, a hand held at times when it was deemed necessary, a shoulder for tears when the terrors surfaced, and, above all, an unwavering devotion for her and Little

Sam. It was a name for the boy that everyone seemed to adopt, rather than Junior.

Without any clear indication of when it began, they were soon inseparable and closer than any three humans could hope to be. Crystal fell under Sambo's spell as predictably as night follows day. They were deeply, emotionally melded, heart and soul, conjoined by circumstance, fate and an abiding love. Without ever kissing passionately or declaring their affections, the three combined seamlessly to form a perfectly harmonious relationship. Their smiles were a beacon for all to see and remark upon, clearly identifying them as persons made exclusively for one another.

Though they conversed openly and often with the people surrounding them, especially Rose and Charlie, it was if they were in a bubble of total seclusion where no outside influence could pierce their unique cosmos. The term 'they only had eyes for each other' did not do them justice. Their world existed for only each other. Apart from the odd occasion when something would spark that shadow to cloud Crystal's gaze, nothing interfered with their total commitment to happiness and love.

On Little Sam's fifth birthday, Crystal and Sambo found themselves alone briefly while Rose and Charlie abducted Little Sam to take him to the pool, still frequented regularly by them all. It was a warm, lazy Sunday afternoon, with Sambo and Crystal casually clearing up their tiny backyard from the aftermath of the birthday party for Little Sam. Sambo threw the last of the streamers and confetti into a large black garbage bag before sitting, while Crystal opened them both a well-earned beer. As Sambo had packed away all but one of the plastic chairs, Crystal wandered over to him with their beers, and, to Sambo's utter astonishment, she sat on his lap, wrapping her arm around him to produce the two stubbies in front of him. Acting as nonchalantly as possible, so as not to make a huge deal of the definitive breakthrough she had achieved, Sambo accepted the proffered bottle with a silent smile. They clinked the two bottles together in a bemused toast, each understanding the implications of her actions in their own minds.

Sambo silently screamed for joy, while trying desperately to control a part of his body with a mind of its own. He was beyond ecstatic, beside himself with a happiness that threatened to overwhelm his senses. Crystal also found it impossible to restrain her smile as she silently sipped her ice-cold beer. The afternoon sun enveloped the pair in a cocoon of warm goodness which neither wished to spoil with unnecessary chatter or awkwardness. It felt too right, impromptu, and perfect to be broken by inappropriate banter.

When the bottles were finally empty, and the sunshine continued to provide a lazy warmth, their eyes suddenly locked in a study of one another, searching for indications of insecurity or fear. Sambo refused to push the delicate boundaries broached by Crystal's advance into his personal sphere. Crystal searched Sambo's deep brown eyes for signs of insincerity or hidden aspects of his personality. Slowly, inexorably, as ponderously as two icebergs meeting on a becalmed ocean, their lips met for their first real kiss.

The melding of flesh between two people so destined to be together could not last long enough for the pair. Captured so fully in the moment, neither gave thought to where it might lead in the near or distant future. That they would be together always never left Sambo's mind. How it would be while they were together was always the question mark hanging over their relationship. Crystal, so damaged internally by her terrible experience, and Sambo so fractured by his inability to practise a love so deep that he feared he might lose her as a result of his waning patience.

Sambo suspected that while it was generally accepted that a man may take the initiative after encouragement, he believed it not to be the case in the present scenario. He intuited a notion that permitted only Crystal to determine the direction and speed of their union, should there be one. He refused to assert his masculinity on the fragility of the woman who required an innate understanding and acceptance from him. He was content to bask in the glow of a kiss that lingered for an eternity before she finally disengaged.

"Sam?"

"Hmm?"

"I want to make love with you, but..."

"I know. In a strange way, I feel almost the same. I am scared of losing you...this. If this is all there is with you, then I will die a happy man for having known and loved in you our special way. Don't get me wrong, I ache for you like I could die tomorrow if I don't share myself completely with you, but I need to know that it will not end if I do."

"Would...would it be terribly wrong if we did not make love today?"

"Not even slightly. To hold you finally in my arms, to feel your mouth against mine, inhale the very essence of you, has fulfilled my every desire in the world. If anything more should come, it will come of its own volition in whatever shape or form it adopts. I will wait for you for the rest of my life if it takes that long."

"I do love you, Sam. I love you more than you could ever know, it's just..."

"I know, Crystal. You do not have to say a word about it."

"After, you know...?"

"Crystal?"

"Yes, Sam?"

"Will you marry me?"

"You can't be serious?"

"Deadly serious."

"But, Sam...I...I have someone else's child. You can't possibly want a wife the likes of me...after what I've..."

"Why? Because you are no longer a virgin? Neither am I, so what? You have a child. Gee, a single mother and you believe that is enough to ensure that I am not likely to want such a tainted woman? That hardly paints me in a very good light, does it?"

"Sam, I may never recover enough to allow a man to enter my body again. A husband has every right to expect and demand a physical union with his wife, a consummation of their marriage vows."

"What most men expect or demand is not how I feel or act. You should know that, Crystal. I neither expect nor demand a single thing from you. I will *accept* anything you offer freely. I accept the challenges and limitations as they emerge. I *accept* everything here and now and that is more than enough if that should be how it remains. I promise to love you, cherish you and protect you unconditionally until your dying breath regardless of the extent of our intimacy."

"I don't...know what to say, Sam. That is perhaps the most touching thing anyone has ever told me. I'm not sure I can even process that right now."

"Crystal, I will give you all the time and space in the world that you need. I will never push you to do anything remotely indecent or unwanted. You will always be in complete control of every aspect of our relationship. I am yours to command. All I ask in return is your hand in marriage. Everything else is entirely yours to include or dismiss at your leisure. Crystal Montague, will you marry me? Please?"

"Are you one hundred per cent sure?"

"With all my heart and soul, yes. I have never been surer of anything in my life. I want to spend the rest of my days with you, on your terms, whatever they be. If you want to exclude me from your bedroom, then that is the smallest price to pay for a lifetime of happiness."

"I hope you do not come to regret those words, Sam, I really do, but, yes, I agree to marry you on those terms. I do love you, deeply. I have always loved you but hoped to protect you from a relationship with me. I don't want to break your heart or disappoint you, Sam."

CHAPTER FIFTEEN

A week spent on Bribie Island counted as their honeymoon, the most affordable option for the newlyweds. Married by a celebrant at a low-key, private function for just the five of them; Rose, Charlie, Crystal, Sambo and the celebrant, whose name was promptly forgotten by them all, at the Ithaca pool. It was a joyously casual affair with attire consisting mainly of swimsuits. The owners closed the pool off to the general public out of respect and fondness for the loyal family unit.

While traditional consummation of their wedding vows did not take place on their wedding night, Sambo and Crystal acquainted themselves intimately with each other's physiognomy for the first time. For Sambo, lying nude next to his bride brought as much satisfaction as he dared hope for. The fact that the intimacy did not end at that delicious state reduced him to quivering jelly as Crystal explored his nether regions with skill and delight. He, in turn, discovered the wondrous anatomy of his ideal woman, previously denied his investigation, though the ultimate act of union did not occur.

Sambo felt a deep-seated contentment known only to those who have the absolute certainty that they have made the right decision. The tingles running through his system like an electric current told Sambo all he needed to know in that regard. His déjá vu signals were pinging off the charts from the moment she accepted his proposal.

Sambo supposed that anyone with enough of an education in their respective theologies and ideologies could soon ascribe any number of parallels within their beliefs to explain his experiences. Sambo did not require explanations. It was enough to acknowledge them, accord them sufficient weight, and act on them. He knew that he was guiding himself. How, he could never adequately explain.

He felt as though his own spirit, his essence, was ever-present, gently nurturing his conscience to accept the subliminal messages and the physical, spine-tingling instances that made him aware of the path.

The fact that they were only able to afford a week away, on an island connected by a land bridge, told Sambo that he had best start earning a decent living with his card-playing or seek normal employment. It was not enough to simply subsist on what he made, he needed to 'up the ante' to successfully provide for them all. Rose had quit her job to become Charlie's full-time carer, bringing in enough in government benefits to scrape through each week. It was up to Sambo to provide the rest in case of emergencies, always a probability with Charlie, and some savings for a rainy day.

While Sambo had passed his apprenticeship at poker, learning the ins and outs of professional play, especially the underbelly of the game, he had yet to put his stamp on the local scene. Stalwarts and old hands at the game saw him as a mark rather than a true player. He had not established any contacts with whom he might partner in order for both parties to look out for one another. There were many cheats to be watchful for in the game. Anywhere there is money to be made, there are underhand tactics and treachery involved.

After several years spent exploring the intricacies of the game and the players, Sambo felt it was time to elevate his status to that of a high-roller in the illegal world of gambling. Many years later, an officially-sanctioned casino would be built out of the old treasury building at the end of Queen Street in the city. Before then, it was all secrecy and stealth in organising and hosting the many games around Brisbane. One such game, found in The Valley, Sambo had been deliberately avoiding due to the proximity of Crystal's nemesis, Tommy Duggan.

Sambo did not fully trust himself to be caught anywhere near the area frequented by the man that sadistically and methodically tortured, raped and subjugated the woman he held dearest. If he were to come across the evil miscreant, he doubted his ability to remain in control of himself. He had harboured many visions of inflicting the greatest possible harm upon the person he hated most in the world. Crystal had to restrain him often when she elected to reveal some titbit of information about her ordeal with the monster. No amount of cajoling or insistence would convince Crystal to lay charges against the man for his vile acts against her and many others.

Sambo was often so incensed by what he heard that it was all he could do not to simply rush to the house on the hill where Crystal had been held against her will, and burn it to the ground with all occupants inside. He knew they slept until well past eleven o'clock nearly every day. He had surreptitiously surveilled the house on numerous occasions, planning his revenge in minute detail, down to the number of matches he required. Of course, he could do no such thing. It went against every fibre of his being. He could no sooner commit cold-blooded murder than he could stop breathing. Sambo was not a man of easy violence or deceit, despite his illegal nocturnal gambling, which could be viewed unfavourably.

Affected by the euphoria of his wedding and the subsequent honeymoon, Sambo accepted a rare invitation to play in a poker game being held near enough to The Valley to be dangerous. He justified his less than cautious acceptance because of the opportunity to raise the stakes from his usual game limits.

It was not uncommon for Sambo to leave games with around five hundred dollars in profit. Unfortunately, there were so few games to be had in Brisbane that it was difficult to survive on such meagre sums, including the odd occasion when he would lose an equal amount. Sambo was very strict in his adherence to a self-imposed limit of five hundred dollars lost or won. Once that figure was reached, either way, he would leave the game.

Oxlade Drive in New Farm, even in the early days, showed a certain prestige in real estate terms. Many multi-million-dollar mansions and fully-preserved colonial Queenslanders adorned one particular section of the street, with direct river frontages. One such Queenslander, immaculate in its preservation and renovation by the current owners, heralded the first game to be held by the owners with a voracious appetite for gambling, made doubly attractive because of its illegality. Marty and Hiram, a couple of drag queens from a Valley 'entertainment' club, very much under the radar, pulled in every favour and marker owed them to host the poker game with a stake of twenty-five thousand dollars.

The buy-in, representing less than a month's earnings to the entertainers, demanded a respectful consideration nonetheless. To Sambo, it was most of what he had saved. If he failed at the game he would be forced to continue in the smaller games for another year or more. He watched from the kerb as the guests arrived in a bevy of limos or souped-up Australian muscle cars, discharging glamorous escorts in their latest haute couture, accompanying the straight male guests. Champagne flutes were handed to every guest as they arrived, and valets appeared to park their vehicles in an underground carpark beneath the stately house.

The front yard was illuminated ostentatiously, with spotlights and strategically-placed coloured lights festooning the large Moreton Bay fig tree in the centre of a roundabout, accepting the flotilla of prestigious metal floating through the wrought-iron filigree gates. Sambo felt entirely under-dressed, out of place and out of his league among the glitterati entering the compound. Most of the parties unfolding from their limousines were ushered to the rear of the house facing the river, where they were entertained by an orchestra and an army of waiters with silver platters of hors d'oeuvres and more champagne.

The hosts, wearing subdued male attire of Italian provenance in direct contrast to their usual evening attire of sequins and glitter, fluttered among the guests with effete wrists dangling limply at every opportunity and kissing cheeks while brazenly ogling every male lustfully. Their naughty shenanigans entertained the superficial crowd, quite used to their flamboyant display of bonhomie, normally nuanced with more than a smidgeon of catty bitterness. It was always cleverly veiled with such a magnificent smile and nonchalance that the intended victim was seldom aware of the vicious intent.

Homosexuality, though only tolerated at certain levels at that time, always accepted in affluent men, flourished in the seedy atmosphere of The Valley. Openly announcing one's proclivities in that regard had not yet become acceptable in the eyes of general society in Brisbane. In fact, it was denounced publicly by the politician and clergyman of the day as dirty, illegal and almost inhuman. Homosexuality was against the laws of the state, the people, and most definitely against the church, by far the worst offenders! Leave it to the church to preach the loudest against something so inherently ingrained in their hierarchy that cover-ups would eventually rock the world when finally exposed.

Sambo ambled up to the gate to produce his gilded invitation upon request by the butler leering down upon the suspicious gate-crasher. With a sniff of contempt obvious to all but the blind and deaf, the butler reluctantly allowed the unescorted invitee to enter the hallowed grounds. Without a comment or direction for the flustered guest, the butler turned abruptly away to await the arrival of more prestigious persons deserving of his special attention.

Venturing onto the manicured grounds surrounding the enormous buttressed fig enjoying centre stage, Sambo began to feel less and less confident about the origins of his invitation, wondering how he could possibly have gained the attention of such a crowd. He did not associate in affluent or homosexual circles. He was in entirely alien surrounds, never having experienced the type of life afforded by the well-to-do. It was as foreign to him as the cucumber sandwiches making their rounds atop the highly-polished silver platters.

Sambo had already decided to forego the game when he was buttonholed by the hosts each sashaying in his direction in a race to be first. Hands, lips and cheeks were presented for shaking, brushing lightly and pecking, in that order. Otherwise, the hands meandered to places he would not have imagined possible during the course of normal introductions and light conversation. He had to brush aside an errant hand on more than one occasion when it ventured too close to prohibited areas. Sambo felt as though he were trying to avoid a bloody great octopus while standing in the yard facing the river, talking to the hosts.

"Darling, we are so glad you could make it. Naughty of you not to répondez, s'il vous plaît, Samuel," said Marty, *or was it Hiram*? They were dressed in identical suits which made them hard to distinguish.

"Huh?"

"Never mind him, darling. We're just glad you could make it. You are here for the game, I hope? We have been so looking forward to...playing with you," said Hiram.

They both tittered insouciantly while Sambo was left innocently pondering the joke. He felt entirely ill at ease with the pair of sycophantic ponces, their wandering hands and their less than civil intentions.

"Now, you must go right on upstairs and see Pierre, who will be the dealer tonight. Such a dear, dear man. He will take your stake and supply you with a receipt, which you can redeem for chips when the game starts. The game will begin at ten o'clock sharp, no late-comers allowed. Pierre has come highly recommended as a scrupulous dealer with a very good eye for any...below-board antics. Not that we are entirely against certain antics of that nature, just that we get to dictate and choose which," said Marty.

"I, I thought I might give the game a miss tonight, gentlemen. I don't think I am the right sort of player for your gathering," announced Sambo with alacrity.

"Nonsense! Marty, I want you to take this young man by the...arm and show him directly to Pierre. Under no circumstances are you to deviate from that purpose, understood?"

"I hear and obey, oh exalted one. Shall I fetch you anything upon my return?"

"Just bring him back here in one piece so that we might continue with our conversation and have a little drinky-poo."

"What'll it be, sweet thing?" asked Marty.

"Umm, just soda water, thank you," answered Sambo.

That response caused such a calamitous stir between the pair that Sambo decided on a cold beer to augment his thirst on the warm evening and assuage his hosts' displeasure. He was then unceremoniously escorted up the central staircase to the regal entrance of the old house. Sambo stared in awe at the grandeur of the old lady in all her astonishing beauty. The interior of the house gleamed with polished hardwood floors, all original, and tastefully stained tongue-and-groove vertical wall panelling, adorned by the an array of Australian art. Original Pro Hart and Ken Done, as well as landscapes by Hans Heysen and Aboriginal artists, Albert Namatjira, and Emily Kame Kingwarreye were just a few that Sambo recognised from his reading, the closest he thought he would ever come to the precious art.

Pottery and clay sculptures, vases and glassware in an array of glass cabinets, wooden carvings of African animals and masks, indigenous Papua New Guinean artefacts, feathered costumes and bizarre phallic pieces littered every available space on counters of polished red gum, ironbark or spotted gum. The entire house and contents were a testament to Australian and islander art as well as Australian timbers. None of it seemed over the top or pretentious: all had been done with meticulous care and sensitivity. Sambo had never been more in awe of his surroundings, nearly overwhelmed by the sheer extravagance and majesty on display. The house deserved to be enshrined as a permanent museum.

If Sambo had felt out of his league before entering the house, he was now utterly bereft at his ordinariness amid such opulence. He saw himself as a country bumpkin suddenly thrust into the middle of a beauty pageant, unable to disguise his ugliness, inadequacy and awkwardness. Marty ushered him forward with a pat on the behind to get him moving. The hand lingered a fraction longer on his derriere than courtesy permitted, with just the slightest pressure of a finger exploring the groove therein.

Sambo stumbled forward into a room off the main seating area that was impossibly austere in comparison to the rest of the house. In the room was a large round blackwood table, with green felt baize at its centre, surrounded by seven matching chairs. Cup holders were evident by the circular indentations in the polished wood, cleverly lined with cork to prevent stains or heat blemishes. It was a superb piece of bespoke gambling furniture, with cushioned leather chairs displaying all the signs of being entirely comfortable. A low-hung fluorescent light shade similar to a billiards lamp, with the ubiquitous fringe, offered a well-lit card-playing area where all movements could be observed clearly.

It was not the dimly-lit affair that Sambo usually experienced. Of course, dull lighting allowed any number of shenanigans to go unnoticed by the novices. It was harder to pull the wool over the eyes of experienced campaigners, but in muted lighting even the professionals were sometimes pressed to identify the shady methods of the various players at the table.

Sambo was simultaneously relieved and perturbed at the inclusion of a professional dealer. Relieved that there would be only one player to watch as a dealer. Perturbed that the single dealer might be found to be cheating in some respect and impossible to accuse in such a setting, openly or otherwise.

The walls were covered in a tasteful flocked wallpaper reminiscent of a river paddle-steamer's gambling rooms. Mirrorless and otherwise devoid of any shiny glass-covered etchings or other artwork, they reduced the possibility of viewing an opponent's cards. In a show of admiration for the table, Sambo ran his hands lovingly around the circumference, secretly investigating the possibility of hidden trapdoors or electronic devices on the underside woodwork.

He had personally uncovered one cheat who had cleverly devised a trapdoor in his table whereby a small section fell open beneath his guarded hand holding his cards, allowing the cheat to exchange a card or two at any opportunity. Sambo discovered the ploy when he heard a clicking sound several times during play. The spring-loaded trapdoor made a very small sound each time it was activated, and only a detailed investigation of the underside during a break in the game revealed the ruse.

When the game resumed, Sambo insisted on changing positions at the table, declaring a non-existent superstition to playing in the same chair all night long. After a minor objection, it was agreed by the majority to alter positions; others being all too aware that something was not quite kosher. Remarkably, the owner and host of the corrupt table ended up being the big loser for the evening. Everyone shook Sambo's hand with extra vigour upon leaving, offering a wink or two while they shook. Sambo suggested in a cool, calm voice before the game had concluded that the owner might benefit in future games with a replacement table. The subtle warning was taken very seriously.

Pierre appeared from somewhere behind Sambo to accept the twenty-five thousand dollars in cash as the entrance fee to the game. Sambo received a beautifully inked card with his name, address and other particulars in perfect script as a receipt.

His face gave away none of the panic he felt at handing over the huge sum representing most of the money he possessed. Sambo reflected, not for the first time, on the wisdom of his choices. While the exorbitant sum would hardly dent the coffers of the elite patronage assembled that evening, he was about to risk all. His subsistence and his reputation were at stake.

Sambo carried the signed receipt close to his heart while he impatiently awaited the appointed hour. Purposely avoiding the hosts and anyone closely associated with the pair, Sambo stuck to the background, silently blending into the scenery as much as his physique allowed. His imposing stature and obvious strength exuded a commanding presence in most company. Among the effete of the upper echelon of Brisbane society, he stood out like the proverbial sore thumb, attracting more than his fair share of unwanted attention.

Sambo made his way to the pontoon at the end of the gangplank, mooring the host's yacht, glowing splendidly in the ambient light. The single-masted schooner showed superior sleek lines redolent of the racing yachts Sambo recalled from the Sydney to Hobart yacht races he watched on TV each year. Not a sheet nor line was out of place, not a cleat un-shined, a wooden board not scoured and polished to within an inch of its life.

The wash of the river against the wooden hull created a gentle susurration in Sambo's ear as he seated himself on the single bench seat atop the pontoon, gazing into the waters flowing past the yacht. Sambo resigned himself to the embarrassing fact that he was about to be entirely outclassed, and relieved of a vast sum of money. He was not a member of the elite, nor did he care to be. He had foolishly assumed that status held no command in the game of poker, only the stake and the play. He was a little confused about the amount required to participate.

Twenty-five thousand dollars, a veritable fortune to him, meant little more than play money to the other members he saw. He decided to deliberately lose any winning hands, not draw second cards to a hand of fruit salad (a hand with a mixture of suits and denominations adding up to naught), and betting stupidly on any good hands, thereby giving away his chance to win a decent pot. He would feign an unlucky streak and excuse himself from the rest of the game after having foolishly thrown away about five thousand dollars; the least amount he thought would be acceptable to the other players when he withdrew from the game. With his plan firmly cemented and his brain attuned to that outcome, he bravely marched up to the house just before ten.

CHAPTER SIXTEEN

"...Winner takes all," Pierre stated as part of the house rules governing the night's game.

Sambo had not considered the possibility of a game where the last man standing won everything, similar to a Texas Holdem tournament. His plan had suddenly been scuppered by the house rules. In his exuberance and joy at having received an invitation to join a big game, he had not thought to question the type of game to be played, believing it to be identical to the pub versions he generally attended.

Sambo had to completely alter his previous mindset to play with all his wits about him. He could not afford to lose the entire sum at stake. He foolishly believed that if he feigned bad luck for the evening, he would be able to withdraw politely to play again another day. The last-man-standing rule jolted him upright in his chair. Each player had to continue until they lacked the funds to see/call a bet, or afford the next ante, at which time they would be asked to leave the room.

The game was announced as five-card draw with jacks or better to open. This meant that a completely dead round of cards, where no one could open the betting, would be rejected to increase the pot with subsequent rounds of antes. With an ante of one hundred dollars a hand and a minimum one-hundred-dollar bet, the pot would soon build in the event that no one was able to open for a few deals. Sambo would have to go back to his standard game plan, playing the players and not the cards.

Pierre, the dealer, sat almost directly opposite him. On Sambo's immediate left and right sat the hosts, with Marty on his left. Next to Marty was a man introduced as Harold Symes, a portly fellow with an enormous handlebar moustache, which Sambo was inclined to assume would come into play at some point. He nicknamed

Harold, Hardy because next to him was the Laurel of the pair. The rake-thin man, known as Gordon Pane, with a nervous tic in the left eye, was the quintessential opposite of Hardy. The dealer, Pierre, was next, then came an Asian person called, of all things, Manny. Sambo supposed it was short for some complicated oriental name which was hard for an Australian to pronounce. Manny was most likely of the same crowd as the hosts, appearing to be less than manly with flamboyant gestures, an obscene lisp and a rather frilly blouse under the suit. Then came Hiram and himself. Both Marty and Hiram had removed their coats to sit in shirt sleeves, losing all affectations to take on new, serious personas without the slightest hint of their former frippery.

Hardy and Laurel were both swigging generously from snifters of brandy, while the hosts had champagne. Manny was sipping delicately from a small vessel containing what Sambo assumed to be sake. The dealer and he were the only persons not imbibing. He had ordered a soda water for himself that had not yet arrived. Breaks in the game would be called every hour to replenish drinks or attend to ablutions. He supposed the waiter, unable to gain entry until the first break, would then bring him his order.

Sambo observed every movement at the table with a practised eye, especially as the pack of new cards was opened in front of them. Pierre deftly fanned out the cards in a perfect arch to indicate to all the players the complete, unaltered deck, first face up, then down. After removing the joker, the remaining fifty-two cards were jumbled upon the green baize surface in a haphazard manner to break up the suits as randomly as possible, before being gathered to be expertly shuffled.

Sambo only seriously started paying attention to his hand after deliberately staying out of the first five hands. During that time he had picked up on a couple of indicators for Hardy and Laurel. As predicted, Hardy's moustache came into play if he had what he felt was a winning hand. Laurel's tic increased with his level of excitement. Hiram seemed to sigh when receiving a bad hand, or not gaining the improvement he desired with the second round of cards. Marty had yet to reveal any indicators, and the poncy Asian showed the most dead-pan face Sambo had ever seen.

On the sixth round of cards, possibly the last before a break was called, with Sambo down over six hundred dollars, he received a pair of aces in his first round, accompanied by a three, a two and a five, of varying suits. Playing conservatively would have Sambo keeping the high pair to discard the other three in the hope of gaining a third ace or another pair, making for a fair hand. Otherwise, he would ditch one of the aces for the chance of a four to make his low straight.

Manny, opening the betting with five hundred dollars, elected to keep all five of his cards, indicating the possibility of a straight, full house, a flush or better...or nothing, a bluff. If Manny was not bluffing, then the lowest of his possibilities for keeping all his cards was a straight. Sambo's chances of getting his own straight were low: beating Manny's straight with his low one should he achieve it, unlikely. Hiram folded. Sambo decided that a possible straight was simply not going to cut it. He could have folded as well, but a hunch told him to continue. He matched the bet (called), and asked for three new cards. He did not touch them when they landed in front of him.

Marty elected to remain in play by matching the five-hundred - dollar bet and asking for two cards. For Marty to remain in play against a possible straight or better meant he had at least three of a kind, and was hoping for a fourth or a full house. Hardy folded with a loud harrumph, probably meaning he was throwing out a reasonable pair that he would have played if not faced with a player keeping his five cards. Laurel asked for one card after matching the bet without raising. Sambo concluded that Laurel held either two pairs or four cards of a straight. His increasing tic action indicated some excitement, which ended abruptly after he received his new card.

All eyes were on Sambo, who had yet to peer at his new cards, laying face down on the table as they had been dealt to him. Manny placed a further thousand on the table as his next opening bet. Sambo raised him hundred, still without knowing his full hand.

"You really need to look at your cards, dear boy," offered Marty before placing eleven hundred dollars in chips before him. "I don't think you have me, Manny, so I need to see for myself."

Manny smiled knowingly. Laurel increased the bet by five hundred after placing the initial eleven hundred in the centre. Manny's mouth curled downward ever so slightly. Sambo believed he had Manny's hand pegged, especially when Manny reluctantly raised the bet by another thousand. Sambo believed that Manny had nowhere else to go. Sambo placed sixteen hundred in chips before him, effectively raising the bet by another hundred.

The room erupted in perturbed banter as everyone insisted that Sambo look at his remaining cards. Sambo peered about him in a relaxed manner as he sat through the protestations.

"Samuel, my boy, you simply mustn't keep raising the bet without knowing your hand. I thought you were a better player, we all did. That sort of recklessness will see you retired from the room in no time at all, and I rather fancy having you by my side," said Marty, placing a hand far too high on Sambo's thigh.

"Please remove your hand, Marty. I doubt you will receive the rise you desire. I will look at my cards when I am good and ready. If that means that I lose the hand or the game and end up leaving the room, then so be it. At the moment, I am content in knowing what I have and what everyone else has."

The laughter in the room broke the tension, as everyone realised what an amateur they had mistakenly invited to their game. The hosts, in particular, were dismayed at the possibility that they had provided such poor sport for their other guests. Hiram then sat upright.

"Very well. I have a suggestion to make, and possibly a way for us, or the lad, to make up for his silly play. Let's play the round to completion, then have a private bet at the end before cards are revealed. You will tell us what you suppose each player has in his hand. The rest of us will bet against your guesses. We win, you pay us even money. We lose, our money goes to you. What do you say? Time to put up or shut up, dear boy."

"I will accept, with the proviso that your bets are no more than one thousand dollars each with a maximum of five thousand for five players multiplied by the three remaining hands in play. That comes to about what I have left at the moment?" suggested a worried Sambo.

"I think we had better all see him so that he doesn't have the chance to raise any more? What do you say, players?" asked Marty, who placed his sixteen hundred in chips forward. Laurel placed his eleven hundred, followed by Manny reluctantly parting with another hundred.

"Very well, everyone has agreed to see you, Samuel. Let us start with the first player left of the dealer, shall we? I will be the first to bet the maximum: one thousand dollars says that you do not know what Manny has in his hand," said Hiram.

The other players all followed suit. Sambo would have to pay them each a thousand dollars if he did not predict Manny's cards.

"I am going to assume that you need only the hand one is playing rather than specific suits or denominations? That would be impossible, of course," offered Sambo. The others at the table nodded gravely. "Well, Manny did not ask for any cards, but I believe he was bluffing. He has no hand to speak of. Nothing above a single low pair is my best estimation."

Manny's face dropped significantly, eschewing the usual bland veneer. Without a word, he tipped over his hand, revealing fruit salad at best, to the astonished faces of everyone present except Sambo and Pierre.

"Manny, you sly old fox! I thought you may have had a flush," exclaimed Marty.

Everyone handed Sambo a thousand dollars in chips, which Sambo kept in a separate pile beside his own.

"Round one to you, big boy, well done. I think it was a lucky guess, though. Manny played that hand magnificently, had us all fooled every step of the way," said Hiram.

"Had he bet less than five hundred the first time I would have been duped as well. Anyone with a straight at the start needs to lure us in with a smaller amount to create some doubt in our minds. Going big off the bat like that told me he was bluffing. I would like to guess Gordon's hand next, if that is all right with you?"

"I don't think the order of your guesses will make any difference to us, boys?" asked Marty. "Very well, I bet one thousand that you have no idea what Gordy has." The rest followed his lead.

"Sorry, Gordon, but you were easy. You asked for one card and, despite acting as though you were disappointed, it was easy to tell you had improved. You had either the makings of a straight, a flush or two pairs in your hand to begin. You believed Manny had a straight, so I couldn't see you taking the risk of getting a better straight than you believed he had, so I surmised that you had two pairs. I think you were given the extra to make a full house, albeit a lower one than you were hoping for. If I *had* to guess, which I believe I don't, I would say that you received a third card between two and five instead of a third to add to the high pair you had, possibly kings."

When Gordon laid down his hand of three fours and two kings, the table became deathly quiet. Once more, five thousand dollars in chips was pushed quietly toward Sambo, where he merged it with the first lot. The players all peered about them uncertainly, stopping when they came to Sambo.

"Before you place any more bets against me, I will tell you that Marty probably had more reason than anyone else to believe he had the winning hand. He began with three of a kind, queens, for sure. Gordon and Marty both had to have full houses or better in order to bet against Manny, who they believed to have a straight. It was the only reason they would continue. Marty received another pair to add to his three queens, giving him a beautiful and probably unbeatable full house in his mind, except he was confused about me and the way I was betting."

"Is he right, dearest?" enquired his partner.

"Unbelievably," confessed Marty.

As the other players listened to the conversation, all became increasingly agitated with growing suspicion.

"Are you telling us you know what those cards are? The ones you have not touched since they were passed to you?" demanded Hiram, rising from his chair.

"Yes," admitted Sambo.

"How could you possibly know? What are they?" shouted Marty. "How dare you..."

"Care to tell them, Pierre, or shall I?"

"What! How dare you bring Pierre into this! What are you saying?" commanded Hiram.

"I had a pair of aces to start with, as well as the makings of a little straight if I split the pair. I'll bet everything in front of me, including your money, that I have another pair of aces under the remaining cards. Ask Pierre if you don't believe me. For some reason he wanted you all to lose rather badly with this hand. I thought at first he might be working for you, building me up a little to fleece me later, but I kept getting one good hand after another, which I promptly threw away at first.

"He was giving me cards from the bottom of the deck where he had expertly relocated them, to provide me with some stunning hands. First one was a flush, then a straight, another straight, followed by a full house and another flush. First five hands, all winners. When I finally received only a pair in the sixth hand, I thought he had given up. He knew exactly which cards he had given everyone, so he was very surprised to see Manny betting so furiously on nothing. He made sure everyone else remaining in play received a great hand, with mine being the best."

"He is talking ze bullshit! You know me, mon cherie. I am honest dealer. You hire me for zis," argued Pierre pompously.

"Your argument would only have appeal if I had touched my cards, Pierre. That is why I deliberately left them where you placed them. Everyone here knows you were the last person to touch those cards. Don't get me wrong, you are gifted. It took me all five hands to finally witness it. You are very fast and accurate, but, when I finally saw it, I knew what to do. Go ahead, Marty, show us all the other pair of aces."

Marty reached over to flip the three cards face up, revealing a pair of aces and a jack.

CHAPTER SEVENTEEN

"What on earth could he have gained from making you the big winner of the evening?" asked Hiram, as they sat around the table with replenished drinks after Pierre had been suitably ousted from their presence. Several of the host's rougher friends were teaching the man a lesson as they spoke, with strict instructions to ensure that Pierre's hands were never again to retain the ability to relocate a card.

"Blackmail, most likely," answered Sambo. "He would have fronted me soon after the game with some spiel about revealing my duplicity to you all unless I gave him all or most of my winnings."

"Why you? Whatever did you do to piss him off like that?" enquired Marty.

"Nothing. I don't know him from a bar of soap. He would have picked me as his mark because I didn't fit in with the rest of you, the odd man out. No one was going to believe me, the outsider, when I protested my innocence, because I was such an unknown quantity. With the particular rules you enforced, the one man left standing holding all the chips had to be me for his plan to work. Thing is, if he hadn't acted so soon I may not have twigged to it. Getting five fantastic hands in a row right at the beginning of the evening had all my alarm bells ringing. He must have been panicking when I threw away hand after hand in those first rounds."

"Will you please accept our deepest apologies for choosing that dreadful man, Samuel? We had no idea. In truth, we only invited you here as a little bit of eye candy. Hiram even postulated that we might persuade you to stay on afterwards to join us in a little fun if we managed to get you drunk enough. We had absolutely no idea you could actually play. Forgive us, darling?"

"Nothing to forgive. I was feeling pretty outclassed, though. And I did wonder why I was sent an invitation, not knowing any of you, that is. How *did* you get to know about me?"

"As a player, word gets around quickly about who is who, and who is upcoming. We were just told that you played the smaller games and were an absolute knockout. Our information was woefully understated in that regard. You are, without a doubt, the most gorgeous man I have ever set eyes on. Couldn't keep my hands off you. I don't suppose there is any way we can entice you over, is there, sweetie?" pleaded Marty with an ostentatious sigh.

"Not on your life. Recently and happily married to the most wonderful woman in the world. It would take ten horses and a stick of dynamite to separate me from Crystal."

"Oh, what a waste." Hiram lamented melodramatically, slapping the top of his wrist to his forehead.

"By the way, I want you all to take back the money you bet on me. It was rigged and I don't deserve the money like that. I wouldn't mind the chance to win it honestly, though."

"Listen to him. You were the one feeling *you* were out of *our* league? My dear boy, we are simply so far below your level it would be like taking candy from babies playing against us. I think I'd have more of a chance by throwing my money into the river than playing against you. At least the wind might blow a dollar or two back my way on the river.

"You take that money as well-earned, and we can all be thankful that horrible person didn't fleece us of the rest. Never fear, he will never manage to play another game in his lifetime. Angel is the most stunning man in a frock you're ever likely to see, but he is fabulously strong and thoroughly conversant in martial arts, positively brutal, darling. If I weren't so allergic to pain I would have him beat me every other day. Ooh, such a virile young beast."

"Hush now, Marty. You're embarrassing him," suggested Hiram.

"Nonsense, pet. I have the feeling young Samuel has seen a thing or two in his time. Awfully clever of you to see through the sham. I thought Hiram and I were ever so observant in spotting such things. Absolute rubes, aren't we, sweetheart?"

"Never spotted a thing out of place, and, believe me, I was looking. Should we introduce him to Steven, do you think?"

"Oh, really? You think he's up to that level?"

"Made a fool of us, didn't he?"

"Come on guys, fair go. Pierre was bloody good, and I only just managed to see how he did it after five hands. And only then because he started from the beginning. I sincerely doubt I would have suspected anything in the second or third period after breaks, if I'd lasted that long."

"Samuel, we do this for pure fun. We let ourselves get serious for a few hours and just relax and enjoy the atmosphere. I don't suppose we'd ever like losing all our money, but it wouldn't really hurt our bank account...if we had one. Our money? All cash in the clubs, and lots of it. That's just the legitimate stuff in front. What goes on behind the frocks and make-up...well! You are in a class well above us when it comes to cards, I assure you. Yes, lover, I think you're right, we should introduce him to Steven," said Marty.

"Who's Steven?" Harold asked, speaking for the first time. Despite his considerable girth, his high voice came as quite a shock to Sambo, hearing him speak for the first time.

"Oh, you remember him from the opening night at the gallery a few weeks ago? At Margo's exhibition? Tall, hairy and so, so straight. Like this one."

"Are you all...you know?" asked Sambo uncertainly.

"Camp as a row of tents, of course!"

"Even Manny?" Sambo asked.

"My dear boy, Manny, short for, Manuela, is a woman. Full post-op!"

"Sorry?"

"Chop, chop? Sex change, Samuel. Overseas, of course. No such thing here in Aussie. Had it all lopped off and tucked in to give him a fine looking fanny if you are into that sort of thing," stated Marty.

"Which none of us is," asserted Hiram.

Sambo grimaced. "Ouch! Really? Gone?"

"Hated it with a passion, the poor boy. Ever so confused growing up with a willy instead of a pussy. Tried to lop it off himself once. Earned him a stint in a nuthouse."

"I can't imagine," admitted Sambo.

"No, not many of you can, more's the pity."

"Where is he...she?"

"Oh, she just had to see what they did to Pierre. She has a real penchant for drama and violence, that one, especially against men. Hates all the straight ones with an absolute passion. Took all of our collective persuasion to allow you to play tonight. Why do you think she hardly said a word? Then you had the temerity to discover her beautiful bluff! Oh, that really was the last straw for you, dear boy. It was lucky you gave her another target for her anger, otherwise you would have copped a bucket-load of the proverbial. I doubt we would have been able to restrain her. She does get into a lather, poor dear. Copped such abuse growing up in Japan with all the traditional bullshit they foist on their children. Honour, face, loyalty and on and on. Such a load of dreary nonsense!"

"Marty, you do go on, love. Tell us about yourself, Samuel. We only know that you are unavailable, straight, and a card player of extraordinary talent."

"Not by half, Hiram. I am a rank amateur compared to some of the top players I have seen, and I doubt that I have even seen the best. I admit that I have studied everything I could about the types of cheating entrenched in the game. I spent most of my time training my eyes in the early days to catch out the sharps. A truly talented sharp is very hard to spot. The best would not have required their plant cards to come from the bottom of the deck, they would have been good enough to relocate the desired cards to the top, where they would be dealt accordingly and in the order they wished. Pierre was good, but far from the best I have seen.

"Me? Nothing much to tell, really. I have a younger brother with brain damage from a car accident, married to a very sweet girl who cares for him diligently. I literally married the girl of my dreams a short time ago. We all live together in an odd and comfortable arrangement that suits our disparate lifestyles."

"Oh, you simply cannot leave it at that. You said you 'literally' married the girl of your dreams? Spit it out, do tell. Do we need popcorn?" urged Hiram. Harold and Gordon (Hardy and Laurel), both nodding their heads eagerly, joined the hosts in pushing Sambo to reveal all.

"I don't suppose I could take a rain check on that? I'm a bit tired. It is almost one in the morning."

"Hah! Still way too early. We don't usually go to sleep until at least six or seven. Of course, we are in bed before then, though. If you wanted to join us I'm sure we could make an exception for you? Want to go to bed early, lover?" asked Marty.

"Honestly, Marty, you are going to scare the poor boy to death. Don't want to give us queers a bad name, love. Heaven knows we cop enough now," argued Hiram.

Sambo reluctantly proceeded to tell them the story of how he met Crystal at the pool and the subsequent near-drowning incident, walking her home, the pre-existing carving in the pole and the accompanying dream. He deliberately kept descriptions of the house and other facts as vague as possible. Halfway through the story, the door opened to reveal the austere Manny returning to the group with a satisfied smirk on her oriental features. Toward the end of Sambo's tale, Manny could be seen to show particular interest in the story despite her avid aversion and distaste for all things associated with straight men.

"Positively spooky. The hairs on the back of my arm are standing on end. You sure you aren't having us on, Samuel? Spinning a bit of a yarn for us old queers? We might be a bit gullible, but we aren't exactly stupid, you know?" remarked Marty.

"I swear it's the truth. Our initials were already there."

No one noticed Manny surreptitiously leaving the room with a look of steely determination marring her features. She remained unobserved as she made a telephone call from the wall-mounted phone in the kitchen, surrounded by the movements of many waiters and chefs at work.

Sambo refrained from answering a litany of questions bombarding him from the gathering. Barely managing to stifle a yawn, he offered his apologies before making his hurried exit. Flush with extra funds from his evening's sojourn, he decided upon a casual walk along Oxlade Drive to revive himself in the fresh air flowing from the river. Mindful that he was carrying an inordinate amount of cash on his person, he nevertheless elected to walk off the evening's events while enjoying the peaceful ambience of the night.

His tranquillity was soon disturbed when a beefed-up Holden Monaro roared towards him, illuminated in an orange halo by the ambient street lighting. The burbling V8 motor pushed the vehicle past Sambo at a breakneck speed. Sambo noted the car squealing to a halt outside the gate of the house he had just vacated. Without paying any further attention to the car or its occupants, he continued his stroll down the tree-lined street.

Sambo elected to venture across New Farm Park after crossing Brunswick Street, on his way to a friend's house in Dixon Street, rather than making the effort of going directly home. He doubted there would be too many taxis available at such an early hour, especially in The Valley. A poker-playing friend had invited him to stay on many previous occasions when they were both tired after a game, so he thought he would presume upon the generosity of that friend once more. In the back of his mind, Sambo registered the return of the noisy Monaro, tyres screeching at the end of Oxlade Drive to enter Brunswick Street, where it swiftly resumed its state of haste.

Sambo happened across his friend, Peter Sutton, just as he entered the street. Peter, returning from his own game, where he had not fared as well as Sambo, waited at the front gate when he saw Sambo under a streetlight. He waved him over in a friendly gesture that saw Sambo respond with confidence. Sambo was pleased to know his friend was home. He would welcome the chance to have a coffee and a chat with his poker buddy about the events of the evening and warn him about a new cheat in town.

They shook hands and greeted one another at the gate before proceeding up the stairs to Peter's modest Queenslander, in need of some tender loving care. Inevitably, the conversation led to a friendly game while they enjoyed their coffee and conversation, Peter listening intently to every word about Sambo's experiences that evening.

Peter was a tall, no-nonsense sort of bloke with a larrikin approach to life. He was never short of a joke or a helping hand. Salt of the earth described him best with his sandy-coloured hair falling roughly about his shoulders in the unkempt fashion of the day. His clothes were perpetually blue jeans and flannel shirt, despite the torridly humid temperatures that beset the city from time to time during the long summer. He wore ankle-length Jim Boots, as they were known back then, basically just a sandshoe with elevated sides running up to the ankle.

"You staying?" asked Peter.

"If that's okay with you, Peter? Too buggered to go home tonight."

"Not a problem. You know that. Always have the spare room set up in case of a visitor. How many times you stayed here?"

"Yeah, often enough. I don't like to assume, you know?"

"Nah, bullshit! You always have a bed here, mate. I owe you for sorting out that bloke for me."

"Hey, no way. Blind Freddy coulda seen that one."

"Well, this bloody Freddy didn't. You always seem to spot 'em, Sambo. Never seen anyone like it. You saved me a ton of dough that night and I don't forget. You're welcome here anytime night or day, you hear? Give you a spare key, too, so I don't even have to be here. Anytime! Okay?"

"Okay, okay, I accept your magnanimous gesture."

"Nothing magnetic about it, I owe you. So, them poofs invited you?"

"Shouldn't call them that, mate, they're all right. Yeah. Didn't know them from a bar of soap before tonight. Think I heard a whisper about them one time. Bit on the touchy-touchy side, but harmless enough."

"Dunno how you could stand it. Fucked if I'd want one of 'em types touching me."

"Well, they wouldn't, would they?"

"Huh?"

"Well, you aren't exactly...pretty...are you?"

"What's wrong with me?"

"What, now you want to be attractive to them?"

"You said they was all hands wiv you."

"Well, I *am* pretty, Peter. At least, that's what I'm told. You, on the other hand, could only be considered visually appealing by your mother."

"Thanks a bunch."

They both laughed at the joke. Peter was under no illusions as to his ascetic qualities. With a freckled, gnarled face and a body evidencing his years on the rodeo circuit, he was hard-pressed to *pay* for a root nowadays. Though he possessed a heart of pure gold, his outward image presented a formidable and scary presence few ventured to accommodate. Older than Sambo by only a year or two, Peter resembled an old man already, with his worn-leather face and gnarled hands protruding from his long-sleeved flannel shirt. In the V of his shirt stood a shock of pure white curls against a darkened, wrinkled tan.

"How did you go tonight?" asked Sambo.

"Bout even, I reckon. You?"

"I ended up very much in front despite not playing a proper hand. Watch out for that bloke I told you about, though I doubt he will be in any condition to deal cards for a while."

"Pierre, eh? Never heard of 'im. They done 'im over then, did they?"

"Yeah, they weren't mucking around, I tell you. They might seem like they're weak, the way they talk and all, but I wouldn't want to get on the wrong side of that Angel-bloke. Built like a brick shithouse with muscles on his muscles, even when he wears a bloody skirt."

"Fair dinkum? A skirt? Now, why would a bloke want to go around wearing a sheila's get-up?"

"Each to their own, I say."

"I'm pretty whacked, Sambo. You?"

"I could use a few winks. You sure you don't mind me staying here?"

"Jeez, leave off, will ya? You know where everything is. Help yourself to brekky in the morning. I'm sleeping in so don't bother waking me. Let yourself out and I will probably catch up with you at Bert's, day after tomorrow?"

"Yeah, I'll probably go to that game, as long as Jim's not going to show up. That bloke's a real pain in the arse."

"Thought you was straight?"

"Very funny. He just can't play for shit and thinks he's better than everyone. Christ, I hate the way he boasts about his cards all the time. The problem is, he never bluffs and he keeps on getting one good hand after another. If I didn't know better I would swear he was cheating. Only, I know he is too dumb and clumsy to cheat."

"On that note... Night, mate."

"Yeah, night, Pete."

CHAPTER EIGHTEEN

It was just before ten in the morning when Sambo stepped from the taxi in front of his home in Rosalie. He was feeling quite refreshed and glad he had opted to stay at Pete's for the night instead of disturbing Crystal and Little Sam after the game. The boy had been suffering a bad flu recently, giving Crystal a hard time and precious little sleep. It was not unusual for him to sleep over at either the venue for the night's game or a cheap motel if the game was across town and the venue did not sport enough rooms for the number of players staying.

Hosting the games proved to be a profitable venture for the hosts, who asked a small percentage of the overall pot and a reasonable rate to hire a room for the evening, breakfast included. They also provided refreshments during the game for a small profit, which no one minded. Most vices were catered for, such as cigars, cigarettes and booze. While Sambo did not partake of anything other than water during a game, others were not quite so inhibited. Drunks were tolerated as long as the punters remained affable and relatively cognisant of the game. Money was money, after all.

Sambo yawned as he walked to the door, which stood slightly ajar. He muttered to himself to warn Rose about leaving the front door open: too many dangers awaited Little Sam and Charlie outside on a major thoroughfare. Sambo walked through to the kitchen expecting everyone to be taking a morning nap. He had thought Rose might be around, though. She was not one to normally take a nap with Charlie.

He turned on the kettle for a cuppa while he stashed his extra money into a biscuit tin he kept under a loose floorboard under the sink. He didn't like to keep so much cash in the house, but refused to place his money in the bank, a direct result of his past experiences. While he was on all fours in front of the kitchen sink, he noticed a discolouration on the linoleum. When he tested it with his finger it came away sticky. He would have passed it off as strawberry jam had he not known that they were out of Charlie's favourite jam. On closer inspection, he decided that it was a drop of blood. Obviously someone, most likely Charlie, had cut a finger or something. Were it not that the hairs on the nape of his neck were standing on end, Sambo would have dismissed the discovery with a shrug.

Sambo became deathly still, slowing his breathing as he soaked up the atmosphere of the house. Subtle, foreign, lingering aromas foretold of strangers having entered the house. The silence may have been caused by all occupants of the house sleeping, but Sambo did not accept that for a moment. With a sudden urgency, he lurched to his feet, ran to his bedroom and threw open the door. Bright red spots of blood on the white sheets of their shared bed caused Sambo to gasp. He cast his eyes about frantically to take in the scene.

An overturned bedside table and a smashed porcelain lamp threw his mind into immediate turmoil, thinking his wife and child, because he saw Little Sam as his own, had been harmed or murdered by thieves. Yet he saw no evidence of bodies. He raced quickly to Charlie's and Rose's room, discovering them tied and gagged upon their bed. Rose was crying bitterly as Sambo rushed to her side, tearing the tape from her mouth. Only then did Sambo recognise the all-too-still form of his brother whom he would have expected to be thrashing wildly in panic and confusion. Then he saw the pool of blood in which his brother lay.

Rose became hysterical the moment she was free of the restraints, clutching at Charlie, beseeching him to be alive. Sambo stood aside for a moment, unsure of himself, not knowing what he would do in the event his brother was no longer alive. Stunned to inaction, he watched as Rose sobbed wretchedly with Charlie in her arms. When Charlie coughed up a clot of congealed blood, Rose initially thought it was a reflexive action caused by her hugging. Then, when Charlie spluttered and inhaled loudly, both Sambo and Rose exclaimed loudly their sheer joy. Sambo rushed to embrace

Charlie and the trio remained in that pose for some time before Rose was able to pacify her quaking giant of a man.

Upon settling Charlie into a relatively calm composure, she was able to answer Sambo's questions. She explained that they had awoken to the sound of glass breaking in the early hours of the morning. Two strangers wearing ski masks had entered the house through the living-room window. Rose had been asleep there while watching a late show. She woke as one of the men grabbed her by the hair, dragging her off the sofa and up the hallway to Charlie's bedroom. Charlie was still asleep, but the man knocked him on the head with something, causing Charlie to moan. He then dumped her on the bed, tied them both up with cable ties and gagged them with duct tape.

"What happened to Crystal and Little Sam?"

"I don't know, Sambo. I don't know. I didn't see them. I only saw one bloke grab me while the other one went into your room. Crystal had seen Little Sam to sleep after he was up coughing and running a fever for most of the night."

"Jesus! When was this, Rose? What time? We have to call the police. We..."

"The one that grabbed me warned me not to call the coppers. He said they would kill them if they detected cops."

"Who? Who said?"

"I don't know, he didn't say. He had a funny accent, though."

"What? What kind of accent? Think, Rose."

"I, I don't know. One of those Pommy-type accents."

"English?"

"No, sort of....wait a minute. Like that fella down the road here, the garbo."

"Patrick? The garbage man?"

"Yeah, like him."

"Irish...shit!"

"What, what is it?"

"It's bloody him, for sure."

"Who, for Christ's sake? What are you talking about, Sambo? How could you possibly know who it is?"

"Left you and Charlie, didn't they? Took Crystal and Little Sam, with an Irish accent. So it had to be the boy's father, that Duggan bloke. Tommy Duggan. Fuck, this time he'll kill her. Fuck!"

"You know where he lives, Sambo."

"Doesn't matter, she isn't there."

"How would you know that?"

"I can feel it. She isn't there, isn't even here in Brisbane. He's taken them somewhere."

"Where?"

"Nowhere close, that's for sure. South...is what I'm feeling."

Rose turned to Charlie, who was still shaking and sobbing pitifully. "Charlie, are you okay?"

"I'm, I'm okay, thanks, Rose."

Sambo and Rose both shouted together..."Charlie!"

Charlie sat up, rubbing his head where he had been hit so hard it made him bleed. "Sambo?"

"My God, Charlie, you...you're speaking normally!"

"Rose, it hurts so bad."

"Okay, Charlie, I'll get you something for it, then we'll bandage that head up, eh?"

"Stay here and look after him Rose. I'll get the first-aid kit from the bathroom. Charlie, I, I don't know what to say except...welcome back, brother. I hope, I really hope this means what I think it means for you. I couldn't be happier...and sadder at the same time. Shit!"

That sadness changed to rage when Sambo tumbled to the notion that might explain the predicament in which they found themselves. As soon as he had seen to Charlie's injuries and calmed everyone down, he would have to pay a visit to a certain someone. A whirlwind of emotions assailed his troubled mind when he followed that thought through to a probable conclusion: a conclusion that led inevitably to himself and his big trap.

He cursed at his stupidity, and berated himself for not following

Crystal's instructions to the letter. She had warned him often enough. She had made him promise and his inadvertent betrayal had led to her capture and possibly her demise. He would never be able to forgive himself if anything happened to her or the boy. When he returned to the bedroom with the first-aid kit, he had to remove such thoughts to concentrate on the miraculous transformation of his brother.

Rose was talking softly to him, soothing him with her calming tone. She immediately relieved Sambo of the kit as he entered, dextrously and expertly applying the bandages. Her experience at caring for Charlie's numerous accidents about the home placed her in good stead to quickly stem the flow of blood from the gash in his head.

"Charlie? How are you, buddy?"

"It hurts, Sambo."

"Wow, Charlie! Your voice is like music to my ears, mate. It's a bloody miracle!"

"What happened, Sambo? How can this be possible?" asked Rose with a frown.

"No expert here, Rose, but I reckon those blokes knocked him on just the right spot to reverse whatever happened all those years ago. Some synaptic connections that were loose suddenly came good again. It's all I've got. I can't explain it, although I do remember reading some medical journal where similar things have happened. The terminology they used was too complex for me to follow. We can only hope that this new condition is permanent. So you need to wrap him up good and make sure he keeps relatively still for a few days as he heals."

"What are you going to do?"

"I have no option but to begin searching for her and Little Sam. She is everything to me. Sorry, Charlie. I would love to stay here and get to know you all over again, but I couldn't live with myself if I didn't do everything in my power to find her."

"Find her, Sambo. Bring them back to us. We're family," said

Charlie.

"Love you, brother."

"Love you too, Sambo."

"Rose, I am going to take some, but there is a biscuit tin with money under that loose floorboard under the sink. Take whatever you need while I am gone."

"I don't understand, how long are you going to be?"

"I don't see a quick fix to this one, Rose. My gut is telling me I have a long search ahead of me. I will send you more money when I can, okay?"

"But, Sambo..."

"I can't give you the answers you want, Rose. I don't know how long I'll be away. I just know that it will be quite a while, maybe even months. I have to follow her no matter where the search takes me or how long it may be. First thing I have to do is find out where a certain Asian deviant lives. She is going to wish that she had never seen me or heard the story I stupidly told. She likes a bit of sadism and violence, I hear, so I will see that she gets her fair share when I catch up with her."

"Her? Sambo, you wouldn't hurt a woman, surely?"

"No, Rose, I wouldn't. In fact, she isn't, or won't be anymore. I am going to rip out her new pussy, jam it on her head and make her wear it as a fucking fur hat."

"Sambo?"

"Never mind, Rose. Long story. I will try not to let my anger get the better of me, and, at the very least, I will make sure it doesn't come back on you two. If you get a call or a letter from me telling you to hightail it, do it immediately without question. All right?"

"But..."

"Don't argue with me, Rose. You saw what this evil prick is capable of. You saw Crystal when I brought her home that first night. That mongrel has her and there is no telling what he will do. I have to find him and put a stop to this once and for all. He's too smart to go back to his house, even with all the muscle he has in his employ. He wouldn't take the chance that if I called the cops I would get hold of one of his cronies. He can't afford to take her back there. I have to trace him."

"How? What do you know about searching for anyone?"

"I have something better than the best detective working for me; tingles."

"Sambo, don't be ridiculous."

"I know you don't believe me, but it is the truth, Rose. I can feel her in my heart and my mind. At this moment I know she is travelling in a southerly direction; by air. I just have to find out where the destination might be. I have a feeling that a certain Asian bitch will be able to provide that information or suffer the consequences."

"What if she goes to the police, Sambo? It's not going to do anyone any good if you end up in jail!"

"Her type doesn't call the police, Rose. Likely to receive more from the *cops* than me. Nah, not an issue, I reckon. You two take care of each other."

Sambo left the room without looking back. He quickly threw a few items of clothing and toiletries into a backpack, retrieved a wad of cash from the tin under the loose floorboard, then left the house. He did not take the car because Rose and his brother would need it. He figured Marty and Hiram would still be at home, given the early hour of the day. He walked to the little shopping centre in Rosalie, where he caught a cab to New Farm.

"My dear, you only just caught us. We're going to a rehearsal. If you want to talk, talk to us on the way. We're late as usual and Lolly is going to have kittens if we don't show up soon."

Sambo was bundled into the back seat of a big Yank guzzler with more fins than a school of fish. The opulent leather seat fairly swallowed him as he sank into it. Marty and Hiram moved in either side of him, looking washed out and harried. The chauffeur slammed the pedal down the moment they were all in, causing Sambo to sink farther into the seat than he believed possible. If he sank any farther he would either be in the boot or under the vehicle. The big V10 motor roared loudly as the tyres squealed on the asphalt of Oxlade Drive.

"You have about three or four minutes to explain yourself, young man, and be thankful we owe you one for last night, or I would have had our man throw you out on your beautiful behind," said Marty.

"Yeah, sorry to barge in on you like this, but it really is a matter of life and death. I need to know where I can find Manny."

"My dear boy, we simply do not hand out information on our guests. Our reputations..."

"I don't give a flying fuck for your reputations, as if you ever had any. Now I want you to listen carefully. I have lost the person I care most about on the planet, and if you two don't tell me what I want to know I am going to tear you a new fucking arsehole and it won't be a pleasant experience. Tell me where I can find that piece of shit, NOW!"

"How dare you..."

Marty did not get a chance to say any more. After Sambo knocked him out with a vicious blow, he turned in the opposite direction to face Hiram, who was cowering against the door, too shocked to call out to the driver.

"I will hold you and your lot personally responsible if one hair on my wife's head is harmed, Hiram, I kid you not. Now you invited that fucking freak to the game and 'it' went and told a very bad man the story that I related to you. Now you are going to tell me where to find her before I really lose my temper. You want to keep those looks you have?"

"What, what are you talking about? What has gotten into you?"

"I don't have time for this. Tell me where I can find that demented piece of shit you call Manuela. I'm not playing games, I will hurt you real bad if you don't tell me."

"I don't know where she lives. We..."

Sambo twisted Hiram's arm so far behind him that Hiram

believed it would snap off at any moment. With a high-pitched scream, Hiram tried in vain to squirm away from Sambo.

"Tell me!"

"Okay, okay. Stop, please, you're hurting me."

"I'll do far more than hurt you. Start talking."

"Lutwyche, somewhere in Lutwyche..."

"You'll have to do far better than that," said Sambo, twisting Hiram's arm at an impossible angle.

"Oh, you are in soooo..."

"Where, Hiram? I swear I will break your arm. I will tear the fucking thing from its socket if..."

"Wilson Street. Wilson Street, Lutwyche. Number ten, I think. That's all I know. Marty is the one with the memory who organises all our shindigs. I can't tell you anything more, I promise. Please, let my arm go."

"Tell your driver to take us there, no funny business. Push the button and give him his new directions. You can drop me off and get back to your rehearsal or whatever."

Hiram, wincing with pain as he retrieved his aching arm, did as he was directed. When the driver began to protest, Hiram stopped him short with a shouted instruction to do as he was told or else he could find employment elsewhere. The car swung onto a new heading through Bowen Hills and onto Gympie Road where it immediately slowed to a crawl in the heavy traffic. Anytime, night or day, Gympie Road, which was also the beginning of the Bruce Highway, meant a high flow of traffic along the northern arterial, the main highway out of Brisbane before the gateway arterial was constructed.

Sambo watched the driver carefully as he showed signs of grave concern for his employers. Marty was beginning to stir, moaning loudly as he touched his jaw tenderly.

"Hiram, what, what's happening?"

"Are you okay, precious?"

"I'm not sure. It feels like my jaw is broken. If you have

damaged my teeth..."

"Marty, shut the fuck up, or I'll job you again."

"Well!"

"Don't provoke him, dear, he really is a nasty piece of work. He nearly broke my arm. I don't know how I'm going to be able to rehearse..."

"Would you two ingrates knock it off? Consider yourselves lucky that I haven't done much worse, considering what that friend of yours has done."

"Can we at least know what it is that she, and we, are accused of?"

"While I was telling you the story about Crystal and me last night, that sack of shit was plotting a sort of revenge for me spoiling her fun at poker. She lit up the moment she made the connection and must have gone out to make a phone call. She would have told the Duggans what she suspected. They kidnapped my wife and the boy in the early hours of this morning. When I got home, she was gone, and my brother and his friend were cable-tied and gagged in another room."

"Oh, my God, did you say the Duggans? Tommy Duggan and his old man?"

"Yeah. Trust you to know a piece of shit like that."

"Know *of* him. Anyone who works or plays in The Valley knows of the Duggans. Shit! I didn't make the connection as you were telling the story. *The* Crystal? Tommy Duggan's slave woman? I'm sure the scuttlebutt said she was dead. You can kiss her goodbye right now if they are involved. They are the nastiest things that ever left the emerald isles, starting with the grandfather."

"I'm well aware of their reputations and capabilities. I was the one who found and rescued Crystal when they left her for dead. Took her months to lose the scars of that night. Some of her inner scars will never heal. Now especially."

"I don't think Manny would have anything to do with that lot."

"Oh, no, Marty. You're wrong, dear. That Tommy is a real

twisted thing. Doesn't know whether he is or isn't, if you know what I mean? I think Manny fell for him at one point, while she still had a willy. Mixed messages coming from Tommy had the poor dear in such a state. I think she would do anything to get on the right side of him. Offering him information about his slave would have been her way back in," explained Hiram.

"Oh, dear," said Marty.

"And Sambo here just gave her the perfect gold pass to Tommy's affections, or so she thinks. Tommy's too ashamed of what he is to ever have anything to do with her. If she pushes the wrong buttons with him, she will end up in the Brisbane River as eel bait. Well, you can forget about getting to Manny. She has the very best security system. You'll never get in," said Hiram.

"Maybe not, but you can," muttered Marty.

"Oh, Marty, when will you learn to shut that mouth?"

"Never heard you say that before, lover."

"Knock it off! I don't want to hear any more of that rubbish. You're right, though, she will never let me in once she sees me. Does she have a closed-circuit video on the front door?"

"And the back door and every room and window, alarmed, the works," said Marty smugly.

"Hmm..."

CHAPTER NINETEEN

"Go away, I'm not interested," came the disembodied metallic voice from the speaker next to the call button.

"Manny? It's Marty, dear. You simply must open the door so we can speak to you, love. We are in quite a pickle."

"Why are you all dressed up?"

"That's the reason we need to talk to you, pet. Doing a dress rehearsal and Lolly just up and leaves us. Such a hissy fit; you have no idea. We need your choreography skills, scrumptious."

"I'm tired, Marty, and who is that with you?"

"New girl, Sally. That's why we are desperate, sweetie. Lolly was supposed to teach her a whole new routine for tonight's show, now she... Look, can we talk inside like normal people, Manny?" said Marty, losing patience.

"Can't you find someone else? I am really tired after last night."

"Manny, I swear, if you don't open up and let some old friends in who've supported you through all your troubles, we will simply wash our hands of you," said Hiram, ending with a loud harrumph.

"Oh, all right. Come on up."

After an electronic buzz, the entry to the foyer opened. The threesome made their way up the stairs in their high heels as genteelly as possible. Their footsteps clacked loudly in the concrete stairwell and all the way along a narrow balcony fronting the road, to a door about halfway along the length of the set of twenty brick flats. Manny poked her head out to ensure no other persons entered at the same time.

"Well, if it isn't Princess Paranoia. Really, Manny, is this any way to treat lifelong friends?"

"We haven't been lifelong friends. I've only known you for a few years." Manny stepped aside to allow the three flamboyantly dressed guests to enter. Manny, wearing a spectacularly bright silk yukata, followed them down a narrow hall into a sitting room. The moment she entered the room she received a stinging slap across her face by Marty, looking fit to kill.

"You horrid little bitch! How dare you embroil us in trouble? How dare you take it out of the house? You really are a sorry mess, you know that?"

"Marty! What...?"

"Don't you 'what' us, dearie. We've been around the block a few times, so don't try to pull the chenille over our eyes, tart!" admonished Hiram.

"Stop this at once or I will..."

"Will what? Call the cops? I don't think so, Missy."

"Marty, what is this all about? I really don't know what you are upset about."

"Really, Manny? Did you think we wouldn't find out that you went behind our backs to make trouble for one of our guests? You know damn well our policy that 'What happens in the house, stays in the house'. Not only did you flout that policy, but you also brought that awful demon into our lives, that...Duggan fellow."

"How..."

"Him, that's how."

Marty pointed directly at Sally, who was in the process of removing her wig to reveal short-cropped hair. Sambo stepped out of the voluminous hoop-skirt he had been forced to wear in order to gain entry to Manny's flat. It was not difficult to tell who it was underneath the heavy layer of foundation disguising his stubble. Manny gasped and staggered backward as she recognised him.

"Honestly, Manny, how could you? How could you involve this young man in all that? Especially with that evil monster you are stupid enough to fancy?" asked Marty.

"We've all heard the talk about that girl he literally enslaved, and how she must have suffered under his rule. How could you tell him where she was? How could you even know where she was?"

"He, he...."

"He, he what? Made a fool of you? That wouldn't be hard. You've been doing a fair job of that all by yourself, you dismal little thing. It's about time you let go of all that baggage you have been carrying around, otherwise you will end up a lonely, lonely little tramp. Oh, Manny, we took you in and this is how you repay us?"

"I...I'm sorry Marty, Hiram. I just..."

"Yes, yes, yes, we know what you just... You just wanted an 'in' with that vile piece of rubbish so you could continue a relationship with him. Shame on you! You have absolutely no taste in men. Your hatred of straight men really has to stop, Manny, after all, you are a female now and you need straight men if you want a fuck now. Samuel has lost his wife, thanks to you, and who knows what that animal will do to her now. Samuel?"

"He's taken her, Manny. Came into my house, kidnapped Crystal and her boy after clubbing my brother and terrorising his wife, then tied them up. I need to know where he took them."

"How did he know where to find them, Manny?" asked Hiram.

"I, I saw the address on the invitation you sent him, he had it lying on the table at one point. I have no idea where he would take her, back to his house, I guess."

"No, he didn't." Sambo was adamant.

"You've been there?" asked Marty.

"No."

"Then how could you know he didn't take her there?"

"The same way she has been in my dreams for so many years. I just know. I feel it. Besides, even if this Tommy Duggan does have a few cops on the payroll, he can't own them all. If I went and made an official complaint, the cops would be forced to act on it. I very much doubt he would get away with kidnapping, assault and possible torture. No, he took them away. They have gone south, Victoria, I think. Melbourne, it feels like."

"Positively spooky, my boy. If what you say is true, then you could probably just feel your way to them without Manny's help," offered Marty.

"No, it doesn't really work that way. I have a general impression of where she is, but I can't narrow it down no matter how hard I try. This...person, has to know something. Talk, NOW!"

Far from feeling cowed by the tall man, Manny fronted him with a martial arts stance, preparing to attack. She let loose a kick without the luxury of full freedom of movement within the restrictive yukata. Sambo easily avoided the kick aimed at his throat and grasped Manny's ankle, swinging her around in an ungraceful arc until she tumbled to the floor.

"Really, Manny, you mustn't make this more than it has to be. Trust us when we say that this man can swing a pretty mean punch," admitted Marty, touching his jaw. "Tell him what you know."

"I don't know anything."

"That's a shame. If you don't tell me where I can find Tommy I am going to mess up that face of yours so no one will ever want you again. I'm not fucking around here. Crystal means more to me than my life and I have no reluctance whatsoever to do everything in my power to get her back. And if she or the boy dies as a result of you turning her over to him, I will offer you the same treatment. You can try to hide all you like, get as much security bullshit as you can afford. I will bide my time and I will wipe that slimy smirk off your face. You have no idea what I am capable of."

"I would listen to him if I were you, dear. He might not look all that scary in high heels and makeup, but he is all muscle and very powerful. I doubt that even Angel could match him for strength," said Hiram.

"How could you side with him?"

"You leave us no choice, Manny. Not only do you use something you overheard while you were at our house, but you risk our peaceful existence by exposing us to that diabolical maniac and his father and grandfather. We have existed side by side in The Valley for years, each leaving the other alone. You have now threatened our lives and our livelihoods with what you've done. We have no special connection with Samuel here other than finding him a beautiful specimen. Sure, he did us a favour last night, but that would have been the end of it. I did not appreciate his use of violence to get his message across to us, but I doubt we would have listened to him or believed him.

"No, Manny, we are not on his side at all. We are on our side, and you have done our side considerable harm. We paid the Duggans a fee to keep the status quo and now that is ruined. Don't you see? Tommy and his mob are going to start poofter bashing again in The Valley because we had a part in playing a game of poker with the man who stole his slave, whether he left her for dead or not, according to Samuel. None of us will be safe in The Valley any more, thanks to you. I hope you're satisfied. Now, if you know anything at all about where that piece of shit could be, you need to tell him. At least, if Samuel is successful, we may stand a chance of surviving."

"Sorry, Hiram."

"Bit late for that now. Tell him you're sorry. You've ruined his way of life, his family, possibly forever. Deserves an apology and any information you have, don't you think?"

Feeling very contrite for perhaps the first time in her life, Manny looked deep into the eyes of a stranger, a man she would normally detest with all her heart. She sighed heavily as she struggled to rise from the floor. She sat down solidly on the cream velour sofa.

"I once heard Tommy mention a holiday house his grandfather owned in Frankston. That's somewhere in Melbourne, isn't it? It's all I can tell you, the only one I know about other than the house on Given Terrace. I am very, very sorry. I never meant to cause anyone..."

"Skip it. Yes, you did. You did mean to cause harm. You are a sadistic prick who gets enjoyment from seeing other people get hurt. Maybe some people deserve it for having mistreated you all your life, but my Crystal doesn't deserve it. She almost died once already because of that evil bastard. He caused her so much pain and grief that she may never recover from her previous treatments, let alone what he may do to her this time around. I will keep my promise to you. If she dies, whatever methods they use, it will be nothing compared to what I will do to you. Whatever you may have suffered in the past, child's play."

He turned to Marty. "I think I'd better come with you to your club so I can wash and change back into my old clobber."

"Sure you don't want to come over to the backside? You are looking thoroughly delectable in that gear."

"Don't you mean the dark side, lover?"

"I know exactly what I meant, Hiram, dear. Oh, very well, come along, young man."

"Marty, Hiram...?"

"You are never welcome at our house, our club or in our presence again. If either of us sees you anywhere near us, we will allow Angel to do with you as he wishes, and his wishes are many, dear, many!" said Marty.

"Thank you for all your help, fellas," said Sambo when they were once again in the car.

"What are you going to do? Fly to Melbourne?" asked Hiram.

"No, he will be monitoring the airports, I reckon. I will get a car from somewhere. Hire it or buy it, and hightail it down there as quickly as possible. Damn, how do you wear these things? These heels are killing me."

"Welcome to our world, honey. It ain't easy being queer, let me tell you. We have five hours of gruelling rehearsals to look forward to after this, in full costume under very hot lights. How I'm not as light as a feather, I'll never know. Listen, after you change at our club, let Candy drive you back to our place. In the garage is a rather beautiful and fast car, a 1964 Jaguar E-type, series 1. The 4.2-litre model, capable of one hundred and fifty miles per hour, darling. Keys are in it. Take it and do try to bring it back in one piece, won't you? We are awfully fond of it."

Three hours later, Sambo had the windows rolled down on the

sleek English sports car on his way up to Armidale in New South Wales. From there he would head to Dubbo, where he would probably stay the evening. Going by his map, he would then head toward Echuca, then Seymour, on to Yea, down to Lilydale and through Ringwood. He would have to use one of the highways to get across to Frankston, located on the other side of Melbourne.

The moment he entered the mountain country around Armidale, the weather turned quite frigid. He immediately realised he had not dressed or packed for the colder climate of the southern states. He had heard about the atrocious weather in Melbourne, that it could experience four seasons in one day, but had never ventured there. He decided to purchase some warm clothing the moment he found a suitable store.

While the vehicle in which he was travelling looked the meanest machine on the road, with handling and road-hugging abilities attributable to a high-performance sports car, it was far from the most comfortable ride he had ever had. The sports suspension ensured his ability to take sharp bends at preposterous speeds safely, but it provided little comfort to the driver. Sambo felt every bump and pothole the neglected roads had to offer, jarring his back into painful spasms with each jolt because of the car's limitations in adjusting to his large frame.

He decided he would stop for a coffee in Armidale. He wound his window up and turned the heater on to full. The limpid air struggling to reach him had barely a modicum of warmth to it after many minutes. He desperately yearned to stretch his legs after being cramped in a seat that had frozen in one position, suiting a much shorter person. Nothing he tried would budge the seat, which was most of the way forward. Sambo's long legs felt as though they were somewhere around his earlobes as he drove.

When he reached Armidale, he raced to find a store that sold some reasonable cold weather gear. Sambo was frozen to the marrow. It was nowhere near winter, yet the cool mountain air and Sambo's non-acclimatised, Queensland body ensured that his blood was near to solid ice when he stepped from the vehicle. He quickly found a boutique shop selling, of all things, swimwear, and, in the rear, a motley collection of last year's cold weather stuff. He threw on a sheepskin jacket with the label still attached, and grabbed a few essentials - thermal skiing underwear, woollen socks, a flannelette shirt and fleecy tracksuit bottoms.

Armed with a mug of steaming hot coffee, held in gloved hands inside a heated cafe, Sambo thawed sufficiently to begin breathing again. He could not believe how stupid he had been to simply don a pair of jeans and a t-shirt. His teeth had not stopped chattering for the previous twenty kilometres.

He had also dropped his car off at a local mechanic to fix the seating problem. No way could he continue his long trip in that cramped position up against the steering wheel. And he had asked the mechanic to look at the heater if he had the time.

Feeling one hundred per cent better and warmer, Sambo strode confidently down the road to the mechanic's. He picked up a few more items of clothing along the way, as well as a stainless steel thermos, which he had filled with coffee, and he purchased some nibbles for the trip. He stopped at a phone booth to book a motel room in Dubbo.

Although Sambo was in the greatest hurry to reach his destination, he knew that his choice of open petrol stations along the way was limited. Driving on desolate country roads in the middle of the night, pushing to reach as far he was able, would only lead to disaster. He had seen the fuel gauge needle drop dramatically the moment he accelerated to full speed on the straight highways. He would be forced to adopt a sedate speed and proper planning to ensure he did not run out of fuel on an inconvenient stretch of road.

Back on the road, feeling vastly better and immeasurably more comfortable in the seat pushed almost to the extreme rear position, Sambo smiled as the bright red car purred leisurely at a sedate (for a Jaguar), sixty-five miles per hour. The car's heater poured delightfully hot air onto his legs and abdomen, and a radio station played some classics. While the peripherals of his life were on track for comfort and speed, his mind moved over to the more troubling aspects.

Crystal had become for him his entire universe, heart and soul. He could not foresee a life without her presence, nor that of Little Sam, whom he loved unconditionally, despite the boy's origins. His marriage was a final settling of all the tremors he had experienced throughout his life. He was inexplicably drawn to a woman by way of a connection that remained puzzling.

The moment he felt that association upon seeing her that first time in the pool, all of his energy had centred on that ephemeral link, finding her, befriending her, talking, sharing and loving only her for the rest of his days. His body and mind were transported to a different plane of existence when he had finally found her. To lose her now did not bear examination. It tore him to shreds to be parted from her.

Despite his brother's sudden escape from his mental prison, Sambo could not remove himself from the cause that consumed him. Delighted as he was to think that he might once again have a brother in whom he could confide and discuss matters, with whom to share his innermost secrets, he could not avoid his burning desire to locate his other half. Without her, he could never again be whole.

The miles flicked past his window without attracting his attention. The white lines down the centre of the road were guiding him dreamily to a rendezvous with destiny. He concentrated his entire being on the message he was receiving across the ether: an infinitesimal signal leaking into his subconscious, calling to him, urging him onward. Native wattles and gums whizzed by as the sleek car settled perfectly into the cruising, mile-gobbling apparatus it was intended to be. Sambo followed his heart, never knowing that the search would take its toll, year after year after...

CHAPTER TWENTY

"I'll see your twenty thousand and raise you fifty more," said Sambo softly, as the room grew deathly quiet, with the amount in the centre of the table increasing beyond most of the other players' purses.

Sambo and one other player remained in the hand, the rest having fallen by the wayside within the first few rounds of betting, when amounts above the threshold of ten thousand dollars had been surpassed by mutual agreement. The player facing Sambo, a hulk of a man barely capable of fitting his immense frame within the armrests of his chair, blew his cigar smoke directly across the table into the face of Sambo. The huge maw of his mouth chewed incessantly on the battered end of a spit-soaked Cuban, as the monster eyed Sambo through slitted eyes.

Sambo coughed and smiled as he brushed away the reeking cloud wafting towards him. His opponent didn't realise that he had finally indicated his hand to the astute player opposite. Sambo's opponent was left with no choice but to raise the amount with what remained in front of the brute if he wished to maintain a modicum of hope. It had taken hour upon gruelling hour of patience, enduring the stench of the tobacco, to discover the meaning of the occasional affront he suffered. In the end, Sambo knew that the only time the man blew smoke directly at a player was when he had no hand to speak of.

Sambo had taken an enormous risk himself, sitting pat with all five cards on a mere pair of twos. Blackey, as he was known, had drawn four cards during the second round. For Blackey to continue betting, he had either improved dramatically or was attempting the biggest bluff of the evening. The atmosphere was palpable, the tension building among them all, the anticipation on a knife edge. Eager faces scanned the two deadpan visages of the protagonists vying for supremacy in the ultimate gentlemen's game, though few 'gentlemen' played the game in the modern world.

Blackey sucked in a lungful of the foul poison before lowering his enormous paw onto the two stacks of chips before him. Sambo could see Blackey's chips totalled around one hundred thousand dollars. Sambo had a little over fifty thousand remaining. A bead of sweat wormed a path down the craggy face of his opponent while the hushed audience held its collective breath. A squinted eye blinked back the ambient smoke drifting from the tip of his cigar as Blackey paused midway to his chips. He smiled.

"Turk, will you extend me a small loan, friend?"

"You know the rules, Blackey. You play what you have, no borrowing during a game. You agreed to the rules before you started."

"We've already broken the rules about the limits, Turk."

"That can be done with unanimous agreement at any time through the game."

"Well, agree unanimously about this then, damn it!" The brute drawled in a harsh Texan accent, redolent of his rough life lived on the oil fields. When Blackey spoke, others usually listened...and obeyed. Their lives hung precariously from a thin thread should they seek an argument. Blackey was well-used to getting his way, often by a deathly stare with steely blue eyes, or else by the brute force of his fist the size of a ham haunch.

"I will save Turk the trouble of a vote. I do not agree. I have only the funds you see before me on the table, Blackey, and I feel certain no one will loan me an equal or larger amount if I decide to challenge your bet. The bet is yours and I say we play with what we have. See my fifty thousand, or call, as you Yanks say, if you are curious about my hand, raise me with your remaining fifty if you believe in yours...or fold."

It was all over as far as Sambo was concerned. Any last vestige of doubt had been expelled permanently by the latest desperate ploy of his opponent. The spell had been broken and the previous pall at the table had been replaced with concern. The other players knew well the fiery temper of the oil-rig boss whom few men challenged. Those who did usually paid a heavy price. Sambo knew that the game was won. If Blackey had even a decent pair he would not have made such an elaborate effort to frighten his opponent with a show of more money. Sambo smiled when Blackey pushed forward the two stacks of chips into the centre of the table.

Strictly speaking, Sambo could now match the bet of another fifty thousand dollars and raise Blackey for the small amount he had over that sum, possibly as much as another thousand in small denomination chips. At that point Blackey would be left with no choice but to fold according to the house rules of the game, to which everyone had agreed before play. Failure to have sufficient funds at the table to match or raise the bet, or to afford the ante for the next hand, demanded forfeiture of the game for that player. A player could not even reach into his pockets to find another dollar or two.

Of course, that style of play, were Sambo to adopt the ploy, would be considered very ungentlemanly and poor sportsmanship. That Blackey sought to employ such tactics would not absolve Sambo were he to mimic the play. Blackey had been prevented from acting out the underhand ploy and therefore had merely expressed a contemplation to do so, far from having been caught in the act. A mild reproach was all anyone would utter in such an event. Sambo doubted his ability to leave the table alive were he to employ the same approach.

He had been invited to the game among the wildcatters of the oil rigs through a mutual acquaintance who saw him playing in a high-roller, casino-sanctioned game one evening. That night in Vegas, the true gambling capital of the world, saw Sambo losing his stake for the first time in many years. Over-confidence had him floundering early in the game. His cocky demeanour won him few friends or favours around the table. After settling down a little during the midpoint in the game, he managed to regain a few of the dollars he had lost, only to come crashing down in the back straight.

Sambo accepted the invitation afterwards while sitting at the bar drowning his sorrows in a few ales. He was given a card with the date and the address of the game to be held a few nights hence. Gathering what was left of his deflated ego, Sambo attended many games in the meantime to once again hone his craft and curb his ego. Once his humility was firmly established again, and he concentrated on the players instead of the game, his play improved dramatically.

Vegas had been one city in the line of innumerable cities over which Sambo had traipsed for year after year in pursuit of Crystal. From Melbourne, he had received word that his quarry had returned to the city of his origins, Dublin. Firmly entrenched among the loyalists of the IRA, Tommy Duggan lay low on the advice of his da. When Sambo finally embarked the plane heading for Ireland, Tommy had word of it before the plane landed, forcing him to move again.

All over the world, year after year, Sambo pursued the evasive man, who ran away every time he got word of Sambo's proximity. Crystal must have played up Sambo's prowess to such an extent that it had him running in circles, scared silly at the very thought of being caught by the man. Sambo followed his subliminal messages and his physical tingles from one part of the world to another, always without success. During this time he knew he had to keep honing his skill in order to afford the plane trips, accommodation and bribe money used to gain the precious few pieces of information he could gather on the whereabouts of one Tommy Duggan, Crystal and the child.

The price of information on the notorious gangster came at a premium. Not only was it highly expensive, but it also tipped his hand most often, alerting his prey to his presence. Then the chase would resume as his quarry fled yet again to another port, another continent, another city, where he inveigled his way into the seamier parts of their urban sprawl, their ghettos. The squalid rooms Sambo discovered after they fled became worse the longer he pursued them. It seemed to Sambo that Tommy Duggan did not have a never-ending supply of cash. There appeared to be limits to his expenditure, indicating perhaps that his father and grandfather did not support his flight of fancy.

Sambo had his own problems in that regard, having to delay flights often for lack of funds. He sought the poker games he required to see him sufficiently fed and housed in reasonable lodgings. Money for clothes, flights, cab-fares and other myriad sundries forced Sambo to the card table more and more. His skills were honed to a razor's edge, and his ability to defend himself against most assaults arising from disgruntled opponents increased exponentially.

For the last year, he had been cruising along all the highways he had heard about covering the great American continent, trailing always a month or two behind his quarry. He had never come closer to catching up with them than when he first landed in Dublin. Unfortunately, a snitch forewarned the ever-lucky Tommy Duggan, enabling him to scamper to the safety of a ferry en route to England just hours before Sambo arrived at his place of hiding. Sambo tracked down the snitch to school him in his error of judgement. Once he gained sufficient funds, he made his way to England.

The rest of the time had simply blurred into a seamless string of poker games and different transports to far-flung destinations around the globe. Most of the time he was relying on nothing more than tingles and common sense to guide him if he failed to gather any useful intelligence. A decade of fruitless searches and mindless meandering led him to higher stakes and even higher associated risks.

A mixture of thoughts and emotions cascaded about Sambo's mind as he met Blackey's eyes across the table, with a veritable fortune resting in its centre. If Sambo managed to win the pot and exit with his life intact, an evens bet at best, it would suffice to see him through a number of years without attending further dangerous games.

"Blackey, I know you don't want me to call. I know you don't want anyone at this table to know what you are holding. If I am reading your body language right, you want me to fold and accept defeat so you can save face. I can't do that. I don't believe for one moment that you have any sort of a hand to challenge mine, so I am not just going to fold my hand and slink away into the night with my tail between my legs. I won't do something as stupid as raise you, though. That would be more than my life is worth, I get that.

"I may just be some dumb Aussie from across the globe, but I wouldn't do that to a fellow player, so I am going to call with my last fifty thousand...unless you want to change your mind? I am offering you a gracious exit without anyone seeing either your cards or mine. You can take back that hundred grand and fold. You don't end up losing it all and I get to breathe more easily a little longer. What do you say?"

Sambo believed that everyone at the table had held their breath again and leaned backward in their chairs as if to avoid whatever reaction was about to erupt. Had they believed it would be acceptable, Sambo felt sure the others would have vacated the table and possibly the room. Sambo stared unblinkingly at Blackey through the fug of cigar smoke enveloping the man's face. The silence in the room became deafening. The veins on Blackey's neck bulged in rhythm with his elevated heartbeat.

For an interminable period in which not a man spoke or breathed Blackey stared a hole through Sambo's head.

"You really gonna call, match my fifty?"

Sambo nodded.

"You swear that's what you is gonna do on a stack-o-bibles?"

"No, I won't swear on a stack of bibles, Blackey, because I don't believe in religion or God. I will swear to you on my own life, because that's what's at stake here, that I am going to match your fifty thousand-dollar raise to see your cards if the bet stands. You will lose the hand by folding, but you won't lose anything else."

"Whatcha mean by that?"

"Well, if I pay to see your cards and it turns out I've outplayed you, you are going to lose face, lose your temper and your life, in that order."

"How you figure I lose my life, matey?" asked Blackey, with a knowing smile.

"Notice how one of my hands is resting on my lap just below the table?"

"Yeah, what about it?"

"Have someone else take a peek at what I'm holding in that hand," suggested Sambo.

Blackey nodded towards Turk, the equally large oilman to his left. Turk slowly bent low to peer under the table. Nodding his head as he rose, he said, "Ain't his dick he's holding."

"Now, you wanna explain to me why you would come to a friendly poker game armed, boy?"

"Same reason you have one in your boot, and Turk has one at his back, tucked in his belt. Michael here to my left has a knife the size of my arm under his coat, and Jules has a pair of knives and a piece in his jacket pocket. Don't know about Brody there, but I'm guessing he has one somewhere. I'm in America, fellas. I know everyone is packin' in America. I would be one dumb son of a bitch if I didn't have one, *boy*!"

"Got the *cojones* to use it, though?"

"Why don't you test me? We'll see if you have any *cojones* left after the bullet smashes into your package, where the gun is aimed. Now I don't figure on leaving here alive if I shoot you, Blackey. I'm not fast enough to get everyone else before someone gets me, but I will shoot your nuts off without any problems at all before anyone touches anything. One of these bloke moves a muscle you can say *hasta la vista* to your manhood."

"You think we gonna let you walk outta here alive after you threaten us?"

"I think that you are man enough to accept if you are squarely beaten. If not, then I have misjudged you. I made a magnanimous gesture in allowing you to retrieve your last bet, to rethink it. More than any other person would be willing to do, I'll wager. I will even go so far as to allow you, and you alone, to see my cards if that is what you decide. Otherwise, let the bet stand. I will match your bet to see your hand and this will all play out as I have described...in the loss of your parenting abilities and further bloodshed, all because you got outclassed by some little upstart from Australia."

"That the way you see this goin' down?"

"Not if you man up, act like a gentleman and accept that you will not always win. What is worse in your eyes? These fellas watching you come unstuck and a whole lot of shooting and blood for fair play, or losing with some dignity which everyone can live with?"

"You about done with all that speechifying?"

"Reckon I am. Ball's in your court; pardon the pun."

All eyes were glued on Blackey, waiting for his final decision. They prepared themselves for the inevitable eruption, each one figuring out his best options to remain alive. All the other players had experienced his legendary temper at one time or another. No one made a fool of John James Black and lived to tell the tale. His explosive nature was usually measured on the Richter scale. No one had ever bested Blackey in a fair fight or not so fair fight in anyone's recollections. They all knew him as a wildcatter who brooked no nonsense from the men under him, but never sent a man to do anything he was unwilling to do himself.

He had earned his respect from years of working the rigs as a hand, then a leading hand, foreman and on up to an independent operator who struck oil with his first hole. His instincts about where to drill were as legendary as his ability to whip any man who gave him a reason. He could be relied on just as strongly to help any man that found himself in trouble doing his job. Blackey would place himself in harm's way to save the life of any worker in his employ, and had done so on numerous occasions.

Blackey looked about him at the men he knew so well; they were close he supposed. Not that Blackey could call anyone close as such. As a boss, he knew he had to keep a certain distance between himself and his men. It never paid to become attached in their profession. Blackey would never like to see these men witness him having to back down, yet he couldn't see any other way out of his foolish betting. He was so used to bluffing the bejesus out of his workers that he had mistakenly assumed the young pup would fold when he began betting big. He had been losing for much of the evening with one bad hand after another, and reckoned he would manufacture a bit of luck for himself. He figured the size of his body and the bet would be enough to scare the younger man off.

If the fellows at the table saw him either take back his bet or erupt when he was fairly beaten, he would be hard-pressed to regain their respect and loyalty. He stood to lose a fair sum, but it was far from making a dent in his financial standing. The worst outcome would be, as the young man said, the loss of face when it was revealed that he had been outclassed by a brash young bloke from the 'ass-end' of the world. He worked alongside the fellows and played hard with them as well. Turk, for one, would not be amenable to seeing him lose it over fair play.

"I want everyone to breathe right now, and let us calm this here situation down a mite. Sambo? That's yer name?"

Sambo nodded. "Well, here's what I think we should do. I want you to put away that little thing you're holding so we can all rest a mite easier. I give you my word that neither me nor anyone else is going to do nothin' rash. Y'all hear me now? I mean it. Don't none o' ya bring out no weapons, no matter what. Got me?"

Head nods and mutters of agreement followed.

"We got ourselves a right little Mexican stand-off here, don't we?"

"I guess so."

"You gonna take my word that nothin' is gonna happen?"

"Gun's already tucked away. Before you get someone to check on that, I'll just say that I can reach it fast if I have to."

"Why don't you take a peek, Turk? Just to keep things on the up n up. We good?" he asked Turk, who nodded.

"All right then. Now, y'all gave me a chance to take back my bet, and that was right kindly of ye. I wouldn't be much of a man if I did that. Reckon these boys might think twice about our future games if I did that. They might think less o' me if I acted up after bein' beat square-like as well. So, I am gonna play the hand like I was gonna, let my bet stay. I raise you fifty thousand dollars. Whatcha gonna do?"

"I'll see your fifty thou," said Sambo, pushing two equal stacks of chips into the centre with his other hand, one still resting below the table.

"Well, see. I got me a ace, king hand," said Blackey, laying down what Sambo liked to call fruit salad. An ace, king hand might win against another useless hand by sheer strength of its legitimacy as a hand in most casinos. If a dealer drew an ace, king hand it was deemed in play, and any guest hand beating it was paid accordingly. If a dealer failed to achieve even an ace, king combination, the hand was null and void and bets were returned equal money, regardless of how good they were.

When Sambo placed the pair of twos face up and the rest face down, there was silence again at the table.

"What else y'all got?"

"That's it."

"A pair o' stinkin' deuces? You bet all that money on a pair o' stinkin' deuces?" Blackey was so stunned that his cigar stub fell into his glass of bourbon.

"Normally, no. I would never have bet all that money on any single pair, let alone twos."

"So why on God's good earth would you bet on them tonight?"

"Because I knew you had nothing."

"And, pray tell, how would you know any damn such thing, less-n you was cheatin'?"

Everyone sat up a little straighter in their chairs, became a little more animated, secretly wishing for the mountain to blow its top.

"Well, seeing as I probably won't be invited to any more of your games, I guess it can't hurt to reveal it. You know what a tell is?"

"We all know what a goddamn tell is, and I know I don't have none."

"Took me a while, but you do...sorry."

"No way. I heard about all that malarkey at professional tournaments and I control everything I do at the table. No way have you found no tell with me."

"I could inform you in private if you don't want anyone to find out."

"Listen to him. You think you found a tell with me and now you think if you reveal it to these lunkheads that they will start beating me? Go on then, spit it out. If-n what y'all say is true, then I just have to stop it, don't I?"

"Fair enough. When you're bluffing, you blow cigar smoke in your opponent's face before making a bet. Every other time, it goes up in the air."

The group looked at one another with bemused smirks as they tried to dredge up memories of past games where evidence of such behaviour might be substantiated. Blackey, especially, grew silent with careful introspection, eyes squinting as he pushed his memory hard. The anticlimactic nature of the straightforward revelation had everyone scratching their heads and looking for confirmation of the fact.

Finally, Blackey turned to his left. "Turk?"

The man scratched his chin with a studied air.

"Don't rightly know fer sure. Might be. Reckon not many o' us ever called yer bluff to find out."

"Think maybe he gotcha there, Blackey", said Brody. "Seed it once when ya blew smoke in me face just 'fore ya slapped a pile o' chips in the guts. Last spring some time, I recollect, some other feller matched ya bet and all you had was a pair o' nines. Never thought nuthin' of it till now."

The rest of the players slowly nodded their heads as they came to the same conclusion. It was to be a crucial turning point for

Blackey if he was able to accept the truth, the embarrassing truth with a good dose of humility instead of his usual display of outright violence. He had organised the small gathering of workers and himself for a bit of R & R in Las Vegas. His boys had been working around the clock with little relief from the back-breaking labour in bringing in the new well. That they hit pay dirt with a gusher came as little surprise to his crew, but that only meant they had to work longer and harder.

They didn't usually accept outsiders to their private poker games, but Turk had made the contact and figured the fellow as an easy mark. It would give their boss another target for once, at games in which they inevitably lost most of their wages and even became indebted more often than not.

It came as a great relief to see their boss going toe to toe with the newcomer instead of taking them to the cleaners. What none of them could know was whether the situation would escalate into a war zone with weapons drawn. Even without weapons, their boss had a notorious reputation for inflicting a world of hurt on anyone that got up his nose. Turk foolishly believed that his normal antics might be diminished in the convivial holiday atmosphere they enjoyed during their first week away from the job.

When the enormous bellow exploded from the huge barrel chest it startled everyone at the table. It was the first time any of them had heard their boss laugh. It was an honest laugh rather than the sneering, smirking, belittling mirth he usually displayed. In truth, Blackey was not a likeable man, yet he somehow won over the loyalty of most who came under his influence. A man's man came to mind, a brutal, hard man of strong convictions and opinions, but mostly fair: it was definitely profitable to be in his employ. No other present-day wildcatter had even a fraction of the success Blackey had enjoyed.

The relief at the table was clearly evident among the smiling faces while Blackey continued to roar with unrestrained pleasure. After a while, the noise slowly subsided, with Blackey merely nodding his head with approval. He admired anyone with the fortitude to stand their ground. Against overwhelming odds, it stood Sambo in very high regard.

"Y'all are okay in my books, Aussie. Takes a real man to stand up to anyone like that, specially among strangers. You won fair and square and proved how y'all did it. I can respect that. No one is gonna do nuthin' to upset this young bloke, y'hear? No one touches him or they answer to me. Aussie? Y'all welcome at my poker game any time at all, and I won't be smokin' during a game ever again, thanks to y'all."

They all cracked up at that comment. The game was finished and it was time to get down to the real fun of the evening, drinking till they dropped. The hotel room was fully prepared for the nightly onslaught of drunken, boisterous partying. Housemaids had removed the delicate furnishings and expensive rugs. Management refused to interfere with the rowdy guests because of the enormous revenue pouring into their establishment during their off-peak season.

Any breakages had been amply compensated from previous evenings, while extra cleaning bills were added to the room hire. John James Black was well known as an affluent oilman and hard drinker/brawler. Other hotel guests were kept to the far wing of the hotel where the noise was greatly reduced by intervening walls. Prostitutes came and went at all hours freely. Sambo was invited to stay for the nightly festivities and debauchery. He stayed for a polite drink or two before managing to slip away unnoticed sometime after midnight.

When Sambo stepped outside the hotel's front doors he had an immediate sensation of enormous loss descend upon him. He no longer felt the signal, the premonition that had guided him thus far: it was totally expunged from his consciousness. Sambo felt a crushing sensation as though his heart was on the verge of collapse. The complete severance of that ethereal connection to Crystal was a mighty blow from which he found it difficult to recover. The breath was torn from his lungs as he experienced an anxiety attack like no other.

Desperately sucking in oxygen without any perceivable benefit, Sambo staggered down the sidewalk to his parked vehicle and collapsed inside. Several panicked moments later, when his breathing returned to a semblance of normalcy, he examined his inner psyche, a type of meditation he had adopted many years prior when attempting to hone in on the threadlike filament attaching him to the woman he loved. A favourite song of his by Golden Earring, *Radar Love*, came about as close as he was ever going to come to an explanation for his unusual connection with Crystal.

Across a city, a state, a continent or even the universe, Sambo believed he would always know where to travel in order to continue his search. Somehow that connection had failed. He no longer had any feelings, physical or otherwise, that would enable him to recognise a direction or a place to which he must travel. It pained him beyond endurance to think it may have been caused by her passing. It seemed the only reasonable conclusion, yet he fought hard with himself to reject it.

CHAPTER TWENTY-ONE

"Welcome home, brother," said Charlie, wrapping his older brother in a huge hug.

Charlie appeared totally different. Sambo stood back to admire the clean, mature physique and ambience of the brother he once saw so diminished and damaged. Charlie shone with an inner light that radiated a confidence and warmth that the accident had stolen from him. He watched as Rose placed a protective arm about his shoulder. She glowed equally, with a belly foretelling of another life soon to enter the world. Their first child, a girl they named Cynthia, had been born almost ten years ago, the year Sambo left.

"It's so good to see you both. How are you doing?" asked Sambo self-consciously, for he had been more than neglectful in communicating over the years.

"Why don't you come in and relax, Samuel, and we can all have a cuppa and a chat?" suggested Rose.

"Sambo?"

"Yeah ,Charlie?"

"Did you...? Is she...?"

"I don't know, Charlie. I just don't know, and that has really been eating me up inside, but it didn't make sense to stay overseas anymore. She isn't over there, or I have lost whatever it was that kept us connected. Or...well..."

"Come on, you two. Let's not start getting all morose this soon after the prodigal has returned, eh?" Rose urged.

Sambo allowed himself to be led into the lounge and gently seated on the sofa next to the big lunk that was his younger brother. Charlie had somehow gained a height and weight advantage over his older brother, who used to tower over him. Sambo felt positively minuscule compared to Charlie, almost as insignificant as he felt when standing next to Blackey, who cast a very long shadow.

"So what's been happening here besides you two making babies?"

As Rose departed for the kitchen to make them all coffee, she said, "Charlie has become the bread-winner, Samuel. Remember I told you about his writing?"

"Yeah, the book you wouldn't let me read?"

"Well, Mr Smarty-pants there sent a manuscript to a few publishers and he was picked up immediately. They are children's books and currently pay enough for us to rely solely on his income to pay the bills."

"Wow! That is really something. I am so..." Sambo began to feel quite choked up. "Really proud, mate. Well done. I...shit..."

"Thank you, Sambo. That means a lot to me. I really missed you, brother."

"I did too, mate. There were so many times when I wanted to chuck it all in and return here to help out and...you know, be here? I just...couldn't make myself do it."

"I got angry a lot at you. Rose will tell you that."

"Mm-hmm," Rose verified.

"But, I knew you had no choice. Even though I wasn't completely aware when you left, it all became clearer and clearer as the years passed. I'm glad you didn't come back for us, you would have regretted that for the rest of your life. I'm glad you found your own way here without our help."

"It's a bit weird hearing you talk like this, Charlie, after...you know? What have the doctors said about your recovery?"

"Nothing but embarrassed looks and apologies."

"Apologies! You have got to be kidding?"

"No way. The medical profession has come down about a thousand pegs since you left. No more demi-gods, just men and women performing an enormous task."

"You are completely recovered, no chance of a relapse?"

"I have had a few regressions in the past. Nothing major, just a few memory lapses and ongoing migraines. Never really recovered from the blow on the head in that regard. It may have knocked some sense back into me, but the physical pain I suffer every month or so leaves me whacked for days. Totally out of commission and locked in a dark room in absolute agony."

"Can't you get anything for it?"

"Oh, I used to have to go to the hospital for regular pethidine injections, but that led to an addiction. I now treat myself mostly with meditation, hot compresses, darkness and quiet. That is sometimes impossible to achieve with a kid, let me tell you."

"As long as you two are happy, and Cynthia is healthy."

"Too healthy, that one," said Rose, returning with a tray of mugs and biscuits. She sat opposite the brothers on a single recliner. They all helped themselves to coffee.

"Yum, nice coffee, Rose. So, happy?"

"Couldn't be happier, Sambo. I thought that was obvious enough to not need an answer."

"When is the new one due?"

"New one is a boy. We didn't want a surprise, so we could get the nursery right. By the way, are you...?"

"No, Rose. I am not planning on moving back in. I have enough money to probably buy my own home somewhere nearby if you'll have me as a close neighbour?"

"That's great, Sambo, really great. What are your plans then?"

"Haven't thought it through, really. All this time I have been a part of something so special that it absorbed me to the exclusion of all else, including my loving family. I have been very, very lost, Rose. I am over forty years old and I have nothing to show for my life. You? I mean, you and Charlie intend to remain here?"

"No choice, Sambo. The owner of the house was selling up, so we asked if he would consider selling it to us on vendor's terms. We managed to get a loan for the deposit and he agreed to the terms we offered. So we are stuck here for the long term. Mortgaged to the eyeballs, you might say," said Rose.

"Well, I can probably help a little with that."

"No, Sambo, you have helped us for years, sending us regular cheques. No more, we insist. We are making do and not missing out on anything vital. Struggling to make all ends meet is a normal way of life and no great hardship for us. Character building, actually."

"Wow, Charlie, you are so...fucking mature now! I'm struggling with it."

"Yeah, took me ages to come to grips with it. Pretty freaky," added Rose.

"I have so much to catch up on. Can you guys forgive me for not being here for all the important stuff?"

"Honestly, Sambo, we didn't know what to think about it all over the first few years. It was all just so...unreal, you know? Definitely not normal, so it spooked us a bit. I could understand to a certain extent what was driving you, but it was hard to think well of you. A few years ago we both sat down with Cynthia to discuss it. She adores you, by the way. She gets a real kick out of receiving your few letters, but, of course, waits impatiently for her presents twice a year.

"We all decided that no amount of pleading or insisting was going to sway you. We accepted that you had to return on your terms, Sambo. Yes, you missed out on a lot of good stuff, but that doesn't mean there isn't more good stuff to come. You do have some babysitting to catch up on, though. Prepare for number two child to miraculously turn up on your doorstep a few times when we are simply exhausted, "explained Rose.

"Fair enough. Deal! Thank you, both."

The conversation went late into the afternoon as the small family group caught up with each other and heard the stories of the intervening years. When Cynthia arrived after school, she demanded Sambo's attention exclusively. Sambo was deliriously happy getting to know his niece, though he felt a pang of regret that he had never had the opportunity to father his own child. He believed he would have made a great father. The moment he thought that, however, he realised that he had already enjoyed being a surrogate father to his namesake, Little Sam. The yearning in him for the family he had lost came storming back into his thoughts.

Cynthia, noticing the sudden sadness overcoming her uncle, was quick to embrace him in her chubby young arms. In her room, Sambo read to her from a children's book titled, *Thambo and Thumper*, authored by none other than her doting father. Sambo was pleasantly surprised by the narrative, recognising himself clearly as the inspiration for the main character, a gentle bilby protecting the community from the evil villain, Thumper, a big red kangaroo with attitude.

Sambo felt an enormous pride for his brother, who had come through the anguish of near brain-dead conditions to write such poignant and touching stories for young children. One story was poised to make its debut in cinemas across Australia in the very near future. Charlie had brokered the deal himself before acquiring a suitable agent. Not only had he sold the film rights for a semi-decent sum, but he had also negotiated a royalty percentage from the box office gross. The less than generous upfront payment was sure to be augmented substantially should the film make reasonable profits.

Sambo accepted the couch for the evening when the hour grew too late to bother with finding accommodation. He would set out first thing in the morning to scout for suitable lodgings until he found a house for an affordable price somewhere nearby. He would stop at all the local realtors to gauge the median house prices in the area. Sleep came easily for him as he settled himself onto the relatively comfortable couch. *Staying* asleep proved next to impossible as his dreams inevitably centred on his broken heart and his unsuccessful quest.

He was not yet willing to completely abandon all hope that Crystal remained alive. However, he felt that it was crucial to begin another stage of his life without the spectre of her hovering about him, consuming him as it did. He recognised the necessity in starting anew, to be there as a brother, brother-in-law and uncle for the family that loved and supported him unconditionally. He had missed far too much of their lives already.

The morning saw him waking from his troubled dreams to find his niece standing next to the couch with a satisfied look of affection on her features.

"What is it, princess? Have I been drooling or something equally horrid?"

"No, Uncle Sambo. I just wanted to make sure you were still here. Will you stay?" asked Cynthia in an almost wheedling tone.

"I'm not going anywhere far, I can promise you that. I have to find somewhere else to stay, though. I don't think I will fit into your princess bed if I stay here, do you?"

Cynthia giggled at the thought of her big uncle trying to fit into her bed.

"Morning, Sambo. You, off to your room to get ready for school, madam. I'll have some breakfast for you in a moment, Sambo. Hungry?" asked Rose while she shuffled her daughter in the direction of her room.

"Ravenous. Your special blueberry pancakes, by any chance?"

"Of course. Just a treat, mind you. I don't make them for just anyone."

"Where's Charlie?"

"Working, of course."

"Hmm?"

"He has a desk set up in our room. He rises at the crack of dawn every day, eats breakfast, gets lunch ready for Princess Cynthia and then retreats to his duties as our provider for the rest of the day. He locks the door once I have vacated and nobody can get in until he emerges. He takes his lunch in there with him and hardly ever comes out to use the toilet all day long. If I want a rest during the day, I have to use Cynthia's bed."

"Wow, that's dedication for you. I am so proud of him, Rose...and you as well. I was pretty rough on you at first. I hope you have forgiven me for that?"

"You were only looking out for your brother, Sambo. I knew

that. Nothing to forgive as long as you don't have any further objections to our relationship. Too bad if you did, because nothing would make me give up my man," said Rose, glowing with conviction and pride.

"I think you are the best thing that ever happened to this family, especially Charlie. Not sure where we would be if you hadn't turned up. I can see how happy you all are and nothing makes me happier than observing that and being given the opportunity to share in it."

"You have no idea how ecstatic Charlie and I are to have you back, Sambo. Still going off to find somewhere to stay today?"

"You bet," said Sambo as he rose from the couch to go to the bathroom.

"Back in a sec." He closed the bathroom door.

"Mummy?"

"I thought I told you to get ready for school? You are going to miss the first bus if you don't hurry up, young lady."

"Will Uncle Sambo be here when I get home from school?"

"I don't know, princess. He has a lot to do and we might not see him for a few days, but he isn't going back overseas, if that is what you're worried about."

"Promise?"

"I promise, munchkin. Now off you go."

"Mummy?"

"Yes?"

"He's funny and very handsome."

"Don't I know it, love, don't I know it. He seems to get better looking with age, unlike..." she left off with a sigh.

"Don't you think daddy is handsome anymore?"

"My goodness, you are a perceptive little creature. I am going to have to be very careful with what I say around you, aren't I? Your daddy is still very handsome and I love him to bits, okay?"

"Yes, mummy," Cynthia said as she skipped off to her room, passing Sambo in the hallway.

Sambo entered the kitchen after saying good morning to

Charlie, to sit at the table already set for him with a stack of pancakes dripping with butter and maple syrup that he would be hard-pressed to consume in one sitting. A steaming cup of coffee accompanied the delicious repast. Bright sunshine streamed into the small kitchen, bathing them in a warm, comforting glow. A pair of kookaburras had decided to let loose with raucous laughs in the tree opposite their window. Sambo smiled and ate heartily as the familiar Australian sound grounded him, reminding him of all the moments he had yet to enjoy in life.

Hours later Sambo was taking a casual stroll around the neighbourhood, familiarising himself, soaking up the atmosphere of the warm Brisbane day. Unbeknownst to him on a conscious level, his meandering walk had taken him unerringly in the direction of the telephone pole on Given Terrace. Before he knew where he was heading he saw the pole at the top of the rise. For a moment or two, he was lost in the memories of the dream and the associated feelings it evoked. He wandered listlessly to the pole and fingered the now much-worn carving. He was surprised that the pole had survived so long. Many of the poles were being replaced with steel poles which sported strong halogen lamps to light the streets and the neighbourhood.

A sudden shuffling sound disturbed his trance-like state. He whirled about, expecting to be attacked by the Duggans or someone within their circles. Instead, embarrassingly, he came face-to-face with an elderly woman wearing nothing but a frown. She fastened herself to Sambo with a terrified mewling sound emanating from her pinched mouth. Sambo looked about him in confusion as he tried to find someone to assist. Being the ever-gallant gentleman, Sambo quickly removed his button-up shirt to wrap the naked lady in it as best he could.

Shortly afterwards a man came running down a driveway looking panicked. Upon seeing Sambo and the woman, he was immediately relieved and fearful at the same time.

"Margaret? Margaret, dear, what are you doing out here?"

"I, I, I can't, Morris. I can't go back in there. Please don't make me?" begged the woman, shaking tremulously in Sambo's arms.

"I'm sorry, sir, she...just ran to me like this."

"Thank you, thank you. Oh, I was so worried when I turned around and she had gone. Just finished her shower, you see? Ran off while I was getting some clean clothes for her. Margaret, you mustn't keep hold of the man. We have to get you back inside to get you dressed. Come along."

"No! I won't. I can't, Morris. Please?"

"At least let me take you back into our yard so we can dress you properly? You're naked, Margaret, don't you feel embarrassed?"

Margaret clung to Sambo as if her life depended on it. Without thinking about it, Sambo swung the frail woman up in his strong, protective arms.

"Now, ma'am, we need to get you off the street. All right?"

"Not in the house. Can't, can't go back..."

"Morris, is that your name? I think it would be best if you didn't force her to go back inside for the time being."

"Yes, yes, quite right, young man, wouldn't dream of it. Would you mind bringing her this way? We'll just walk up the driveway, dear? Is that all right? I just need to get some clothes on you, Margey." The man's voice was concerned.

"I am so very sorry you had to see this, young man. It is all..."

"It's nothing, Morris. Nothing at all. Just lead the way."

Sambo was astounded when the man led him up the driveway to the mauve house of the Duggans', Crystal's old house. In the front yard, unobserved by him prior to this, stood a for sale sign by a realtor he did not recognise as having visited that morning. It was an eerie experience to be walking brazenly up the path of the house he had so long kept under surveillance.

He could not see any scenario where the old couple could possibly fit into anything as nefarious as the Duggan clan. Sambo assumed, correctly, that the Duggan family no longer owned the house. He was relieved and rather perplexed as to the reason the house had been sold. The woman in his arms continued to wriggle and murmur, becoming increasingly agitated the nearer to the house they came. Shunning the stairway to the front door, Morris led them to the rear of the house, where there was a small granny flat a little larger than a shipping container situated against the rear high paling fence.

Morris raced ahead to open the door of the small cabin. Sliding the glass door in its aluminium frame, he moved aside to allow Sambo to enter carrying his wife. Sambo gently lowered Margaret into the waiting arms of her concerned husband, who quickly carried her into the bedroom and closed the door. Sambo was left wondering what to do next. He supposed it might be impolite to simply leave, yet he did not want to embarrass the elderly couple any more by staying. He almost decided to leave; then he remembered that he was not wearing a shirt.

Sighing heavily, Sambo took a seat on the settee in the sitting-room at the front of the cabin. As the room appeared to be lived in, Sambo assumed that the woman, Margaret, might be using the cabin to avoid entering the main house. Why she would be in fear of the house, he had no idea. Before he could change his mind about staying, the bedroom door opened to reveal Morris retreating carefully after seeing to his wife.

Returning the shirt, he said, "Oh, I am so very, very grateful to you...?"

"Samuel Border. Sambo to my friends." He offered the man his hand after donning the proffered shirt.

"Morris Plainfield. Pleased to meet you, Sambo. I am so sorry you had to witness that. My wife, you see? Margaret, she, well she is not well anymore. She has become unglued since we moved here a couple of years ago. Nothing helps, nothing. Psychiatrists, medication, nothing. I am at my wits' end. I finally caved in to her demands about moving, but we simply cannot sell this wretched house. We are only pensioners and we cannot afford to simply leave."

"What is it, though? What's wrong?"

"Oh, dear. You are going to think us such foolish old people if I tell you."

"Then perhaps you shouldn't. None of my business, anyway," allowed Sambo.

"Nonsense! Least I can do for the way you helped out with Margaret. Not too many considerate young men like you around anymore. Haunted."

"I beg your pardon?"

"The house, haunted. I know how that sounds, but there it is. Horrible, horrible things happening in that house. Margaret feels it far more than me, but I have seen and felt things in there that would make your hair stand on end. A month after we settled into that house, our lives were shattered. Doors banging for no reason, lights swinging without wind. Noises in the middle of the night, beds trembling and the ill feelings one gets...simply nauseating. Both of us sick as dogs almost all the time."

"Surely it can't be as bad as all that..."

"Oh, worse, much, much worse. My wife has fallen over so many times in that house when furniture has suddenly appeared in the most unlikely places. Middle of the night we hear sounds, we get up to find our door barricaded with furniture on the outside. Go to the bathroom and filthy water comes from the spout. We have had the plumbers in here so often, they refuse to react to our calls any longer. Lights go out, no electrical faults. Windows open when we know we have closed them. I even hammered three-inch nails into a window frame one afternoon. Next thing we know, a violent wind is rushing through it only an hour later.

"Our lives have been a living hell from the very start. Margaret moved out here a few months ago, unable to tolerate being inside the house any longer. She has become quite unhinged, thinking I want to force her to return. I don't want to go back inside either, Mr Border. I am scared to death of where this will all end. Sorry to unload all this on you. It's just...well."

"That's okay, honestly. Sorry this is happening to you. Was there any indication by the previous owner of anything untoward about the place?"

"Hmm, funny you should mention that. Margaret and I were both wondering at our good fortune in purchasing such prime real estate for so little. We never met the owners, but the real estate agent behaved very oddly. He always remained outside whenever we inspected the property. Gave us the key and waited in his car. It was a lovely house and we had not the slightest inkling as to what would occur once we moved in. We both loved it immediately. We felt very comfortable in it. At first, that is. Look, I know it's early, but my nerves are frazzled and I need a drink. Can I offer you one, please?"

Sambo realised that Morris desperately needed some company, even a stranger's. He accepted the offer despite rarely imbibing at such an early hour. They sat outside the cabin on two reclining deck chairs, nursing beers. The sun remained overhead, warming them nicely as they conversed at length. Morris had given his wife a strong sedative to allow her the rest she deserved, enabling Morris the opportunity to reveal everything occurring in the house since they purchased it.

It was a terrible tale worthy of a Stephen King novel. Sambo listened politely as the afternoon unfolded, and arrived at the inevitable conclusion.

"So, Morris, how much are you hoping to get out of the house?"

"Oh, I am at the point of walking away from it altogether. My Margaret means everything to me, and if there is any hope of her getting better by escaping this monstrosity, I will leave."

"What price have you listed it for?"

"A mere fraction of what we paid just twenty-four long months ago. I have asked them to lower the price even more just today. It now stands at fifty-four thousand dollars. We bought it for nearly two hundred thousand, which we believed was under-valued by at least a hundred thousand. If we can get out of it for enough to get into a rented house, we will be happy. Every potential buyer so far has left here running moments after they enter. Many of them make it no farther than the bottom of the front stairs, where they double up and void their stomachs. Twenty or more couples and investors so far, all sick or terrified, moments before or after they step inside."

"I haven't anything like what you say it is worth, but I can comfortably offer you a hundred thousand for it."

"Oh, don't be dense, Sambo. Haven't you been listening to me? I couldn't possibly accept such a generous offer from someone as kind as you. I wouldn't wish this house on my worst enemy."

"I'm willing to take my chances. I have a special connection with this house and I have a feeling I won't be as troubled as others by living here. If I am wrong, worst case scenario, I will do as you have done. I will take up residence in here. It's a comfortable little cabin. I am alone, so it will suit me just fine."

"If you are serious about this, Sambo, and you will regret it if you are, I will agree to sell you the house, but not for one cent more than the current asking price. You either agree to pay me the present price or I will refuse to sell. I have already made up my mind that you are a very brave or foolish man, and I have grown immensely fond of you in a very short time. I hope you do not come to blame me or think us terrible if this deal should backfire. I have to accept your offer; my wife's life depends on it, I feel."

Margaret, upon hearing the news that a potential sale was in the offing, made a miraculous recovery to join the pair as a lucid, untroubled diner within the cabin before Sambo bid them goodnight. Sambo spent the night inside the 'haunted' house without incident as a way of proving both his sincerity and safety to the concerned couple. Appearing at the top of the rear stairs in the morning looking refreshed, relaxed and unscathed, Sambo left Morris no choice but to accept his proposition.

Sambo offered them a little more money for the furniture which Margaret was reluctant to keep, as she feared a lingering taint upon the items. Her features revived remarkably within a very short time. Sambo assisted them in finding a suitably furnished flat in another suburb far removed from the vicinity of the house. He helped them over the following years whenever he could with a little cash or a helping hand. Margaret eventually recovered to become the bright and vibrant person she was before their ordeal began.

For the following evenings in his new home, Sambo kept up a keen vigilance for anything untoward or out of the ordinary. The only regular occurrence was the return of the dream where he met Crystal. The dream always ended at the kiss and was therefore rather benign compared to the nightmares suffered by the Plainfield couple. While his dreams continued to cause him pangs of depression and loneliness, Sambo neither feared nor regretted their visitations.

Oddly enough, over the course of a few months, that dream altered its content dramatically. Sambo found himself ensconced within Crystal's version of the dream rather than his own. He and Crystal appeared slightly older than their ages in his own dream, as well as being dressed in the attire of the mid-forties. He was dressed smartly in a RAAF uniform resplendent with medals and the insignia of the rank of SQNLDR, squadron leader. The smart navy-blue suit cinched at the waist by a belt, and the jaunty angle of the peaked cap, left no doubt about the confidence emanating from the pilot about to embark on his tour of Europe.

Crystal appeared demure and restrained in his dream, with a hint of worry marring her otherwise perfect features. In calculating the risk her beau undertook as a pilot about to head off to war in Europe, she appeared wholly supportive, yet troubled. Her love for him was clearly evident in the glow of her cheeks and the sparkle in her eyes. When the proposal came, it was always accompanied by a mixture of joy and fear. The carving followed, then the kiss, and no more. Sambo always woke with a feeling of delight suffusing his body and mind. It lasted only a moment or two as he awoke fully and then remembered her absence.

Moving into the house had taken next to no time, as he could fit most of his personal belongings into his newly acquired Holden VT

Commodore four-door sedan, considered by most to be their most reliable model ever. Sambo did not require anything fancier than a basic model. Sporting a V6 motor capable of producing sufficient torque and speed for Sambo's needs, the Executive had ample interior capacity to take his brother and his family anywhere together.

Life soon settled into a routine for Sambo. He resumed his casual walks around the neighbourhood and surrounding suburbs, for the exercise and to assuage his curiosity. He also indulged in a new form of recreational exercise, kayaking. He purchased a sit-on-top kayak and suitable safety gear, and invested many hours, testing his strength and stamina against the current of the Brisbane River by paddling as far upstream as Wacol once his strength increased sufficiently. His savings allowed him to forego the poker games for a period. A few wise share investments while in America showed encouraging signs of developing into a source of regular income.

Sambo began to enjoy his time on the river immensely, fascinated by the scenery and activities on either bank as he paddled upstream. As his stamina increased, Sambo was soon paddling significant distances. Often, when nearing one of the turning points in his daily paddles, Wacol, he would rest awhile to enjoy a picnic lunch and refreshment before deciding to return home or venture further upstream on any given day. One place had Sambo intrigued as he paddled by. Set on a large portion of land fronting the Brisbane River was The Park Centre for Mental Health, known previously as Goodna Hospital for the Insane, Goodna Mental Hospital and Woogaroo Lunatic Asylum, to name a few.

Patients were often seen lounging on the grounds by the river, soaking up the sunshine and the healthy goodness of the surroundings. One or two nurses were always on hand to supervise as well as a few burly orderlies in case patients proved cantankerous or obstinate. Sambo often paddled to the opposite bank to observe the poor wretches totally lost in their tormented worlds. The screams and shouts were what first drew his attention to the site. On more than one occasion Sambo witnessed a patient stripping off their clothes to take a plunge in the river, only to be halted in their attempts by the orderlies. Roughly forced back to their outdoor recliners, the patients resumed their drug-addled, mindless recreation.

One such match between the orderlies and a highly agitated patient captured Sambo's attention one day as he paddled nearby. Disregarding the altercation became impossible for him as he observed the commotion from afar. His blood suddenly came to a boil as the orderly dealt his patient a vicious blow that sent her reeling.

Sambo paddled quickly to the river bank from where he could disembark. He maintained his vigil on the pair as the man used his strength and perceived authority to reduce the woman to a blubbering heap upon the manicured lawn. He was still swinging punches and delivering kicks as Sambo arrived on the scene. With one well-timed roundhouse kick, delivered with tremendous force to the orderly's nose, Sambo was able to halt the assault on the hapless patient.

Sambo peered at the woman's phthisic features, marred further by bruising and blood, and discovered an all-too-familiar countenance. Her rheumy, drugged eyes, staring into space, caused Sambo to shake with rage. Without a doubt in his mind, he knew it was Crystal, though she exhibited a highly advanced age discrepancy from when last he saw her. The orderly was rousing himself from the torpor of the stunning blow delivered by Sambo, in time to receive a repeat of the treatment. Other orderlies and an attendant nurse were now rushing to the scene. Sambo hurried to Crystal's side, embracing her with a comforting hug.

"Sir, sir? Unhand the patient. I warn you. We will call the police and have you arrested if you do not do as you're told."

"This is my wife and that man was asaulting her. If you don't want me to bring down this institution with a whopping great lawsuit, I suggest you find me someone in charge!"

CHAPTER TWENTY-TWO

"Mr Border, my name is Doctor Cartwright. May I offer my sincerest apologies for the unfortunate incident you witnessed and may I assure you that it was an isolated one, which we will investi..."

"Save it, buster. I've paddled past here often enough to know it was not an 'isolated' incident. I intend to press charges against that employee and the others I have witnessed treating patients here with less care than animals," argued Sambo, clutching onto the frail and shaken form of his wife.

"I...understand your concern and I can appreciate your wish to see justice done where you perceive a wrong has been perpetrated against this patient..."

"This 'patient' is my wife, legally married in the eyes of our law. Now, I don't know who signed her into this facility, but I am taking her out."

"Mr Border, that will simply not be possible until we have established a few..."

"Listen to me, you smarmy prick. You have detained my wife illegally, without her husband's consent. Your employees have demonstrated highly questionable methods of control, under your purview. That makes you responsible for their illegal behaviour. You will figure substantially in the consequent police interviews when I lodge my complaints."

"I assure you that all the protocols were followed when this woman was accepted into our facility. You have yet to prove your identity and your relationship with...Mrs Duggan."

"Her name is Mrs Crystal Sally Border, nee Montague. I can produce a marriage certificate and any other forms of proof you desire when the authorities show up."

"In the meantime, may we take care of...your 'wife' to see that she is more comfortable, please?"

"Anyone tries to come near me or Crystal, they will rue the day they were born. I will not allow the subjugation of my wife through your drugs and abuse any longer. Now, have the police been called?"

"I believe they arrived a short time ago and are on their way up here. Mr Border, despite your beliefs, you will cause your wife further unnecessary stress if you do not allow us to see to her needs," suggested the doctor, advancing as if to check on the patient's vital signs.

"Back up, arsehole! You do not get to inflict any further atrocities on my wife. She is not now, nor ever will be, in your 'care' again. This...place has already shown its hand in that regard and I will make sure the public hears about it. I heard you say that she was legally signed in? Seeing as that is absolute bullshit, and you do require the spouse or next of kin or a court order to legally have her committed to psychiatric care, then you are acting against the law. Unless you can produce incontrovertible evidence to the contrary? I am her husband, with proof, whereas you did not ask proof of the imposter posing as her husband, who had her committed.

"You are in deep shit, doctor. Your admittance procedures are woefully lacking in security. You have taken into custody a healthy woman and reduced her to this state with incompetence and ineptitude. Have the police been informed about the information they need at my home and where they could find my documents?"

"I assure you that I have followed your instructions in that regard. I pray that you are one hundred per cent correct in all that you say, Mr Border. If the police do not find sufficient evidence to corroborate your story, I will bring upon you the full force of the law to have you arrested on several charges, including kidnapping and assault. The orderly you attacked requires extensive surgery as a result of his injuries."

"How you can even begin to defend a monster who attacks your patients is quite simply beyond my understanding. You are no better than he."

"We have only your word on the events of today. Several others tell an entirely different story."

"Then how do you explain the fresh injuries on my wife? Even an incompetent fool like you could recognise fresh injuries if you saw them. Or are you saying she did this to herself? Yes? Gave herself a few uppercuts then somehow managed to kick herself in the ribs? Amazingly versatile human to do that to herself, wouldn't you say? I'm sure that you have a few ways to explain it, but none of them will be the truth. Fucking doctors! You're all full of shit and believe you are unaccountable. I will make sure *you* are made the exception. You will be held accountable for the actions of your staff if you continue to defend them."

"Mr Border, the...your wife is ill. Whether there was insufficient priority given to identification at registration or not, your wife was gravely ill, showing signs of a complete breakdown."

"Of course she did. So would anyone who had been kidnapped by the most sadistic bastard on earth, torturing and abusing her daily after nearly killing her once before. He obviously has her son, Samuel, whom I adopted. The natural father found where we lived and took them. I chased them all over the world for a decade before having to give up.

"Did you give her a physical examination upon her admittance? Did you notice any abnormalities like past or present bruises, contusions, lacerations, broken bones, especially ribs? That mongrel preferred a cricket bat last time. I am sure you did find these things, but, naturally, you believed the piece of shit when he said she did it all to herself, huh? Some fucking doctor you are. Blind fucking Freddy would have been able to detect abuse with a patient exhibiting those telltale symptoms. How much fucking cash did that cunt throw at you to make you dismiss those observations? Just wait. Just you fucking wait until the cops get here."

"I have nothing more to say to you..."

"Good! Fuck off out of here and leave me and my wife alone. I only want to talk to the cops, anyway."

Doctor Cartwright left his office with a look of serious concern marring his otherwise complacent features. He moved swiftly along the corridor in the direction of the admissions records, kept under lock and key, accessible only to senior personnel. Before he reached the room, however, he was confronted by the arrival of the police, led by a senior nurse. He silently cursed his neglect in failing to conceal the dubious intake records, for which he had gained significant monetary donations. He had made a mental note a year ago to destroy all evidence of the admissions made on vague or spurious grounds.

Doctor Cartwright resigned himself to the fact that an investigation of the centre was unavoidable in the face of the serious allegations facing his staff. He would personally see the moron who threw them all under the bus, out of a job with no reference and possibly in court, as long as it didn't backfire on him. John Grey, the orderly on duty at the time of the patient's admission, had received the token reward for turning a blind eye to the false procedures followed.

They had kept the woman under such a high dose of medications that she had somehow become inured to their effects, requiring ever larger doses to keep her subdued. They often fought with the tenacious woman to make her swallow the cocktail of drugs, resorting to injections when those attempts failed. She had shown remarkable resilience to any form of control, physical or mental. Doctor Cartwright had warned the inept orderlies often about leaving evidence of their control techniques upon the patients, especially that particular woman.

He was paid an inordinate sum to ensure she never again made an intelligible remark, to guarantee her silence. Falsifying diagnosis of mental fatigue and total permanent breakdown was a serious offence, one for which he could be imprisoned for a very long time should it be discovered. He would have to work hard to forestall any such investigation into the hospital records. Thankfully, he had patient confidentiality to hide behind.

"Ah, Detective Saunders, I'm glad you're here. If we can just slip into a room where we can talk privately before..."

"Doctor Cartwright, this the third time I have been called here in similar circumstances over the course of a year. I have in my possession documents proving the man's claim that you have his wife here under false pretences, that you did not pay sufficient notice to the legalities when admitting a patient to this facility. I am going to talk to the witness first. You are to wait in the next room until such time as I need to question you. You will make no moves or requests from your staff towards that records-keeping room in which direction you were heading. I will leave Officer Johnson here to ensure that order is followed."

"Detective, they are highly confidential and private records in there..."

"Which no one will touch unless a search warrant is issued, I assure you. I will be doing everything by the book on this one, and if I so much as smell a whiff of impropriety about this situation I will see that they hang you out to dry...doctor. Now turn around and lead the way. Don't make me cuff you in front of the staff. You do not want to test me today."

"I am willing to cooperate fully with any investigation you desire, detective. My staff and this facility are beyond reproach, as you will soon find out."

"I really doubt that. I have been investigating this centre for the past year and have held some very interesting interviews with former patients, of which there are very few, and former staff members, of which there are many. One of whom you described as a disgruntled employee? She has been most forthcoming with statements and corroborating evidence that will see you thrown out of the medical profession and jailed if I have anything to do with it. Now, unless you have a confession to make, I suggest you don't talk anymore until after I have interviewed the witness. Then it might behove you to contact a very good lawyer when you have the opportunity to use a phone."

The detective, nurse and doctor marched back in the direction of the room holding the Borders. Detective Saunders left the doctor in an adjoining room to stew on his dilemma. The nurse was ushered into the room in the hope of rendering caring aid to the patient.

"Mr Border, I am Senior Sergeant Detective Douglas Saunders. You can call me Doug if you like. I have in my possession the papers identifying yourself and your wife, taken from the drawer in your bedside table, exactly where you informed us they would be. Would it be possible to speak to you alone?"

"Detective...Doug, my wife has been through such trauma that she may well be beyond rescue. I hope with all my heart that it is not the case, but I will not allow any of these...people to administer any sort of assistance whatsoever at the moment. I don't trust any of them, and my wife has suffered enough. I think it best that you ask your questions with Crystal present. I will not let her out of my sight while I am here."

"You understand that we have to investigate this matter and that we cannot simply accept your version of the events. Your wife will be given the utmost..."

"No! She will not remain here. If there is no compromise to that, then I will stay here with her. No one here is to touch her or give her anything. If she has suffered a breakdown as they allege, then I will bring her out of it on my own, at home once she is released. Unless she has acted in a criminal capacity, endangered herself or others, I'm relatively sure that she cannot be legally committed by the state?"

"She will have to be re-examined by another psychiatrist to determine her state of mind."

"That may well be necessary, but not here and not by anyone connected to this facility. I will pay whatever is required to move her safely to another facility while her evaluation takes place as long as I may remain with her, but I will not allow medication of any description, not even an aspirin. Do I make myself perfectly clear?"

"Very well, Mr Border. I think we can accept those conditions for the moment. Now, would you mind giving me an account of what you witnessed and some background information?"

Two hours later, Detective Saunders left the room shaking his head. It was a disturbing tale of torture and abuse of monumental proportions upon the woman, preceding anything that occurred at the centre. He silently whistled at the sheer tenacity and determination of the man, Samuel Border, in traipsing across the globe to find his wife and stepson.

The woman's admission to the centre had taken place a couple of years ago by a man posing as her husband, even having the temerity to name her Mrs Duggan. Tommy Duggan, Shamus, the father, and Paddy Duggan, the grandfather, were well known to the detective, having been denied convictions against them for any number of infractions over the years. Obtaining a false report to have the woman committed was the very least of a long string of complaints against the Duggan family.

Ten years ago Tommy Duggan disappeared from the Brisbane scene. Doug Saunders' colleagues had been unable to trace his whereabouts despite extensive investigations. Their residence, somewhere in Paddington, he thought, had been sold for a very modest sum, considering its prime location, many years after his sudden departure. An elderly couple had purchased it approximately two years ago from Paddy Duggan, who seemed to disappear afterwards. Rumours, innuendo and outright accusations of money-laundering, prostitution and bribery were among the crimes being investigated by state and federal detectives. Kidnapping and assault were simply additions to the litany of allegations against the notorious Duggan trio.

Detective Saunders knew of at least two policemen suspected of being in cahoots with the gangsters. Many more were assumed to be on the payroll. Collecting enough evidence against them or the Duggan clan to bring them to justice was almost impossible. Evidence disappearing from lockers, charges being suspiciously dropped by prosecutors and judges, coroners filing dubious autopsy reports on alleged victims...the list was endless.

If Detective Saunders was able to collect eye-witness testimony for kidnapping, assault and battery, and any number of other charges against the clan, he felt positive they would be able to nail them at long last. Much depended on the woman to come through the trauma and her subsequent treatment at the centre.

He silently cursed Samuel Border for not involving the police when the kidnapping first occurred. The threat against the kidnapping victims notwithstanding, he was negligent in not coming forward at the time. The detectives would have had a decent shot at extraditing Tommy from Ireland had they been aware of his whereabouts. He was not sure what to make of all the other nonsense the husband went on about, dreams, feelings, and...tingles? That caused the detective to feel less than confident about the husband as a reliable witness. *Lawyers would have a field day with that bit*, he thought.

He had already been on the phone to arrange for the Borders to be transported to another institution. He had to pull a lot of strings and call in quite a few favours to allow the husband to remain with his wife. Considering the condition of the wife, Detective Saunders thought it preferable to have her husband nearby, hopefully assisting her to gain a semblance of awareness before too long.

He was going to enjoy watching the doctor, and the staff under his influence, squirm as he applied all the pressure he could muster against them. Two former patients had come forward in the last year to accuse the centre, and, in particular, Dr Cartwright, of wrongdoing, falsifying psyche reports, illegally detaining patients and overmedicating. There were too many witnesses to dismiss when taken together with this new allegation.

CHAPTER TWENTY-THREE

"Hello, remember me?"

Manuela squealed as she was bundled into the alley between tall buildings in The Valley, unable to offer any effectual resistance.

"What do you want? Who...oh, you again."

"I told you I'd be back if my wife came to any harm, didn't I? Here I am."

Sambo spoke between clenched teeth. He slammed her against a brick wall in the tight alley perfumed by the industrial bins overflowing with rotting restaurant refuse.

"Thanks to you, my wife has suffered years of physical torture and now a mental illness. Give me one good reason why I shouldn't subject you to the same treatment?"

"That was, that was years ago. I can't be held respons..."

Manny did not get to finish the sentence. Sambo slapped her brutally across the face, breaking open the Botox-filled top lip. "Try to wriggle out of your complicity once more and I will carry through with my threats, shit-for-brains. I don't care what happens to me anymore. I will kill you without hesitation unless you start cooperating with me unconditionally. No more bullshit, understand?"

"Okay, okay, I promise. Please don't hurt me."

"I know he is back in town. I want to know where he is."

"Who?"

The savage backhand broke open the bottom lip, loosening a tooth.

"Don't play games. Last warning. You don't want to fuck with me. I will break every fucking bone in your body, starting with your right arm if you do not answer my questions to my satisfaction. Got it?"

He received a quiescent nod.

"Where?"

"If, if I tell you, will you promise to leave me alone for good?"

"You are not in a position to bargain with me."

"If you are going to hurt me anyway, then I have no incentive to tell you. Heaven knows he will do worse to me if he finds out I helped you. May as well get on with it."

Sambo punched her heavily in the midriff, making her double up breathlessly. He followed up with a vicious blow to the jaw.

"You don't bluff a poker player, fuckwit! You are going to regret what you did. I..."

"Myrtletown. He's in Myrtletown," said Manny between gasps. "Last house on the right, before you get to the mangroves near the mouth of the river. He and his dad live there; the grandfather died a few years back. That...that's all I know. I swear."

"It makes sense, but why should I believe you? How do you know?"

"I...I followed them there one night. Tommy, he, he saw me, but wouldn't even acknowledge me. Just turned around and went inside after giving me the most awful look of disgust. I don't care what happens to him anymore. They, they have direct access to the river from their backyard. They have a small jetty with a fast boat tied up there. Please, I am telling you the truth and...I'm sorry for what I did. I never meant to cause her any harm, or the child. I'm very sorry."

"Get out of here. Away from this city and these people. I don't want to come across you ever again. If I do, it will be the end of you. I hate you for what you did. I can't stand the sight of you, so fuck off, now."

Manny raised herself to a standing position, then strode awkwardly past Sambo into the streetlight on Brunswick Street. Sambo strode to the mouth of the alley, watching her stagger down the street clutching her midriff. He felt awful. Manny may have been born male, but she was not a male any longer and he was sick to know that he had just assaulted a female. His guilt could not be assuaged by any justifications. He knew he had no choice, but it sucked.

He followed Manny's path down the well-lit street until he came to his car. In his mind, he swilled the situation around to find a plan. *Bloody Myrtletown again!* He detested that dump with all his heart. Nothing good would ever come from that shithole. He would have to find some way to disable any vehicles they owned, then work his way around to their boat to ensure it was incapable of providing an escape route. Weapons created the greatest concern for Sambo. He would be faced with an armed enemy while he remained weapon-less. Apart from a softball bat, he owned nothing of significance.

For the first time while in pursuit of the monsters who had kidnapped his wife, Sambo realised that he had never had the slightest notion of how he might accomplish the task of rescuing his wife once he found her. She was more or less safe from them at the moment, so rescuing her did not come into play. So he had to ask himself the real reason he was contemplating anything at all. He had no right to assume that Little Sam was in any need of rescue, as the boy was with his biological father.

Tilting at windmills had been his sole agenda for so many years that he knew no other way. Attempting his lonely vigilante crusade against the Tommy Duggan across the globe left him with little else to occupy his mind. Despite the wise counsel of his conscience, Sambo continued to plot his revenge. The police were stalled by their lack of evidence against the Duggans, their inability to locate the family, and with Crystal remaining incommunicado. Her first-hand testimony against the family was vital to proceed with prosecution.

When it came right down to it, Sambo's impotent ability to effect change left him raging inside, desperately hoping to procure justice for his suffering wife. Crystal might never recover from her ordeals. She was locked within a fragile shell, not willing to risk emerging into the light of day. She shook uncontrollably while she relived her nightmares day after day. Sambo remained by her side for months, rarely sleeping and eating less and less as time marched on.

Oddly enough, once Sambo moved her to his home, her former home, and the home of the Duggans, where her ordeal began so long ago, she settled considerably. Still refusing to talk or make eye contact with anyone, she at least calmed sufficiently to begin eating and drinking voluntarily again. Far from recovery or exhibiting signs of self-awareness, it seemed almost as if an unknown benefactor was at hand to assist in calming her troubled mind. At times, Sambo caught Crystal muttering while alone in her room as if she were holding a conversation with someone. Secretly and subversively, her interactions halted the moment anyone approached.

Sambo hired a full-time psychiatric nurse to care for her after bringing Crystal home from the second institute, when it became clear that her recovery would be a long-term process, if it happened at all. Doctor Cartwright had pleaded guilty to his crimes under the advice of his lawyer, over a year ago. He was sitting in a jail cell awaiting sentencing. Ten other staff members of the Wolston Centre were convicted of various crimes: they all pleaded guilty to avoid the harshest sentences applicable.

Detective Saunders had relegated the case and the search for the Duggans to the back-burners, pending testimony from the victim, Crystal Border. His hands were tied in that regard, which was what prompted Sambo to begin the search himself again for Tommy Duggan. He paid scant regard to the question of Little Sam's safety, concluding that it was the son they coveted above all else. If an heir was their sole purpose for abducting Crystal in the first place, it seemed wise to assume that the boy was not in immediate danger.

Before Sambo knew it, ignoring his vehicle, he had walked to the end of the road, winding up in Myrtletown. When he finally realised where he was, he supposed it would not hurt to inspect the house, the neighbourhood and the access points. A reconnoitre of the battleground might well be essential to any plan he might devise.

In the back of his mind, Sambo really just wanted evidence that Little Sam was in no danger. He would never forgive himself if that were not the case.

As luck would have it, directly across the street from where the Duggan family were purportedly living stood a vacant house. It had been that way for many years in Sambo's estimation. Gaining entry from the rear, Sambo made his way through the dusty rooms until he was in the main living area facing the street. Through a grimy sliding window set in an aluminium frame, he was able to keep vigil on the house across the road. The hour was late. Sambo assumed that the occupants of the house under observation were about their nefarious nightly activities. Sambo settled himself into a relatively comfortable sitting position to await their return.

Startled awake by the flash of head beams shining directly in his face, Sambo scolded himself for having fallen asleep. The vehicle was in the act of reversing into the opposite driveway, hence the glare of the headlights illuminating the house where he sat. When the headlights were turned off, he was unable to see anything until his night vision slowly returned. His heart jumped a beat when he caught sight of the young man accompanying the two adults.

Little Sam would be close to seventeen, Sambo calculated. In the dim view afforded him by the street lighting, Sambo recognised the features of Little Sam, no longer little by any stretch of the imagination. Tommy Duggan, over forty years old, the same as Sambo, sported a silver streak over the ears, while his old man was nearly bald. He noticed an awkwardness to the old man's gait and a stoop that belied his modest age. At only sixty-five, it appeared that Tommy's father suffered from arthritis or some other debilitating joint/bone deficiency. Sambo estimated that it would not be long before Shamus Duggan would require a walking frame, rather than the cane on which he now relied.

The trio held a brief discussion on the veranda of their home, where Sambo witnessed the first sign that Little Sam was suffering under the oppression of his father and grandfather. Tommy cuffed his son hard over the back of the head when it seemed the boy did not agree to something spoken. Briefly, standing defiantly with clenched fists at the ready in front of him, Little Sam assumed the pose of a defending boxer. Rage tore through Sambo as he watched his adopted son kneed savagely in the groin by his father.

Consumed by anger, his common sense obliterated by the white-hot rage building in him, Sambo threw caution to the wind in an attempt to intervene. Somewhere, somehow, between the front yard of the house in which he had been hiding and the veranda of the Duggan residence, Sambo had picked up a fallen branch.

Before either of the Duggans knew what was happening they were being bludgeoned by a hefty bough wielded by the enraged man. Blow after bone-shattering blow, Sambo unleashed all the pent-up fury percolating within him for over a decade. With a clear picture in his mind of the way Crystal appeared after he had rescued her from nearby, he rained his brutal justice upon the pair of twisted mongrels who had blighted the Brisbane scene for more years than anyone could remember.

Cries of agony and despair finally tore through the screen of hatred blinding and deafening his senses. Sambo leaned against the rail of the veranda entirely spent, gasping for air. Upon registering no movement from the pair at his feet, Sambo feared that he may have actually killed the bastards. Before he could find out one way or the other, another pair of frightened eyes tore his heart out. Little Sam, himself on the floor of the veranda, watched his stepdad with fear and concern etched on his features.

When Sambo discarded the bloodied branch and knelt next to Little Sam with a warm smile, it melted the youngster's heart immediately, assuring him that Sambo meant him no harm. In fact, Little Sam confirmed with that loving smile that his stepdad loved him far more than his real father ever had. Sambo picked up the skinny lad and gave him an embrace that evidenced his wholehearted love.

Without realising it, Sambo believed that he had been grieving the loss of his adopted boy as keenly as his mother had. A gaping hole in his life had suddenly been filled to the brim. Tears streamed down the faces of the pair as they hugged furiously, unable to release each other. Only a groan escaping one of the men at their feet alerted them to the fact that an exit was highly desirable at that point. Without a backward glance, the pair left the yard, exited the suburb of Myrtletown for good, and headed home.

Little Sam was not seriously injured, just bruised, but neither wanted to cut short their time together as they walked back to the car discussing the events leading up to the scene they departed. Sambo delivered the news of the boy's mother with great care. Thankfully, Little Sam was aware only that she had suffered a nervous condition of some sort. Sambo neglected to give his boy a complete rundown, believing that he and his mother were going to be healing tonics for one another.

Sambo listened closely as the lad related the tale of their abduction and the constant flights in a mature voice, convincing Sambo that he was no longer the child he remembered. He told of his increasing torment at the hands of his father and grandfather upon their return to Australia, each competing with the other as to who could be more tyrannical and brutal in their treatment of the troublesome boy. The boy had become a serious bone of contention between the two Duggan men. The grandfather did not believe that Little Sam was a Duggan, while Tommy suffered for his incompetence at allowing the mother to live in the first place.

When Tommy was finally able to convince his old man that Little Sam was his child, he suffered all the more for his ineptitude. At times, Tommy believed he would have been better off not pushing the fact at all. He would definitely have been better off ignoring the bothersome person, Manny, because of the years of abuse he copped after kidnapping Crystal and her whelp. He still found it difficult to believe that the boy was his, given the ultrasound evidence which angered his father and grandfather to near apoplexy so many years ago.

He quailed when they forced him to launch into an attack on the woman for the audacity of providing a female child instead of an heir. Although he was no stranger to inflicting pain on a woman, especially his woman, he did not want to go so far as killing her. He did not want that for several reasons. Mostly, he did not want that because he could not face the prospect of finding another incubator for his seed. He was so ill at the prospect that he became totally impotent, no longer caring for sex, babies, heirs or anything else connected to the act of furthering the Duggan line.

Then the years spent on the run, always just one step ahead of the persistent man dogging their heels, left a deep rift in the family's unity. His father and grandfather communicating to him from Australia, were in a delirium of ownership about his child once they accepted his birthright, like nothing else on earth mattered but the safety and continuity of their lineage. Protecting Little Sam against discovery, and possibly having to surrender the child to the adoptive parent, forced him to run and his father and grandfather to hide. The inexplicable fear his father exhibited in that regard had Tommy confused. He always believed his father and grandfather feared nothing, controlled everything and killed anyone who didn't like it, starting with their wives.

Little Sam, with his stepfather's arm around his shoulders, fought back the tears as he revealed his traumatic tale. When money started running out, he was often left hungry and filthy, hiding out in ever-worse hovels in Tommy's despicable company. It seemed perplexing to his young mind that someone who acted so tough and indomitable should fear his stepfather or the police in Australia. According to the boasts he overheard, the Duggan family had many members of the police force in their pockets.

The boy could not be aware of the implications facing the Duggan clan should a full investigation of their lives and close examination of their house take place. The Duggan family's skeletons were not hidden in a closet, nor were they all relegated to fish hooks in search of eel, they resided underground, specifically under the soil beneath their home on Given Terrace. With Tommy's impulsive move to kidnap his son and woman, he had inadvertently invited more trouble into their lives than his family wished. Worse, evidence had been interred along with those bodies, murder weapons, fingerprints, DNA, everything a halfway competent prosecutor required to put them all away for several lifetimes.

When Tommy brought home his son and the mother of his child, the household was thrown into complete chaos. Grandfather Duggan was all set to do away with his imbecile of a grandson and his useless father. He knew all too well that they were under constant surveillance by the federal police and elements of the local constabulary not under his control. They needed only a whiff of a scandal such as kidnapping to bring all merry hell down upon them and their comfortable lives.

A confrontation between the members of the Duggan household escalated through the long evening until it was finally determined that Tommy would have to leave the country. Naturally, the best place for him to stay under the radar for a while was back in the old country of their grandfather's birth, Ireland. Though still entrenched firmly in the conflict between the IRA and England, Ireland represented the only place where the underworld would protect and hide them, where they knew people.

When Tommy received word that someone was hot on their trail, he fled Ireland for England, then other parts of the UK, always only a few steps ahead of his pursuer. Several attempts by operatives in his employ to waylay the vexing follower met with severe punishment. His resources slowly dwindled over the years, with no money forthcoming from Australia, until he was forced to commit crimes in order to survive. Once the crimes began he came to the notice of local authorities, forcing him to move on earlier than he wished. In the end, it seemed as though the entire world was chasing the him.

He could not know who to trust any longer. Money was insufficient to provide reliable protection and silence. Word of mouth among the underworld society branded the Duggan family as 'too hot to handle', making his contacts retreat into the night when approached. Safe houses were denied him, transport and protection were impossible. Eventually, he was left with no choice other than to return to Australia, where at least he knew he could make a dollar or two, albeit illegally. His grandfather had sold the family home before Tommy's return to dissuade interest in the property by the authorities.

Little Sam related the story of his great-grandfather's illness and protracted death, felt most keenly by his grandfather. Tommy did not care a whit for the old man. He had been tormented by the family too long to have any feelings for the despicable tyrant. He was told of Tommy delivering his mother to the Wolston Centre after she suffered a nervous breakdown. Little Sam had been kept separated from his mother for so long he had trouble remembering her face. It was all he could do to simply stay alive under the brutal thrall of his father and family.

While it was difficult to remember clearly what his stepfather looked like after a time, it was all too easy to recall the great affection of the selfless man. When Sambo came barging onto the veranda of the house that night with murder etched on his features, he was totally stunned at first, frightened and worried for his own life. Then the big man calmed enough to look down at him cowering on the deck. When Little Sam saw that warm smile on the big man it triggered a flood of memories that immediately told him he mattered, that someone cared. Devoid of any real affection for so long, it stirred a great emotion in him to know that he was not hated altogether.

Upon questioning, it became clear to Little Sam just how much he mattered. That his stepfather crossed the globe in pursuit of him and his mother caused him to glow inside. It also made sense to him to understand why Tommy had to move all the time, just as he was getting used to one place. He made a lot of connections as Sambo revealed the details of his decade-long search and how he finally lost all contact.

"What was it, dad? What kept you going all that time? How could you know where we were?" asked the young man.

"A long time ago, I had a dream with your mother in it. I then met your mother for the first time at the Ithaca Pool. Messages, physical tingles and haunting dreams continued relentlessly until I found her again on the night of your birth. If I empty my mind of everything else, I am able to hone in on her signal. I get a sense of direction when that happens. I instinctively know where I must go and what I must do to get closer to her. I am connected with your mother in a way that leaves me both perplexed and breathless at times. I can't explain it any other way and, whenever I try, it is woefully inadequate."

"So what happened? Why did you eventually stop?"

"I lost it, Little Sam. Sorry, I better start calling you Sam, huh? Not so little anymore?"

"I prefer Little Sam, actually. Mind if I call you dad?"

"Chuffed, Little Sam. Just really..." Sambo choked back some tears.

"So, you were saying...?"

"Um, yeah. About a year and a half ago, I simply lost all contact with her. Nothing came, no matter how hard, or not, I tried. I had no choice but to return. Her breakdown may have been the cause of the disrupted signal. It may sound really strange to you, Little Sam, but I spoke to Crystal in my mind. I heard her laugh and talk and I saw her smile all the time. That picture just blinked out one day. I thought the worst, of course. I should have known better. Something had to be guiding me to take up kayaking on the Brisbane River all of a sudden."

"Huh?"

"Oh, you don't know any of that, do you? When I returned to Brisbane, I actually bought the house in which Crystal lived with her father for a time before the Duggan family bought it...again. It was years after they bought it that your mother was seduced by

Tommy Duggan and kept there as a sex slave until the night she was nearly killed and abandoned at Myrtletown. That was the night I found her again after a very long time, and also the night you were born. Your mother never told you any of this?"

"Tommy kept me from her almost all of the time we were on the run. I was too busy ducking blows to be all that concerned about her whereabouts, you know?"

"Sorry, Little Sam. I am so, so sorry you had to go through all that. I will do everything in my power to keep you safe from now on. Anyway, I started kayaking up the Brisbane River just for exercise and fun really. Or so I believed. I was eventually drawn to a section of the river overlooking a park-like setting where people were lounging around in the sun with other people supposedly looking after them.

"After a bit of research, I found out what it was and returned there a few times just to observe. I saw a bit of rough treatment at times. The staff of the centre did not act professionally and, when I saw them abusing a lady one day, I decided to do something about it. Turns out the woman was your mother. Once more I was drawn to her without knowing it. I had lost the pictures of her in my mind, could not reproduce them, but they were there after all."

"What, what is going to happen now, Dad?"

"First things first, we take you home to reunite you with your mother. Be gentle with her, Little Sam. She might not recognise you at first. May never recognise anyone again for that matter. She has been subjected to more misery and suffering than any person ever should."

"You really love her, don't you?"

"More than my life. More than anything in the world. She is so much more than a mere external physical presence to me. I will love and protect her with every ounce of my energy for the rest of my days. Trouble is, though, I may go to prison for what I did tonight. You are going to have to care for your mother in that case. Are you up to that?"

"I'll try."

"That, that's all anyone can ask, Little Sam."

"Thank you for...everything. I hope you don't go to jail because of me."

"You stop thinking like that. It was my temper that did that. The moment I saw them hurting you I just lost it...again. I should not have done what I did, and I only have myself to blame. It is wrong to hurt people like that, no matter what they are guilty of. Hatred and violence just end up being perpetuated when either party refuses to let it go. How are you feeling, by the way?"

"I'll live. I've had far worse from those two. Ran away a couple of times but didn't get very far. Never knew where I was most of the time."

The night air turned chilly as they made their way along the streets. Sambo was worried about a future for Crystal and Little Sam if he were locked away. If either man died as a result of the beatings delivered by Sambo that evening, he knew he would have to plead guilty to murder or manslaughter charges. He would not contest the charge no matter how justified his actions may have seemed to him at the time. He was a big enough man to face up to his responsibilities. He had already noted Crystal as sole heir in his latest will. Little Sam was listed as the next recipient to inherit in the event his mother was incapacitated, with a proviso that all her needs were taken care of.

He peered at the young man walking by his side, strong, albeit with a slight limp, determined and proud. He felt sure that Little Sam would fare well in this world, with or without anyone's help. Although the lad did not remember his mother as well as he should, Sambo believed that their reunion would accomplish that task. He only hoped that Crystal was able to respond eventually. The nurse he hired did not envision a happy ending where Crystal was concerned. It appeared to her that Sambo's wife had retreated completely into her own mental hell, from which she could not escape.

The constant physical and mental torture she had endured forced her deeper and deeper into a state of denial, where the rest of the world ceased to exist. No one could expect anyone to survive such a protracted ordeal. The loss of contact with her son had been the final catalyst, driving her into oblivion. Unable to accept reality any longer, her mind simply retreated into a place of comfort and ignorance of her surroundings. She might no longer be capable of existing in the present.

Sambo could only guess where she might be, what she might be thinking. He wanted to believe she was lost in their shared dream, in that moment of their first kiss, albeit a fantasy image, a truly happy moment for her. There were still occasions when he caught her whispering to herself or an imaginary friend. She maintained the glassy-eyed vacant stare but seemed to be holding a genuine conversation at times, not that Sambo could catch a word.

The house in which she had been detained failed to impinge on her character, failed to hold any significance for her one way or the other. Sambo was truly concerned that she would digress further, being in the location of her worst experiences. In fact, quite the opposite seemed to occur as Crystal drifted aimlessly through the house when she managed to become ambulatory. Most often she kept to her bedroom, sleeping soundly under the watchful gaze of her nurse.

Tilly - Matilda Case - ensured that her charge was cared for in the best possible manner. She talked to Crystal all day long, explaining what she was doing at all times. This way, Crystal was never surprised or frightened by anything Tilly did. Crystal had been easily spooked by any number of things when she first left the centre and then the other facility upon her discharge. The doctors all advised Sambo against removing her from the facility once it was established beyond a doubt that he was her legal guardian and next of kin, and that they had no legal right to detain her any longer.

Sambo's long experience with doctors made his decision an easy one. Regardless of their sternest warnings and threatened consequences should Crystal be removed from professional care, Sambo bundled her up the moment he was free to do so in the eyes of the law. Detective Saunders had delivered the news himself that Crystal was no longer a ward of the state. Though he saw the difficult road ahead for Sambo, he did not advise him on how to proceed, knowing full well that the man would not listen.

CHAPTER TWENTY-FOUR

"Mum? It's me, Sam Junior...Little Sam. You look...so...I mean, wow! I had no idea you were such a knockout. I only seem to remember how awful you looked most of the time. You know? Black and blue, puffy eyes and swollen lips? I don't remember much of my time with you and Sambo before my fifth birthday because I was so young. The few times Tommy allowed me to visit with you, you were always banged up and on some sort of drugs or something."

Sambo watched from the doorway as mother and son were finally reunited. Crystal showed no signs of recognition or change from her usual vacant stare. Tilly watched carefully for signs of her patient becoming overwhelmed with the enormity of the situation. She hung back at a respectful distance but monitored the exchange closely. Sambo backed away, feeling foolish. He half expected his wife to light up the moment she saw her son again. He should have known better. He returned to the living room where Detective Saunders was waiting for him.

"You can take me now if you like, Detective."

"A bit premature for that, Mr Border. Both men are in the hospital at the moment going through several surgeries to set bones and suture cuts. Tommy Duggan has a split scalp which required more than fifty stitches and it is unclear whether he has suffered brain damage at this point. We won't know more until they have recovered sufficiently to talk, if they do. You voluntarily handed yourself in when you called me about tonight and until someone either dies or recovers enough to press charges, I am willing to allow you to remain here. I will ask that you do not attempt to leave town or come near the hospital where the, ah, victims were taken."

Sambo nodded his acceptance of the conditions. "That is very generous of you."

"Considering that assaulting people is becoming a habit with you, you better believe it. I do not want to hear anything more of this nature in future. Do I make myself very clear on the matter, Mr Border?"

"You have my word on that. Thank you."

"How is the boy holding up?" asked the detective as he relaxed somewhat.

"Not bad. Better than I would in his shoes. What a mess! I don't know if either of them can ever come back from that. What sort of a life is it going to be for him?"

"The very best that you can make of it for him, I hope? He deserves every opportunity you can provide to see him through it all. He will need some schooling to get him caught up to start with."

"Yeah, private tutor, though. I don't think he will be up to school, public or private. I want him home with me and his mother. They both need as much time as possible with each other to start healing. Listen, Detective..."

"Doug."

"Doug. I can't thank you enough for doing this. Are you going to get in any trouble on my account?"

"Listen, Mr Border, the law is the law and I have to follow it as much anyone else, but there is very little compassion floating around for that pair of mongrels. Regardless of their condition and your possible implications in that regard, they are facing a long list of charges thanks to Little Sam's testimony, if they recover fully, that is. That alone will see them behind bars for a very long time. I will be making a not so subtle inference to the pair that any charges filed against you will ensure harsher penalties for them both when it comes time for their trials. We have them now, Mr Bor..."

"Sambo."

"Very well. We have them by the short and curlies, Sambo. This house will be kept under observation the moment they start waking up. You and your family are under our protection until these gangsters are placed behind bars. I sincerely hope you do not join them, but you will understand if I have no choice?"

"Already told you that you can take me now if you want. I understand that what I did was wrong. I lost it, I told you, and I know that is neither a good reason nor a defence. I surrendered myself because I believe in the law, Doug. Goes for me just as much as those two. I can hardly expect them to be brought to justice for breaking the law then hope to escape it myself. I will cooperate with anything you say and any condition you place on me. I just ask that you keep an eye on Crystal and Little Sam for me if I get sent away?"

"You have my word on that. You are a good man, Sambo. Look after that family of yours, they need you desperately, and we will speak soon."

CHAPTER TWENTY-FIVE

Thirty-seven-year-old Samuel Gerrard Border Junior stood before the gate leading to his parents' house on Given Terrace. The house looked grand, sporting a new coat of green paint and the front garden was resplendent in spring blooms. He halted before pushing through the gate to delve into his sad memories of the house, and, in particular, one of its occupants. He was here to introduce his parents to their new grandchild, Tatyana Mia Border, as well as celebrating his mother's birthday turning sixty-two, a year younger than Sambo.

Little Sam's wife, Natasha, stood impatiently beside her husband, dreading the encounter with the woman who had never once acknowledged her presence or responded to her grandchildren. Thankfully, their two eldest, Mitchel and Connor, were unable to accompany the family because of sporting commitments: both of them featured predominately in the track and field events for their inter-school sports carnival.

Natasha, who had inherited her grandmother's Slavic short temperament, fought to quell the knot of anguish she felt tightening in her stomach. A bitter row had seen her husband succeed in shaming her enough to attend the birthday and pay her respects to his beloved mother. Little Sam had championed his mother, despite her permanent condition, to Natasha's extreme frustration for longer than she could remember. The ensuing arguments, often leading to full-scale battles, had seen the pair visiting a marriage consultant several times throughout their tumultuous union.

Her one triumph culminated in her right to name their third child. Natasha chose the name of her great-grandmother, who died at almost the moment her daughter was born, just two months ago. She adored her great-grandmother, who cared for her when her mother passed away at childbirth, and her grandmother was too busy at work to pay her any attention. Even as a third generation

Australian, Natasha felt her foreign roots deeply enmeshed in her psyche.

Little Sam peered sideways at his wife, cradling the infant, his baby girl, in her arms, fidgeting annoyingly to show her frustration at having to attend the ceremony. He smiled and sighed inwardly, knowing that another argument would ensue that night. It was inevitable. He was looking forward to seeing his uncle and aunt, who had a pair of their own, the pigeon pair. Cynthia Celeste Border was now nearing thirty-one years of age, and Graham Charles Border was ten years her junior.

Neither of his cousins would be present as they were both overseas. Cynthia, a lawyer for a top Sydney law firm, was brokering a deal for her clients that would see her in New York for the next two years. Graham was enjoying himself immensely in Italy with the parents of the boy his own parents billeted as an exchange student years beforehand. Young Roberto and Graham had become best friends during his stay and remained in constant touch when he departed. Reunited with his friend, Graham was considering remaining in Italy.

Little Sam sighed again before finally pushing open the small, knee-high gate in the front fence to walk his family to the left and up the driveway to the rear of the house. He and Natasha would be staying in the small granny flat in the backyard. He hoped it would be as soundproof as he remembered it when he stayed there to finish his schooling, because he knew they would be making a lot of noise that evening. He wished, not for the first time, that he could enjoy a relationship like that of his uncle and aunt, or even his stepfather and mother.

At moments like those, he winced as he remembered that he was not the blood relative of those people he so admired, other than his mother. Though he desperately wished otherwise, he knew he was not a Border, but a Duggan. He unwillingly surrendered to the knowledge that he was not of the same substance as his step-dad or uncle. He quailed at the thought that he might one day show an inferior side to his character, a Duggan trait. He could think of nothing worse than turning out like his natural father.

He had gone to visit Tommy once during the man's long incarceration, only to find a pitiful shell of a human being. Tommy Duggan and his father, long dead, had suffered greatly as rapists and child abusers in jail. Though they were locked in a protection prison, they gained the scorn of other inmates nonetheless. Each day behind bars had them fearing for their lives. Slowly, the constant tension and the fights had taken their toll on the pair. Beaten neck and crop, Tommy appeared at the window of the visitors' room before his son in a cowed and suspicious manner. Little Sam left without a word being spoken. It was the last time he had seen his father.

Tommy was denied parole twice, solely on the moving testimony from the victims of his crime, namely Sambo and Little Sam. He resigned himself to serving his full sentence of eighteen years. He had been released two years ago and neither had heard from, or of, him since. A police presence had been established upon Tommy's release but was withdrawn a week later when it seemed the infamous Tommy Duggan had shown none of his former menace or arrogance.

Holed up in his halfway house, it appeared Tommy had succumbed to the inmate hell known as institutionalisation, where he feared being on the outside. When people are locked away for a lengthy period, and required to follow a strict set of rules governing their every move, they soon come to rely on those parameters, fearing any alteration to their routines. An inmate is sometimes known to stand before an unlocked door once released, with no understanding that they may pass through the door without waiting for a guard to open it. They become so ingrained in the routine and procedures of their incarceration that they are incapable of adjusting to freedom.

Two years after his release, Tommy Duggan remained within the halfway house, slowly devolving into a miserable old man incapable of functioning in a normal capacity. Police believed it was only a matter of time before he would be taken away to live out his days in the same facility where he had placed Crystal. Under new management, the centre had shaken off the scandal surrounding the shamed Dr Cartwright and several staff members associated with the inquiry.

Sambo had been urged many times to place Crystal in a similar institution over the years while she remained in a perpetual state of incommunicado. Even Little Sam had pleaded with his stepfather to make peace with the fact that his mother was beyond reach, that he needed to live his life. Sambo never once contemplated such actions. While it seemed so sad for everyone who knew him, Sambo was a happy man. He was more in love with Crystal every day, if that were possible, and patiently fended off any arguments to the contrary.

Truth be told, Sambo did have a glow about him and a contentment that affected all who came in contact with him, enveloping them in its comforting familiarity. Only a few moments spent in Sambo's company left you with little doubt as to the sincerity of his happiness. His smile ignited a room with its pure and genuine bonhomie. The indefatigable patience and care shown to his wife immediately allowed everyone to relax within their company. Though Crystal never showed the slightest recognition or sign of affection, Sambo persevered as though nothing were amiss or in the least unchanged from their previous time together.

Little Sam often wondered whether his dad was in a state of denial, yet had to accede to the fact that Sambo appeared to be living a full and happy life. He also knew that their marriage had never been consummated, which puzzled him. He knew how important the act of making love was for himself, so wondered at the strength of character portrayed by a man willing to forego those pleasures to remain faithful for so many years. To the best of Little Sam's knowledge, his stepfather had never strayed nor sought companionship elsewhere.

His suspicions that Tilly had played a part in their relationship came to naught when it was revealed that the woman's sexual proclivities did not run to the male of the species. Tilly remained with them to the day, ever present, ever caring and ever peripheral. She came in the evening before Sambo went to his nightly game at the casino, and left in the morning upon his return. The routine suited them all and no change was forecast, although Sambo had accrued enough in savings and investments to enable him to retire permanently, something he proposed to do in the coming year.

Sambo greeted them warmly at the top of the back stairs after they unpacked for their brief stay. Natasha had been quite besotted by Sambo from the moment she had been introduced to him by her fiancé. She managed to hide her infatuation unconvincingly whenever she was reacquainted with the large, regal gentleman. He never failed to exude a rugged earthiness while maintaining a serenity and distinguished poise that left her breathless at times. Had she met the father first, she felt sure she would have pursued the older man to the end of her days. She had never met Little Sam's real father and had no desire to do so.

That there was a disconnection between Sambo and his wife afforded her an unrealistic hope that she might one day fulfil her fantasy. Were it not for that vague notion of an impossible union, she would not allow herself to be talked into the yearly visits on the occasion of her mother-in-law's birthday. She presented her lips to be kissed rather than her cheek whenever the opportunity arose, much to Sambo's annoyance. He put it down to a foreign tradition of which he was unaware. It always felt decidedly awkward for him to do so.

Sambo took the young baby from Natasha's arms while they entered the house. All the drapes and blinds were always open fully to allow the maximum amount of sunlight to flood the house with its brilliance. For some reason, unbeknownst to Sambo, Crystal always seemed more relaxed in that atmosphere. She tended to show a morose, depressed nature whenever the house was darkened during the day. The proud grandfather walked into the living room, following the young couple.

Sambo regretted bitterly the missed opportunity to father a child of his own, and so lavished much attention and love on his step-grandchildren, nieces and nephews. He never failed to mark a birthday or other occasion where his kin were concerned. Presents for the children had proven a difficult task the older they grew. He always knew, with Tilly's help, what to purchase for young children, but not when they grew older. Teenagers were world apart from any living creatures on the planet. He usually ascribed to the voucher theory at those times, allowing them to make their own purchases.

Little Sam went straight to his Uncle Charlie and Aunt Rose upon entering the living room where they were seated. Natasha opted to make herself comfortable in a lounge chair as far away from the depressing form of Crystal as possible. Tilly sat patiently to one side at the rear of the assembled guests so as not to intrude on their family gathering.

"Uncle Charlie, I hope you brought along a copy of your latest book so I can start reading to Tatyana?"

"Little Sam! She's too young."

"Crap! I started reading your books to my other two the moment I got them home from the hospital. Aunty Rose, you look smashing, as always. I reckon you get prettier every year." Little Sam hefted Rose into the air easily in a swirling hug.

"Little Sam, you put me down this instant. I am far too old to be swung around like that anymore. Gosh, are you big! Almost as big as your f...as big as Sambo."

"Aunty Rose, how many times do I have to tell you that I consider Sambo to be my father? He has always been more of a father to me than bloody Tommy Duggan. So, you can say 'my father' when you're talking about Sambo. No need to always stop in embarrassment."

"Oh, I know, Little Sam, but I guess I don't want to look like I am forcing that connection, you know?"

"I understand, I suppose. I just wish we could all get the fact that my real father was a notorious gangster, an evil son of a bitch, and the cause of my mother's condition, out of our thoughts. My true father is, and always has been, Sambo as far as I am concerned. My father rescued me as a baby and again as a teenager, so he deserves all the love and affection I can give him, okay? Now, if you'll excuse me, I have to pay my respects to the woman of the hour," he said as he went to kneel in front of his mother, who was sitting in a leather armchair with a soft blanket draped over her lap.

Crystal stared at a point behind Little Sam's ear with a serene smile creasing her lips. She neither acknowledged nor gave any indication of hearing her son's birthday wishes. Little Sam reached up to peck her on the cheek. He searched his mother's face desperately for any sign of recognition, any minor emotion, only to be disappointed. His mother ate when fed, toileted upon being moved to the restroom, allowed herself to be dressed and walked about the house in a shuffling gait, but showed not the slightest hint of recognition of the world around her.

Only Sambo was aware of rare moments when he observed his wife turning her head and moving her lips to communicate with the air in front of her. Not a sound passed the moving lips, but the eyes had a sharper focus instead of the vacant stare she typically exhibited. A beatific glow suffused her features on those occasions, causing Sambo to believe that his wife might yet somehow find her way out of her mental abyss. Regardless of the passage of time, he maintained his eternal hope that he would one day be reunited emotionally with the woman he loved.

Little Sam peered into her limpid eyes, once so vivid and engaging, only to find the usual vacancy. He sighed as he wished his mother a happy birthday. Keeping Crystal at the centre of their activities, the family hovered about her on her special day, including her in conversations and celebrations. Sambo managed to tip a little champagne into her mouth at the toast, while the others watched. Only Natasha refused to include her mother-in-law in conversations, would not drink a toast to her or even peer in her general direction.

Natasha sat sullenly alone, using her need to feed the infant as an excuse to leave the living room to retreat to their temporary abode in the backyard. Feigning a headache later in the afternoon, she managed to stay downstairs in bed for the remainder of the evening. When Little Sam eventually joined her around nine o'clock, she was remarkably well without the slightest hint of a headache remaining. In fact, she bounced back so miraculously from her affliction, she was able to instigate the row he knew would be forthcoming.

"Why would you leave me alone down here all afternoon?"

"You told us you had a headache, Natasha. I thought it best to let you rest. Are you saying you lied about a headache?"

"How dare you accuse me of lying?"

"I asked you a question, Nat. I didn..."

"Natasha, my name is Natasha. I have told you I do not like this Nat, you call me." She affected a false Slavic accent for the sake of the fight.

"Natasha, keep your voice down, please. I do not want a fight."

"I will not allow you to accuse me of lying. I will not keep my voice down."

"Even if you sound foolish? You told everyone upstairs you had a headache. Now you are proving to everyone who can plainly hear you that you don't have a headache."

"You know I can't stand all that stuff up there and that..."

"Be very careful what you say, Natasha. I will not hear anything bad said about my family, especially my mother," Little Sam warned resolutely.

"Or what? You will hit me? Like your father..."

"Oh, drop it, Natasha. I have never raised a hand to you in all the years we have been together. NEVER!"

Natasha was stunned to silence at the shout from her husband, the first time ever he had raised his voice to her. From their bedroom came the sounds of the baby waking, breaking the stalemate and the weighty atmosphere.

"See, see what you have done? Now Tatyana has been woken by your shouting. You accuse me of being loud when it is you who wakes the baby."

Natasha left the room to settle the baby while Little Sam remained in the front room feeling guilty about raising his voice. He had an inkling as to how a man could become so incensed by his spouse that he might strike her. He had never felt even remotely so inclined, but, in the back of his mind, he knew the malignant impulse lurked. It was the fear of acting on those lurking impulses that bothered him more and more, concerned that Tommy's genes would somehow emerge to transform him into the monster he remembered.

The years he spent travelling with his father had been indelibly inked into his memory. The atavistic, cruel behaviours he had witnessed toward him and other victims left him shaking with dread during his tormented sleep. While he remained a perfect paragon of patience and kindness to his family, friends and work associates, he harboured grave fears for his future if he had inherited even a quotient of his father's personality.

It was futile to attempt to dissuade him from these dark thoughts. Sambo had often rejected the theory Little Sam proposed as pure hogwash. Sambo told him time and time again that he was not destined to become his father, that he had his own life from which to draw his responses. He need not concern himself over false conclusions. Try as he might, however, Little Sam continued to dwell on the possibility that he would metamorphose in his later years.

Little Sam used the interruption as his wife disappeared into the bedroom to postpone the argument. As he stepped through the sliding glass doors he saw a shadow at the top of the stairs. Before he fully recognised the person, he propelled himself forward swiftly, hoping to prevent his mother from falling. He reached her just as she was stepping forward. However, Tilly already had hold of her elbow and steered her gently back into the house.

Little Sam followed the two women back into the living room, where Crystal was decorously returned to her favourite chair. Sambo seemed concerned when they entered the room, having taken a short reprieve to alleviate his bladder. Rose and Charlie had retired earlier to the guest bedroom.

"What is it, Tilly? What happened?"

"Oh, nothing to fret about. Mrs Border just went for a little stroll on her own. That's all. Caught her at the top of the stairs."

"You mean outside?"

"Well, just."

"I've never seen her do that before. You?"

"Oh, yes. Many times."

"Do you think I should place locking security doors at the exits?"

"Keep her locked up, you mean....?

"Yes, I see. That was pretty tactless, wasn't it?"

"What do you mean, Dad?"

"Remember your mum was pretty-much kept prisoner here by Tommy Duggan until you came along."

"Oh! Yeah, wouldn't be right to keep her locked up, whether it was for her own good or not," he said, settling onto a couch near his mother. "Dad, I don't get it. Why the hell would you even think of buying this house when Mum has such bad memories here?"

"She had good memories here, too," said Sambo, sitting opposite and picking up his leftover champagne. "She lived here for a time with her father before the Duggan family purchased the home again."

"What do you mean, 'again'?"

"Well, from what I can work out, your great-grandfather mysteriously gained possession of the house as a young man. His son, your grandfather, was born and then they sold it for some reason, possibly needing quick money. One or two owners had it before Crystal's father purchased the property when she was a teenager. That was when I first met your mum, at the Ithaca pool. She was only fourteen then and I stupidly thought she was much older. The Duggans purchased the house again when the Montagues left for the overseas posting.

"Why did I buy it? Not sure I can accurately answer that. Providence, coincidence, convenience? Take your pick or maybe all three. I was out in front of the place when I met the owners who had it before me. They were terrified of the place, sold it for a pittance. I could hardly refuse."

"Terrified?"

"Utterly petrified of the house. Said it was haunted. So did the realtor, so did everyone else I have spoken to about the house since then. Quite frankly, this house should have a much higher value considering its prime location in relation to the city. Nice city views, relatively large block with a decent Queenslander on it."

"Haunted? Come on?"

"I didn't say I have experienced anything like that. Quite the opposite for me and your mum. I have never felt more comfortable in a house in my life. I hear nothing when I go to sleep at night. And, believe me, I have stayed up many a night when I wasn't playing poker to find out if it was true. Even tried a séance here once with one of those Ouija boards. Load of absolute crap, mate. Nothing haunted about this hou..."

"Yes!"

All eyes turned to Crystal in astonishment. Mouths agape, they stared as Crystal continued to nod her head at the air to her right. Her eyes were seemingly focused on a point approximating the level of a person's head standing before her.

Sambo rushed to her, kneeling and clutching her hands in his.

"Crystal? Did, did you say something?"

Tilly hovered nervously nearby ready to administer aid and comfort should it become necessary. Little Sam leaned closer on the couch at her left to hear anything that might be said. The air seemed to hesitate in its path around the house, while its occupants poised mid-breath in hopeful anticipation. Crystal nodded her head and her lips continued to mouth silent sentences to no one. She then turned her head toward Sambo, her eyes no longer containing the faraway look of the past. Glistening with a drop of moisture, her mouth slowly formed a loving smile for her husband.

"Sydney?" asked Crystal, barely audible.

Sambo flopped to the floor on his backside, suddenly feeling every minute of his sixty-three years of life descend upon his shoulders. Crushed, shattered and utterly bereft, the enormous, impossible weight reduced him to nothing more than an old man living beyond his years. His once vibrant, distinguished features and silver hair turned lustreless, drab and ancient in the blink of an eye. A grief more powerful than anything he had ever experienced caused him to groan inwardly in despair.

The years of waiting and hoping had finally passed with Crystal showing none of the recognition he believed she would regain. His singular obsession to gently nurture his wife back to health, and the sheer certainty that he would succeed, quickly dissolved. He regretted not placing his wife under the care of health workers, feared that he had made the wrong decision, costing Crystal her one opportunity at a life.

Little Sam, watching his dear father at undoubtedly the lowest point in his life, could not bear to see the man he loved and admired falter so. He empathised greatly with his dad, feeling every ounce of weight the man had to bear. That the first word uttered by his wife should be a stranger's name was as heart-breaking as never hearing your baby say Dada or Mama.

"My Samuel? My darling, sweet, sweet Samuel?"

"Yes, Crystal, yes. It, it's me, love," answered Sambo through the surprise. Crystal looked about her to see Tilly and Little Sam on the verge of tears. "How are you, Crystal? Are you okay?"

She peered about her, at her surroundings, recognising them, and nodded her head in approval.

"I'm...okay, Samuel. I, I have something very important to...tell you, my darling husband."

"Oh, God, you have no idea how wonderful it is to hear your voice, Crystal. You..." Sambo could not finish.

The crushing despair of a moment ago evaporated as quickly as it appeared. He was unsure what to do, how to act, what she might recall, or how she would react to everything that had occurred. His mind was a swirling maelstrom of jumbled thoughts and emotions. He rested his head wearily on her lap while she stroked him lovingly. Little Sam placed a hand on his mum's arm just to let her know he was there, but, likewise, was unable to control his happy tears.

"Shush, Samuel. There, there, my beautiful man, Samuel. You must listen. You must hear me. I have something that we need to tell you. Camille and I."

Sambo jerked his head up at that.

"Who?"

"Camille...Sam."

"Yes, Mum?"

"No, not you, my boy. Oh, Little Sam, how you have grown. No, I am talking about Camille Matthews."

"I don't understand, Crystal. Who and where is this Camille Matthews?"

"She's here, Samuel. She has been here all along, watching over us and tormenting anyone who wasn't. She has something to show us. Something very, very important. She just told me it was time, time for you to finally know."

"Know? Know what, Crystal?" Sambo asked, shaking his head in sad frustration, thinking his wife was receding further into insanity or senility.

"The dream, Samuel. The end of the dream. I agreed. 'Yes', I told her, it is time you knew. Time everything was out in the open at long last. Tilly, would you be so kind as to make us all a hot brew? We have a long night ahead. Little Sam, fetch the others if you would, but leave your wife and the baby downstairs. They will not want to hear this."

"Whatever this is, Crystal, are you sure it needs to be done this instant? Wouldn't you prefer to rest first?"

"Why, Samuel, that is exactly what I have been doing all these years. It was only because of you that I was able to walk through my...inner maze. Sorry it took so very long, my love. I hope you can find it in your heart to forgive me?"

"Stop, it...no. Tilly..."

"Hush, Samuel, don't be so modest. You never gave up on me, not once. You went against everyone who told you to place me in an institution, or, at the very least, allow psychiatrists to fiddle with my brain. You stood tall and proud and declared loudly your love for me and that undying devotion called to me. I heard you, Samuel, through the fog, and the distance of a million miles. I heard your voice. I felt you in my heart and my mind, but I couldn't reach you, darling.

"It has taken all this time to travel those many miles to enter the light again, to hear your voice clearly, here and now, in the flesh. But I had other help as well."

"This...Camille?"

"Yes. I can see you recognise the name now. You know her, don't you?"

"I, I think so."

"No, Samuel. You mustn't say things just to humour me. I know you recognise the name and, if you let us, we will explain what happened. We will finish the dream."

"Mum, this is getting a bit weird. Are you sure you are feeling all right?"

"Will you please do as I asked? Go fetch Charlie and Mary-Rose. We must tell them."

"Tilly, is this...you know...right?" Sambo asked as delicately as he could.

Tilly was entering the living room with a tray of cups and saucers.

"I don't know quite what to tell you, Mr Border. It appears to me that Crystal has turned a corner and is functioning quite reasonably. Crystal, you do understand how strange this sounds to us mere mortals?"

"Yes, Tilly, I do know it sounds a little 'out there'. If you would all indulge me for a while, I am sure I can explain it," said Crystal as the others arrived from their half-sleep states, dressed in pyjamas and nightgown covered by robes they fastened as they approached.

"Thamboooo?"

"Charlie, it's okay, it's okay," said Rose, placing a protective arm about his big shoulders.

Sambo also used calming tones to settle his younger brother, who had reverted to his old self momentarily with the fear he felt. Sambo could not know that Charlie had been experiencing a terrible nightmare prior to being woken by Little Sam. Rose, too, had had to shake off the remnants of a disturbing dream. Rubbing the sleep from their eyes, they settled into the living room as Tilly distributed the coffees and teas, each to their own preferences.

"Crystal?"

"Yes, Mary-Rose?"

"Do you know where you are and what has been happening?"

"Mostly. I know we live in my old house, and where I was held captive for a time. I know how you have all helped me over the years, each in your own way. A lot of what was being said around me managed to filter through the layers of haze to reach me eventually, but I was simply incapable of responding in a normal sense. I am sorry for all the worry and anguish I have caused you."

"You were ill and required living assistance. If you had a debilitating physical disease it would have been no different, Crystal. While I am sure we were all concerned for you, we were not concerned *by* you," said Sambo kindly.

"Always the perfect gentleman, Sam. You deserve a medal for your patience and loyalty with first your brother, then me," said Crystal.

"Hear, hear," added Rose.

"Come on guys..."

"No, it's true, Sambo. I would never have survived if it wasn't for you," said Charlie.

"Bullshit! Most of your progress was due to Rose."

"No, Samuel. I helped, but I wouldn't have been able to if you had not made sure that Charlie was home under your care. Hell, they were threatening to pull the plug on him at one point," explained Rose. "You have no idea how much you have sacrificed for others, do you? You are a regular hero, Sambo, to all of us."

"He is definitely my hero, Rose. I know that I would not be alive today if Sam had not taken the steps he did to care for me when he found me half alive. I am also positive that I never would have come through this if I had been placed in an institution. I owe you my life on so many levels, Sam dearest. Little Sam and I have only you to thank for being allowed to live as long as we have. You have touched more lives than you will ever truly realise, my love."

"Stop it, all of you," said Sambo, turning bright red with embarrassment.

"Your humility endears us to you that much more, Sam."

"They're right, Dad. I love you from the bottom of my heart and know that I am here by the grace of your goodness alone. No one would believe the extremes you went to, to follow nothing but a hunch, an itch at the back of your mind, across the world in search of us. I have seen some of the letters you get from all over. Seems you did a lot for many more people as well. You've never even mentioned any of them."

"What none of you understands is that I never made any conscious decisions to help anyone, it was just a blind compulsion, right place at the right time. Had I thought about things long enough I am sure none of it would have happened. Crystal, I could never have given up on you. You are such a part of me that I would have died without you. It is almost like being part of conjoined twins. An inseparable addition to me that I simply and selfishly refused to abandon."

"What no one here knows is that Sam has already given his life for me...for Camille."

"No, Crystal. I'm here, alive and well...now. I may have died without you, literally, but I am here."

"You don't understand, Sam. Let me explain." When everyone appeared to be settled, drinking their beverages and ready to listen, Crystal took a long swig of her coffee before starting her story.

"On Saturday, the seventh of October, 1944, a handsome young pilot, a squadron leader named Sydney Burton, had a date with his sweetheart, Camille Matthews. They were both in their mid-twenties. They had a romantic dinner in the city and then saw a movie in the Regent Theatre on Queen Street. They were very much in love and anyone seeing them that night was left in no doubt that they were meant to be together for the rest of their lives.

"The following morning, Sydney was due to leave Australian shores for his part in the conquest of Europe by the allies. He would be joining a major push to end the second world war, and so they had only that last night to enjoy each other's company. Sydney wanted more than to simply spend a lovely evening with his girlfriend. He hoped to pronounce to the world his undying love and devotion for his sweetheart.

"After the movies, which neither truly saw or remembered, having had eyes only for one another throughout the double feature, they walked arm in arm along the dark city streets. Sydney, ever the gallant gentleman, lit the way with a torch that he had covered with a red handkerchief so as not to present a visible target for any Nazi spy or bomber in the skies at that time. They walked from the city through Roma Street and up to Given Terrace.

"Long before they reached her house in Red Hill, they stopped for a time to rest on a bus stop bench seat. There they sat, under the stars, silently enjoying the simple gesture of holding each other's hands. The night was still when Sydney slowly turned to Camille, nervously smiling as she looked deep into his eyes. Filled with an enormous love for the woman he knew to be just the right person for him, he asked Camille to marry him."

Crystal paused as she wiped a tear from her eye.

"And then they kissed for the first time and the initials were carved?"

"Yes, Little Sam. They kissed for the first time. They had known each other through school, been together as a couple for as long as their families could remember. Samuel and I have told you all this story a few times: however, you don't know the rest."

"You told us there was no more, Crystal?"

"No, not quite right, Mary-Rose. I told you that my memory of the dream ended there, as did Sam's."

"You know the rest now, my love?"

"Yes, Sam."

"So why don't you tell us the rest then, Crystal?"

"You do need to hear it, but are you sure you are all up to it at the moment? Maybe we *could* wait until morning?"

"No, dear, it is time. If you don't do it now..."

"How very tactful of you, Sam. I don't think I am going to regress back to that dark place, my darling, but you may be right. It is time. After Sydney proposed on one knee and Camille accepted, they kissed..."

***

...Sydney was over the moon. When the couple reluctantly parted, it was all Sydney could do to not yell out loud in proud jubilation that his proposal had been accepted. He looked about uncertainly when he suddenly realised that he did not have a ring.

"Oh, crikey, Camille, I haven't given any thought to a ring for our engagement! What are we going to do?"

"Do about what, Sydney?"

"Well, we simply have to tell the world about us. If we can't do that with a ring... Next best thing, eh? Here, you hold this torch for me while I announce our betrothal to the world."

"Sydney, what are you going to do? You can buy me a ring later. You and I both know we are engaged, that's all that matters."

"Camille, I leave for Europe tomorrow...oops! Don't breathe a word of that now. Top secret. Mustn't say a thing, please?"

"I already knew, Sydney. It's all the talk around town, and I knew you were leaving tomorrow. You told me."

"Yes, I was allowed to tell you that but no more. I could be court martialled for letting that slip. You won't tell, will you?"

"Of course not, silly. You just make sure my fiancé comes back to me in one piece, you hear? Oh, Sydney, I am so worried."

"Now, now, pet. None of that. I'm an Aussie pilot, love. Bloody bulletproof, I am. Be back before you know it. Nothing could keep me away from you. Not them bloody krauts at any rate. I'll go and drop a bomb on old Adolf meself, just you wait and see. Now, hold that a sec," said Sydney, handing Camille the torch.

Sydney walked over to a telephone pole. He dug out an old pocket knife he had retained from his childhood. Every kid he knew had a folding pocket knife. The kids often had friendly competitions to see who could keep their knife the sharpest. Each child would test their knife on paper or delicate fabric scraps pinched from their mother's sewing basket until a winner was announced by unanimous decision. Sydney carefully unfolded his razor-sharp pocket knife, then began carving their initials into the hardwood pole. Just as he had finished...

"Looky here, boys. Got us a fancy soldier boy and his...lady love, we have."

"G'day lads, how's it goin'?" asked Sydney innocently.

"Oil be roight foin, thank ye."

"Name's Sydney..." he said, offering his hand for a shake.

The three motley looking lads drew closer when they spied the knife Sydney was holding.

"What ye thinkin-o-doin with that, then?"

"What? Oh, sorry. Nothing, nothing at all. Just a little decoratin' on the post here is all."

"Oil be judge-o-that. Give it here fore ye hort yeself."

"Hey, fair go, mate. Had that little pocket knife since I was knee-high to a grasshopper. Hey, watch it there, mate. That's my fiancé you're...

Before Sydney was able to defend himself, the three young men jumped him, while Camille pounded their backs ineffectually with her small fists. When Sydney had been sufficiently subdued by the trio, he was kept pinned to the ground by two of them while the third, the one doing all the talking so far, grappled with Camille, who had begun to shout for help. The man backhanded her viciously, stunning her to silence.

"I be Paddy Duggan and oi want ta invoit ye horm. Now, ye wouldn't want ta hort me feelings, would ye?"

Paddy laughed as he indicated to his friends to pick up the bloke he'd decked and follow him. He marched the struggling Camille up the driveway of a nearby house, with a hand clamped firmly over her mouth to prevent her from attracting unwanted attention. The group entered the underside of the mauve house, shielded on three sides by the closely-spaced palings, affording the occupants some privacy during daylight hours. The rear of the house contained a small cabin with sliding glass doors in a wooden frame.

While his da had pummelled him to within an inch of his life for perceived indiscretions most of his life back in Ireland, and his ma had long ago perished by his father's hand, Paddy had fought to rid himself of the taint he'd acquired as a result of his upbringing.

He had run away from his beloved homeland when it seemed he could not escape his family curse. When he arrived in Australia, he found his way to Brisbane. Once there, it did not take him long to experience the down-at-heel life of a lowly immigrant with no trade and no future. Before he knew it, he had surrendered to the darkness within, to commandeer a home from an elderly couple who had built the house in the early 1900s. It was a grand dame of a Queenslander, making use of its unique design to take advantage of all available air flow and ventilation during the summer heat.

Mr and Mrs Harrow were now permanently residing beneath two feet of soil underneath the house after being made to sign over the deed to one Patrick Duggan. Paddy had also managed to 'persuade' the Harrows to hand over their life's savings once they retrieved said sum from their bank. Mr Harrow, being the manager of the bank, had no trouble implementing the large withdrawal without undue attention. Most likely he believed the word of Paddy Duggan that he and his wife would be freed once the payment had been made.

Unfortunately, no such promise was kept and the Harrows disappeared from the Brisbane scene completely. Friends and neighbours who dropped by in the passing months were sent packing with a flea in their ear by the redoubtable Paddy Duggan, house owner and landholder, new Australian, with a pretty penny to keep him mightily amused. The only thing missing from his new life was an appropriate woman to bear him children. Unfortunately, Paddy Duggan lacked the basic decency to attract a woman of the correct station in life. He would not settle for some doxy down at the local, slobbering ale over an ample bosom, nor could he abide a tramp peddling her wares to anyone with a cock.

Paddy prided himself in achieving certain standards to which his women must adhere. Mostly, though, he required subservience and total obedience, along with a touch of respectability. The woman he chose should possess a modicum of intelligence and more than a dash of class. Big tits would be nice, but not essential. When the opportunity presented itself right outside his front door one evening, Paddy decided to take advantage of the circumstances.

Something about the house had never sat well with Paddy, so he moved himself to the cabin in the rear, leaving his associates to live in the house. They manacled the unconscious Sydney to one of the stumps beneath the house. To an adjacent stump, out of reach of one another, they tied his girlfriend after stripping her naked. Paddy eyed his gagged and bound prize lustfully. Over the coming weeks and months, he would force her fiancé to watch as he trained the lass to accommodate his every desire.

A year later, barely alive, Sydney sat in his own filth, gasping as the chain about his neck tightened dangerously. Camille sat very still at her stump diagonally across from him, her belly fully extended with the form of her child stretching the skin tight. They were both reduced to mere skeletal figures subsisting on no more than a slice or two of bread and some weak, tasteless broth each day.

Paddy referred to their token repast as Irish stew, but it was neither stew nor broth, nor anything remotely palatable or nutritious. Beaten black and blue almost every day, Sydney could hardly make out the form of his fiancée through his near-permanent bloodshot and swollen eyes. Both legs had been broken many times over the course of the year they spent incarcerated by the evil man and his cohorts. He watched helplessly as Camille was used day in, day out in every vile and disgusting manner possible, first by Paddy Duggan, then his mates, when it was obvious she had fallen pregnant.

Sydney choked himself leaning as far forward as the chain around his neck allowed, turning a vivid blue as his lungs screamed for air. Without the use of his legs, useless sacks of flesh and bone that bore the first signs of becoming gangrenous, he had to use his arms to reach out. A few weeks ago, or months, he could not be sure which, Sydney spied something peeking through the dirt at his left. At first, he was puzzled by the familiarity of the object, but lost for an explanation and unable to reach it in any event.

Only the rough motions of his tormentors kicking and abusing him finally unearthed the small object enough for Sydney to finally understand what it was. Sitting there in the shadowy gloom of the house during the day and the total darkness of the night, having little else to occupy his mind, he concentrated on the object for many days until the mystery was finally revealed. He recognised his pocket knife, which must have slipped from his abductor's trouser pocket when they dragged him under the house. The end of the knife just peering from the ground was enough for him to see the stainless steel blade with the dirty, worn, wooden sides.

Every day thereafter he tried desperately to reach the implement without success: tantalisingly close, yet just beyond his reach. He had choked himself into unconsciousness several times already and was no nearer than that first attempt. Resigned to the futility of the task, he bided his time, planning with what was left of his mind. He steered the daily torture routines in the direction of the partially hidden knife. He flung himself desperately in that direction, screaming into his gag with the effort as his legs flopped uselessly and agonisingly below him.

Yesterday, his assailants had finally managed to kick the knife in its clump of dirt a little closer. Sydney almost cried with relief. His euphoria was short-lived, though, when it appeared the knife remained beyond the scope of his arm's length. With no regard for his well-being, having given up long ago on a life, Sydney struggled gamely to move his arms, bound at the wrists, farther and farther until he believed he heard his shoulder pop out of alignment with the socket. The minute advantage of a few extra millimetres provided Sydney with enough reach to finally grasp the object.

***

"...unfortunately, it did not afford them the means by which to escape their captivity," said Crystal, appearing tired after relating the long tale to her enthusiastic audience.

Tilly had replenished their beverages as the night advanced into the early hours of the morning. The group had come to see the story as more or less real, but still wondered how it connected them to their present situation. Both Tilly and Sambo had inquired regularly throughout the unfolding story if Crystal needed a rest. She assured them that she was up to the task of completing the tale if she had enough coffee and an audience to keep her going.

Charlie seemed to be affected more than anyone else by the violence and malevolence exhibited by the antagonists, knowing that the main character was closely related to his nephew. Sambo and Rose kept a watchful eye for any signs of relapse by Charlie into his private, brain-damaged world in which he often sought refuge against a harsh or demanding environment. Rose, showing no ill-effects of aging as the years progressed, shared everyone's curiosity and concerns over the disturbing tale, wondering how much more their little family could endure if it was somehow connected to them in a real sense.

Sambo displayed more tension than the others as he came to

terms with Crystal's escape from her mental prison and the foreboding tale she narrated. He felt he knew where the story was heading without actual knowledge. It was just an irksome suggestion at the back of his mind causing him to fear the end of the tale.

Little Sam sat next to his mum, often placing a reassuring hand upon hers, especially when she described the terrible tortures visited upon the couple by his great-grandfather, Paddy Duggan. More and more he came to loathe his origins and fear his eventual transformation into an evil monster that seemed to be his destiny, his curse.

"So, did he use the pocket knife to get them free?" asked Little Sam after the small hiatus in the narration.

"No, Little Sam. The small knife was no match for the chains or the padlocks uniting the ends around their necks..."

***

...The night had turned very dark with no moon showing behind a thick curtain of gathering rain clouds. Sydney, nearing the end of his endurance, felt the blow the hardest when he realised he was unable to escape his bonds to rescue his fiancé, or use the small implement as a weapon. He wept in frustration and groaned with the increasing pain in his twisted, deformed legs emitting the first indicative aromas of rotting flesh. He knew they had little hope.

Camille barely registered the struggles and the muted cries of pain coming from her right as her fiancé attempted to reach something on the ground nearby. Her gag had slipped down enough to allow her to breathe properly through her mouth for the first time in weeks. Her nose was terribly swollen from the many beatings to her face, hardly allowing her any intake of air. She heard Sydney speaking softly to her through the haze of confusion and pain.

"Sydney, Sydney?" she whispered so as not to attract the attention of their gaolers. "What is it, Sydney?"

"It, it's no good, Camille. I can't get us out of here."

"My gag slipped, what happened to yours?"

"I found my little pocket knife, Camille. I used it to cut the plastic cable tie holding my gag in place and the one binding my wrists, but it is useless against the padlock and the chain. I failed you, my darling. I am going to get very sick very soon from the gangrene in my legs. I won't last much longer, I'm afraid."

"Sydney, I..."

There was a long pause where the only sound was the sighing of the wind through the palings.

"Sydney?"

"Yes, Camille?"

"You know what to do."

Camille heard the sharp intake of breath from Sydney announcing his understanding of her statement.

"I know that this is not the end for us, Sydney. I know that we will be reunited in love again. We were destined to be together. I feel that in my heart, and know it with every fibre in my body. We will be together. Be strong, my love. I will hum softly so that you know where to throw the knife once you are done. Make sure you leave one good arm to throw with."

"Camille...I love you so very, very much. I..."

"You must."

"The baby?"

"It cannot be allowed to suffer the horror of its father. It must be spared that at all costs. At all costs!"

***

"...exsanguination," declared Crystal as she finished the story.

"What does that mean, Crystal?"

"They died of blood loss, Mary-Rose. Sydney accepted Camille's statement that it was their only means of escape. He sliced open his arm from the wrist to the inside elbow, severing one or more major arteries, the basilic and several lesser veins. He did not slice open both arms, knowing that he needed one good arm to throw the knife to Camille.

"She hummed softly in the dark, so Sydney knew precisely where to throw the small blade. He explained carefully how best to achieve the desired effect to Camille through tear-filled sobs, all the while declaring his everlasting love and devotion. Here, they both lie," Crystal explained as they gathered beneath the house where she was pointing to a place beneath the concrete slab poured somewhere around 1980.

"At least they were buried together, making their beliefs come true that they would be together again," said Tilly.

"No, Tilly. They weren't. Camille was buried here, while Sydney was buried over there.

"Then at least they were finally left in peace..."

"No, Little Sam. They were left in pieces. Paddy Duggan was so furious at being robbed of an heir that he took to the corpses with an axe, chopping them up into chunks no larger than a fist. They were thrown in their graves with the weapon used to inflict the post-mortem carnage. You will contact the police tomorrow, sorry, later today, to instigate a major investigation and excavation to this area under the house and outside in the backyard. There will be more than enough evidence there to put your father behind bars for the rest of his life, Little Sam, and to give closure to the many victims and their families destroyed by those monsters, and for Camille and the others, the opportunity to finally leave this house."

Crystal staggered slightly in Sambo's arms as she came to the end of her revelations.

"I think you and Dad should contact the police, Mum. You deserve to see this come to an end after all you've been through."

The rest of the group were nodding their heads in agreement while Crystal merely smiled knowingly and lovingly at her gathered family.

"Take me back upstairs, husband. I want to sleep next to my man again. It has been far too long since we shared a bed."

Sambo swept up the fragile woman into his powerful arms, not the least bit diminished by his advancing years, and carried her easily up the rear staircase to re-enter their house. After bidding everyone a sincere good night, the group separated to their various bedrooms. It was nearly two in the morning before Sambo managed to climb into bed to join his wife. A small bedside lamp remained on to allow the couple to gaze lovingly into each other's eyes.

"My dear, dear Sam. How wonderful you have been to me. I think it is high time that I showed you just how much I truly love and admire you for all you have done. Make love to me."

"We don't have to do that, love. I'm more than content to have you here by my side again, sharing my life."

"Oh, but I insist, husband. I want you inside me tonight. I want to share my body with you as we have shared our hearts and minds. I want us to meld into one entity tonight and forever, my one and only."

Sambo kissed Crystal lightly. She tasted the saltiness as a tear cascaded gently down his cheek to lay upon his upper lip. Without a word, the couple melted effortlessly into each other's curves, responding with increasing vigour to the deep urges rising from within. They undressed each other seamlessly, each coordinated movement a symphony of love's ballet. The searing heat of their naked flesh touching one another inflamed their desire to a crescendo of masterful harmony.

"I don't want to hurt you but I want you more than I could ever admit," whispered Sambo.

"Don't be afraid, Sam. You could never hurt me. Nothing will ever hurt me again."

When Sambo entered the fiery warmth of his lady for the first time, he became lost in the delirious ecstasy of the moment. He arched his back to ensure his entire length buried itself in the moist and deliciously hot flesh. Crystal writhed wantonly within his arms in the thrall of complete and utter surrender. The two lovers entwined and crushed each other in an embrace that lasted an eternity. Moment after joy-filled moment they shared their bodies, giving generously of themselves in total rapture. When the shuddering climax erupted within them simultaneously, filling them with the explosive effusion of their bodies, they lay panting, entirely spent, and ultimately sated.

Sambo had never experienced anything quite as magical, as enriching or rewarding. He did not believe a state of such euphoria was attainable. That he was admitted to partake of such bliss would fill his heart to the end of his days. That he was able to finally share himself with the woman of his dreams surpassed all notions he harboured of what true lovemaking might be. His one instance where he lost his virginity did not come close to approximating the pure ecstasy of his union with Crystal.

He turned to his side to peer into the face of the angel beside him. Seeing the angelic smile suffused him with its comforting balm. Watching the smile fade as life slowly passed from the woman he loved caused his heart to beat extraordinarily fast, culminating in takotsubo cardiomyopathy, or broken heart syndrome, as it is commonly known.

CHAPTER TWENTY-SIX

"Where are all these people coming from?" asked Rose of the Catholic priest about to walk past them, on his way to greet more and more guests appearing for the small ceremony Rose and Charlie had organised.

"My dear, I think you and Charlie should come with me," suggested the priest.

Frowning, Rose and Charlie left the row of pews at the front of the church to follow the priest down the aisle. When they exited through the huge, oaken double doors at the front of the church, they were astounded at the crowds awaiting entry to pay their respects to Sambo and Crystal, reposing in open coffins at the transept of the church. Rose had organised the church ceremony despite her brother-in-law and her husband's atheistic views. Observing the throngs of well-dressed folks waiting to enter, she was pleased she had won the day in that regard.

She led the ever-quiet Charlie back to their positions in the front row where their children and other family members waited. Charlie had been reduced to a shambling mess upon witnessing his brother and sister-in-law in each other's arms the morning of their passing. Rose had heard him repeat only long "Thambooooooos" in the days that followed. He was inconsolable and caught in a cocoon of misery and grief. Little Sam and she fared much the same. The days following the tragedy were a nightmare. They were all moved to a nearby motel while Sambo's house was practically demolished to dig up the understory and the entire yard, including lifting the backyard cabin with a crane, to excavate the area under it.

The authorities uncovered so many human bones and incomplete skeletons that the forensic department would be kept busy for years. Murder weapons, conveniently placed with the corpses, were tested and printed and DNA harvested to determine the identity of the victims. DNA testing of the Border family and anyone else who had stayed at the house were gathered to eliminate their inclusion in the list of growing suspects and victims derived from the evidence. Many further arrests of persons known to associate with the Duggan family would ensue in the coming months and years as they were progressively identified by the fingerprints or DNA analysis of evidence found on the murder weapons.

The Duggan family and their cohorts were soon named as the worst serial killers in Australia's history: the body count mounted to over a hundred victims. Graves were found on top of older graves. Bodies of children, women and men were amassing the further the authorities delved.

Rose kept the others away while she organised the funeral for their beloved family members. It was decided that once the forensic specialists were finished with the bones of Sydney and Camille, they would be interred along with Sambo and Crystal. Rose and the police were unable to locate any living relatives of the couple who died so tragically beneath the floorboards of the house on Given Terrace.

Rose marvelled at the mass of humanity pouring through the open doors. She recognised but a few among the sea of grieving faces. More than twenty thousand mourners attended the church, the grounds and the street outside, listening to the litany of touching eulogies narrated inside and played over loudspeakers located on the exterior of the church.

People from all walks of life, all stations, all backgrounds and professions quietly gathered, listening to every heart-filled word spoken.

"...Sambo, you saved me from a life of abject poverty and probably criminal conviction had you not so generously given of your spirit and pocket at my time of dire need."

"...Sambo will forever reside in my heart as the most loving and kind person I knew. His constant helping hand and generosity at our mission for the homeless placed many a member in a warm bed on a cold night, and good food in their empty bellies."

"...Sambo would always end a game of poker with a goodwill gesture where he gave away a portion of his winnings to be distributed among the many charities we were known to support."

"...He came to my rescue one night when a man threatened me with a knife."

"...Sambo provided some taxi money and airfare for me to get back home to my parents in Melbourne when he found me one night. I was alone and scared after running away from home..."

"...he selflessly took up the mantle of caring for his younger brother..."

"...taking care of his wife..."

"...assisting when he could..."

Charlie, Rose, Little Sam and Margaret Border wept as hundreds of mourners offered anecdote after anecdote of Sambo's generosity, courage, and kindness to them, all of which came as a complete surprise. They were overwhelmed with the outpouring of love for their wonderful brother, friend, son and confidante. Doctors, nurses and allied health-workers, poker friends, policemen, American oil workers, drag queens, the Queensland premier, Australia's Prime Minister and other people from all walks of life clasped hands in silent prayer and respect for a true man among men and in honour of his selfless deeds. In a heartfelt speech by the Prime Minister, it was announced that Samuel Border would be recommended for a posthumous honour during the Australia day awards.

The initial twenty thousand mourners were soon joined by thousands more as the media caught wind of the event. Long after Rose, Charlie, Little Sam, Margaret, the children and Tilly had left the church, recordings of the eulogies continued to draw in the masses vying for inclusion in the momentous occasion. What started as a four-line obituary in a local newspaper soon turned into front-page news across the continent, as hundreds, then many thousands of Brisbane's residents and persons from across the globe clamoured for positions surrounding the church to listen to the touching words, to pay homage to the hero within receiving the accolades of so many citizens.

It was touted in the Courier Mail as the funeral of the century, surpassing celebrity, politician or monarch. Tributes and flowers from across the country and the world flooded in to cover the church inside and out, and the street, for weeks afterwards. The hundreds of charities and organisations that Sambo had touched were inundated with donations and offers of volunteer assistance. The church where the ceremony was held gained sufficient funds to restore the roof and leadlight windows, which had deteriorated badly over the years.

CHAPTER TWENTY-SEVEN

"Welcome, Detective Saunders," said Rose, as she led the detective down the hall of their Rosalie home.

"Please call me Doug," insisted the detective.

"All right. To what do we owe the honour of your visit to our humble home, Doug?" asked Rose, as she offered the detective a stubby of beer.

As he was officially off duty, Doug happily accepted the proffered beer. Charlie sat at the kitchen table with a look of nervousness spreading across his features. It had taken almost a year for him to shake off the debilitating effects of his brother's death. Sambo had been a very large chunk of his life.

Rose had made Charlie a chocolate milk, one of his favourites. Little Sam had been asked to accompany them at Doug's request. Little Sam, sans wife and children, now that he was divorced, dreaded what the detective might have to discuss with the group. He was seeing another woman and their friendship was just looking like it might develop into something worthwhile. All he needed was more scandal or notoriety to quash his burgeoning relationship.

"I have an...onerous request to make of you all," started Doug unconvincingly.

"Oh boy! I don't like it already," stated Little Sam.

"Maybe I should have said unpleasant rather than onerous? There really is no way of sugar-coating this, so I may as well come right out with it. I want your permission to exhume the bodies."

Deathly silence met his request. It was some moments before Rose stirred.

"Um, what bodies? I mean, whose?" she asked nervously.

"Well, the four of them, actually. The two couples. The early pair you explained about, as well as Sambo and Crystal."

"Thamboooo!!!" cried Charlie, covering his face with his hands and shaking spasmodically.

Rose rushed to her husband's side, scowling at the detective. "How could you even think of such a thing? Why on earth would you want to do that to them...and us?"

"Are you off your nut?" remarked Little Sam, also going to aid his uncle.

"I apologise for upsetting you all. I wouldn't be asking if it wasn't very important," offered the detective, wincing at his own pathetic attempt to placate them.

"Important to who...whom? Your mob, I suppose? Not much help to us or important enough as far as we are concerned, to disturb four people who deserve a whole lot better than have their graves desecrated," argued Rose vehemently.

She fetched a sedative from her apron pocket, always kept handy for Charlie when difficult situations arose. She deemed their present situation as one more worthy of medication than most. Charlie gratefully accepted the capsule, which he swallowed without water.

"It is going to be rather difficult to explain and for you to accept what I tell you without exhuming the bodies to produce proof positive."

"Speak fucking English, will ya? What does all that crap mean?" shouted Little Sam.

"Can we all just calm down and discuss this, please? I promise you that no one will lift a finger without your express permission. It is, in our opinion, vital that we double-check our findings. There are some...anomalies with the DNA samples we collected, something quite impossible to explain scientifically should our findings be corroborated with new evidence."

"For God's sake, spit it out, will you, please? What is it?" asked Rose in an exasperated tone.

"All right, I'll try. Do you remember we had to gather DNA samples from yourselves and everyone who had been in the house in order to help us separate victims and suspects from the residents of the house?"

Everyone except Charlie nodded.

"Well it appears we may have made an error. If it were correct...well, it simply defies all logic no matter how many times the evidence has been verified by different experts. We simply must have new samples from those four persons to establish once and for all that our findings cannot be correct."

"I'll try this again, see if I can't get a better answer this time. What findings? What on earth are you blathering about, Doug? Have you gone troppo or something?" asked Rose.

Doug sighed with resignation.

"It seems, despite exhaustive testing and recalibrating all the systems and highly sensitive scientific instruments, that the two couples in question are identical. I am not talking similar or of the same family, but identical in every respect down to the very last nucleotide."

"Huh?" uttered Little Sam in confusion.

"Nucleotides are what make up the DNA strand which we use nowadays to map the human genome. The nucleotides are arranged in a very specific order for every individual on the planet and cannot be replicated by anyone else. It is an exact science with results standing up in a court of law as definitive and conclusive evidence.

"Camille Matthews and Crystal Border nee Montague, have the same DNA, as do Samuel Border and Sydney Burton, according to our tests. Which of course, is impossible and would set up a calamitous precedent, were it true, for future and past DNA testing. There are no family connections, no reason they would even have similar characteristics, let alone identical. In order to clear up any confusion we are asking if we can exhume the rem ...bodies of your loved ones as a means of..."

"NO!" came the simultaneous chorus from the assembled participants.

"But..."

"No!" Once again the group spoke as one.

"Regardless of your confusion and whether we want an answer or not, we cannot give you permission to disturb our loved ones. They have suffered more than most on this planet and I am sure I speak for everyone here when I say they deserve their rest now. We will not allow their graves to be exhumed and their remains tested until you satisfy yourselves and reach a conclusion we reached ourselves long ago. Seems quite clear to us that they were the same people. How else would we all have ended up in that house? How would Crystal and Sambo have shared exactly the same dream? How..." Doug cut Rose off.

"Shared dreams?"

"Oh, didn't you know about that? You knew about Sambo's dream only then? Crystal and Sambo shared a common dream and that is what drew them toward each other. The night they passed away, Crystal related the entire dream to us all," explained Rose.

"Well, you mentioned the part about Crystal having a conversation with someone and pointing to the exact spot the bodies were buried under the house, but neglected to mention that she shared a dream. Sambo did tell me about his dream and that was hard enough to swallow."

"You would have had us all committed if we told you that," offered Little Sam.

"I may have raised an eyebrow..."

"Aw, come off it. Even now you're giving us weird looks."

Once Rose had finished retelling in great detail the story of Sambo and Crystal, Doug Saunders shook his head in amazement. He could offer no alternative to the collective beliefs of the tight little group so traumatised by the events in their lives. He accepted their refusal of his request to perform an exhumation. He forgave them their certainty that strange things happen, but could not honestly ascribe to their notion of love's destiny.

EPILOGUE

At the precise moment that Sambo breathed his last on the fateful evening of his greatest joy, elsewhere in the city of Brisbane, entirely apart from one another, two babies were born. A girl, named Calliope Elspeth Moorland, and a boy, named Simon Arthur Bowman, were born to loving parents and enjoyed happy, carefree childhoods in their respective suburbs.

A chance meeting of the two occurred on the occasion of their twentieth birthday, when they shared a popular city venue for their individual surprise parties organised by good friends. Naturally, having a birthday on the same day at the same venue became an instant ice-breaking introduction for the pair. They soon became good friends.

A year later, still dating regularly, they were strolling along a street when they happened upon a bus stop bench placed conveniently along their path at the most opportune moment in their perambulation. While a first kiss had long ago become part of their cherished memories, the advent of a golden ring with a single diamond at its centre elicited surprise and great excitement by the recipient of the gallant proposal.

The young, newly-engaged couple, continuing their casual stroll, came across a curious phenomenon. The telephone pole they passed had inscribed, within a heart, a set of initials mirroring their own. Gratified that fortune had seen fit to grant them a carved declaration of their promise to one another, they ventured on, only to stop at a realtor's sign nearby.

Sitting atop the neglected property stood a derelict Queenslander in desperate need of care and attention. With but a brief moment staring at the propitious sign, the couple agreed instantly to approach the realtor with an offer if the asking price was within their budget. Within another year, the house had been transformed into a paragon of the renovator's art. A small cabin residing in the rear of the property was soon treated to as meticulous an overhaul as its nearest neighbour, transforming it into a delightful apartment which the young couple wisely rented to a single executive gent working in the city, thus assisting them to pay off their mortgage.

Many, many happy years were spent in their first home, where they were joined by a new baby in each of the first three years. The family of five continued to live in the house on Given Terrace, and often made the trek to the Ithaca pool on Saturday afternoons. They were soon introduced to a lovely octogenarian couple by the name of Mary-Rose and Charlie Border while attending the pool. The families became good friends despite the wide age differences, with Charlie often reading to the three youngsters from his tremendously successful *Thambo and Thumper* series of children's books.

Mary-Rose and Charlie were often seen by Calliope and Simon with mysterious smiles and a wink or two whenever they were enjoying their company. The two families became inseparable and were often found in each other's homes, where the Bowman children and the Border grandchildren played congenially. The Bowman family lived a happy and uneventful life into their eighties, long after the Border couple had passed away peacefully, within two days of one another, both well into their nineties.

The End.

Author's Note

Thank you for reading my novel. As an Indie author/publisher, the only means of promoting our product if we do not spend a great deal on advertising, is by word of mouth. The easiest way to achieve that is for someone who appreciated the book to write a favourable review. If you enjoyed reading my book as much as I enjoyed writing it for you, please take the time to leave a review on whichever platform you used to acquire the book.

If you would like to follow me on facebook or wish to know when my next book will be available, navigate to my website where you may contact me via the contact page or follow the link to my facebook page.

http://lakesidecaravanpark.wixsite.com/josef

https://www.facebook.com/Josef-Peeters-Australian-Author

OTHER BOOKS BY THE AUTHOR

Fiction
Dumped

Action/Adventure

Nothing takes the fun out of a vacation faster than a plane crash. Except for a confession of infidelity just before the oxygen masks drop. Read **DUMPED** to see who survives.

See Josef's website for purchase links to all major retailers.
http://lakesidecaravanpark.wixsite.com/josef

Daintree Denizens

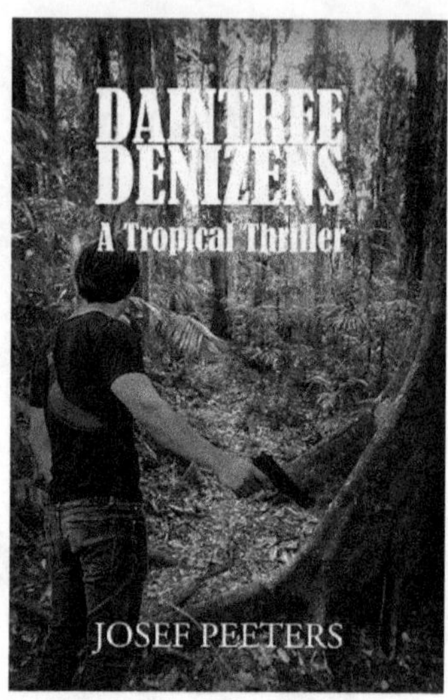

Thriller/Mystery/Suspense

When Barry Ottoman's idyllic, solitary, lifestyle is shattered by the appearance of interlopers with a mysterious agenda and intent on harm, he must call upon his vast knowledge of Australia's northern rainforest's flora and fauna, to effect an escape from a deadly pursuit.

See Josef's website for purchase links to all major retailers.
http://lakesidecaravanpark.wixsite.com/josef

Non Fiction
Wood Whisperer Volume 1

Finding the courage to go against the grain of popular convention, one man discovers his true passion for a lifelong kinship. Join Josef as he deigns to venture into the art of woodcarving.

See Josef's website for purchase links to all major retailers.
http://lakesidecaravanpark.wixsite.com/josef

Wood Whisperer Volume 2

Continuing my self-taught journey into woodcarving. Exploring the methodology and thought processes involved in producing commissions and exhibit pieces.

See Josef's website for purchase links to all major retailers.
http://lakesidecaravanpark.wixsite.com/josef

Wood Whisperer Volume 3

Dare to dream. Dare to be yourself. Allow imagination to soar above opposition along your path to creativity. Be inspired by Josef on his wood carving journey to find the spirit within the wood and himself.

See Josef's website for purchase links to all major retailers. http://lakesidecaravanpark.wixsite.com/josef

ABOUT THE AUTHOR

Josef Peeters, born in Dusseldorf Germany, in 1961, immigrated with his parents and two brothers to Australia in 1964. He became a naturalised Australian soon after his eighteenth birthday. After a lacklustre education spent in numerous schools across Queensland, Josef left at age fifteen to begin work as an assistant projectionist in the original Regent Theatre in Brisbane, before it became a multi-screen complex. Josef has followed artistic pursuits in performance, literary, and sculptural genres. He now continues to write and self-publish for his own benefit and pleasure while maintaining a Caravan Park business with his second wife at Moulamein NSW, Australia.